A Hidden Witch

Debora Geary

DEBORA GEARY

Copyright © 2011 Debora Geary
Fireweed Publishing
Print Edition

ISBN: 978-1-937041-05-2

To my daughter.

May you always touch
the magic that lives
within you.

DEBORA GEARY

Chapter 1

It wasn't the first time in her life Elorie had wished for magic of her own, and it likely wouldn't be the last.

"Sean James O'Reilly, you'll be walking the plank, matey." The illusion spell that had just turned her into a pirate came complete with growly voice and glinting teeth, so all she accomplished was sending Sean and his two classmates into hysterics.

She couldn't really blame him—witch history lessons tended to be a little long-winded. Gran had dealt with plenty of witchling pranks in her years of teaching, but she'd also had enough power to magically counteract the more embarrassing stunts.

Elorie was not so blessed, but there was more than one way to handle a ten-year-old boy. She walked over to the bookshelf in the corner of her living room and pulled out the thickest volume of witch history she could find. *The Trials and Tribulations of Edward C. Millgibbons, Hedgewitch, on his Journeys about the Countryside.* That seemed like a suitable weapon.

She set the tome down on her coffee table, pulled out a piece of paper, and began to write in large letters. HOMEWORK. Then she looked at the book, looked at Sean, and let loose an evil pirate laugh.

Sean looked at the book in horror. "You can't give us homework, Aunt Elorie. It's summer!"

His twin brother, Kevin, looked at the book with interest. That figured. He was probably out of stuff to read again. She'd slip him the book on the sly later, after it had done its job in encouraging Sean to rethink his spell. Elorie put on her best pirate scowl and tapped the paper with her hook. Nice touch, the hook—very realistic. Sean's spells were improving nicely.

Six-year-old Lizzie was no dummy. "You better turn her back into a regular person, Sean. Momma says girls don't get mad—we get even."

Out of the mouths of babes, Elorie thought.

Sean was beginning to look concerned. "There might be a little problem with that."

Uh, oh.

Kevin shook his head. "You don't know how to reverse it, do you?" He punched his brother in the shoulder. "Idiot. I'll go find the spell workbook."

Lizzie hopped down from the couch. "That will take too long. I'll go get Granny Moira." Lizzie was at least one generation and a couple of cousins removed from being Moira's actual granddaughter, but in the Nova Scotia witching community, those were minor details.

Moira was matriarch and witch historian. And while she had a not-so-secret soft spot for witch pranksters, her tolerance for poor magical judgment was a lot smaller. Sean was right to look concerned.

Elorie went to put a kettle on the stove. Gran would want some tea. She also took a moment to look in the mirror. It wasn't every day you had a grizzly beard and an eye patch. She grinned at her reflection and headed back to the living room just in time to see Lizzie bound in the door, Gran following more sedately behind her.

Elorie kissed Gran's cheek. "Thanks for coming."

Moira giggled like a small girl. "Is that you, Elorie dear? I assume young Sean is responsible. Lizzie said he's having a wee problem reversing the spell."

"Aye, matey," Elorie growled, and then added more quietly, "and sweating about it now."

"A bit late for that." Moira headed into the living room.

Sean was sitting on the couch beside Kevin and looking very subdued. "Hi, Gran. I think I need help. I didn't mean to turn Aunt Elorie into a pirate."

That earned him dubious stares from everyone in the room. "Well, I didn't mean for her to get *stuck* that way. I just wanted to do it for a minute, but I must have goofed somewhere."

Moira looked at him sternly. "What's the first rule of magic, Sean O'Reilly?"

"Do no harm." Sean hung his head and missed the twinkle in Moira's eyes.

"And what do you think life would be like for Elorie if she were a pirate forever?"

Sean looked forlorn. "Well, it would be hard to make her jewelry with a hook for a hand, and Uncle Aaron might not want to live with a pirate."

Elorie thought Sean underestimated her husband's fondness for the absurd. She also hoped Gran was about done torturing the poor boy—the eye patch was getting itchy.

Moira sat down beside Sean. "So, tell me how you set the spell, and we'll see about how you might undo it."

"Can't you just fix it, Granny Moira?" asked Lizzie.

Moira looked very serious. "No, my dear, I can't. Sean here is quite talented at spellcasting, and I'm not strong enough to reverse his spell." She laid a hand on Sean's shoulder. "With power comes responsibility to use your magic wisely and with good judgment."

Kevin, who had been scribbling furiously in a notebook, looked up. "I think I know what he needs to do."

Both Moira and Elorie nodded with approval—it was good for witches to develop a strong sense of communal responsibility. Kevin laid his book on the coffee table. He'd drawn some sort of complicated flow chart. Elorie's eyes crossed just looking at it.

Kevin and Sean started talking and gesturing in some sort of incomprehensible twin-speak. Lizzie sat in Moira's lap and played with her antique pendant. Finally Sean looked up. "Okay, I think I know what I need to do now, but we're gonna need a circle."

Moira rubbed his head. "Indeed. It often takes more power to undo a spell than to cast it in the first place. Best you be remembering that. Shall I be joining your circle, then?"

"Yes, please." Sean's face shone with pleasure, and Elorie felt the same in her heart. It was a rare thing for Gran to join a training circle these days. They all tried to pretend she wasn't getting old.

Their circle assembled with the ease of long practice, and called to the elements. They pushed power to Sean and held it steady for him to start casting the reversing spell. Everyday magic at work.

Elorie watched from outside the circle, feeling the usual small ache of exclusion. The sense of accomplishment was newer. She'd almost entirely taken over Gran's role coordinating witchling training in their little corner of the world. The next generation was coming along very nicely, and she could be proud of her part in making it happen. It had taken a while to find her purpose and make peace with it, but she'd found her way to belong.

As she watched, Sean's fingers began to flutter, and she knew his spell reached readiness. A slight shimmer in front of her eyes, and she assumed from Lizzie's grin that her pirate self had been replaced by plain old Elorie.

The kettle in the kitchen started to whistle. "Sean and Kevin, go make Gran some tea. Lizzie, you can get cookies out of the tin for everyone."

The witchlings scampered off, and Moira winked at Elorie. "That's a nice bit of spellcasting by our Sean, and some lovely circle work as well."

Elorie grinned. "Aye, aye, Captain."

~ ~ ~

Moira smiled as she walked back into her cottage. Elorie was a wonderful witchling trainer. Others in the community could handle the training of specific magics, but Elorie was the glue that held it all together. It was a true shame her granddaughter had no power—she would have handled it well, with respect and a solid sense of tradition. Too many modern witches forgot their roots.

Aye, and old witches resisted using modern tools as well. Moira laughed gently at herself. She sat down in front of her laptop and made the now-familiar clicks that would take her to Witches' Chat. Young Sean's antics had delayed her a few moments, and Nell and Sophie were likely already waiting.

"I seek the ones who share my gifts,
To talk, to learn.
This portal will my power discern,
And let me in, as one of three.
As I will, so mote it be."

<u>Sophie</u>: Aunt Moira, welcome!

<u>Moira</u>: Hello to you, Sophie, and Nell as well. I'm sorry I'm a wee bit late—we had a spell that needed reversing.

<u>Nell</u>: Uh, oh...

<u>Moira</u>: Just witchling pranks. Young Sean cast a pirate illusion on Elorie. It was quite good, actually—she looked and sounded quite ferocious.

<u>Sophie</u>: He's got plenty of talent.

<u>Moira</u>: Indeed he does, and we haven't anyone who can keep pace with him for long. I have an idea to propose to you, Nell.

<u>Nell</u>: I'm all ears.

<u>Moira</u>: How would you feel about bringing some of your young ones on a little trip this summer? I'm thinking we could have a bit of a summer gathering and do some intensive witchling training. Sean could use some lessons from a talented spellcaster—you'd be perfect for that job.

Nell: Sure, give me the troublemakers :-)... Nathan has a pretty busy summer, but I could definitely bring the girls and Aervyn. Let me figure out when we might be able to make the trip.

Moira: That would be lovely. It's an open invitation—anyone who would like to join you is welcome, including you, Sophie. Elorie's thinking about starting a website to sell her jewelry; I know she'd love to borrow a bit of your expertise.

Sophie: She's welcome to create her own site, but I'd be delighted to sell her work on mine. There's certainly magic in all that sea glass she collects, and it would be a nice expansion of my current wares.

Moira: It would be a joy to see my girls working together again.

Sophie: One step at a time, Aunt Moira.

Moira: Just tucking a little seed into the dirt, my dear. There's much love between the two of you yet, but I know it's complicated.

Sophie: Consider it planted.

Nell: Speaking of your site, Sophie, I was thinking of a couple of enhancements to our fetching spell for Witches' Chat.

Sophie: I thought it was working quite nicely. We've had some delightful witches join us in chat lately.

Nell: We have, but they've all been actively practicing witches. I was remembering back to when we pulled Lauren in, how she wasn't aware she had power.

Moira: She's been a wonderful addition to the witching community.

Nell: Exactly. I was thinking that maybe we want to find more like her.

Sophie: You're a brave woman. Supposing we wanted to, how would we do that?

Nell: I looked at the power signatures of the witches we've been chatting with lately and compared them to Lauren's early readings. Hers were strong, but much less disciplined.

Sophie: That would make sense—she'd had no training.

Nell: Right, and I think we can use that. I can tweak the spell to seek those with less-disciplined power traces. We'll either find witches with less training, or those who aren't aware of their gifts.

Moira: That was a little rocky last time around, Nell. It's all turned out for the best, but I think we were fortunate Lauren didn't slam the door in our faces.

Sophie: I agree, but it's tempting—we know there's a need for it. We'd definitely want to have someone on tap to go evaluate them, like Jamie did for Lauren. There's a lot more to helping an untrained witch than simply finding her, and we didn't have much of a plan last time.

Nell: The girls and I are working on a virtual scan so we could assess someone remotely, but we haven't finished it yet. And Jamie isn't free to travel this time—Nat's been dealing with morning sickness, and I don't think he'd want to leave her.

Sophie: Someone should have mentioned she was having trouble. I have a couple of crystals that will help, and I'll blend her some tea.

Nell: That would be great, Sophie. I need to send Ginia out to train with you—we're really short on healers here, and I'd love to know if she's got that talent.

Sophie: With her earth power and affinity for plants, it wouldn't surprise me at all.

Moira: Bring Ginia this summer, Nell. We've healers here, especially with Sophie coming to visit as well. If Ginia's got healing talents, that's just one more reason to gather in one place for a time.

Nell: A week attempting to laze on the beach sounds good to me. Just let me work out the logistics. In the meantime, should I tweak the fetching spell to find witches who aren't actively practicing the craft, or leave it alone?

Moira: If we're having ourselves a training gathering, then it seems like fortuitous timing to find someone who might be untrained.

Sophie: When can you have the spell adjusted, Nell?

Nell: I think the girls have been working on it in secret. There's an encrypted folder on our network called Codename: Hidden Witch.

Sophie: Ginia's turned into an awesome spellcoder. She's kicking all our butts in Realm.

Nell: That's my girl. I'll see what they've got, but it wouldn't surprise me if we're ready to go in time for our regular chat tonight.

Moira: In that case, I'll have myself a wee bit of dinner and talk to the both of you in a couple of hours.

~ ~ ~

Elorie could feel her hands cramping, and the natural light was getting dim enough that she had to squint to see the delicate silver wires she was twisting together. This particular piece of sea glass was one of her favorites, a brilliant blue that made her think of Venice.

Blues were the rarest of her beach finds and she hoarded them, only dipping into that jar when she wanted to make a particularly special piece. This was a necklace for Gran, and it didn't come any more special than that. Gran shared her love for the history and resilience the sea glass represented.

Elorie liked to imagine the long life of each treasure she worked on. She held the bit of glass up in the dying light, studying its shape one more time. Perhaps this one had been part of a bottle sitting on the dressing table of a fine lady in Venice, or one crossing the Atlantic on a ship. It might have been tossed overboard, or the ship come to an untimely end. And then the broken pieces of glass had tumbled in the ocean waters, fighting with pebbles and sand to come to rest at last on a lonely Nova Scotia beach, perhaps waiting centuries for her eyes to find it.

Elorie made a mental note to have some friends over for dinner soon. Getting all misty-eyed about her glass was a sure sign she'd been too much of a hermit lately. It was for a good cause; she had a growing pile of gorgeous new work ready for the Art Fair in San Francisco.

It was rare for her to venture beyond the borders of her home province, but under Aaron's gentle pressure, she'd submitted her designs to the continent's most prestigious art show and been selected for one of their emerging artist slots. It was a high honor, and quite a bump in her nice, stable life.

Truth be told, it was rather terrifying.

Since the natural light was now entirely gone, she gave up trying to finalize the setting for Gran's necklace and began to tidy her workspace. She always left one work-in-progress lying on her desk as inspiration for the next day. With a last touch to the jewel-blue glass, cooling now without her fingers to keep it warm, she started the more mundane tasks of organizing her tools and sweeping the floor.

Her laptop pinged with an incoming instant message, Aaron's solution to having to leave the inn to get her attention. Seemed a little silly when a shout out the back door would work, but evidently she'd ignored one too many of those. Dinner was probably ready. She sat down at the computer to let him know she'd be up to the house shortly.

<u>Nell</u>: The spell is fetching someone now... her name is Elorie.

<u>Sophie</u>: Hello, Elorie, and welcome to Witches' Chat. We're delighted to have you join us!

<u>Elorie</u>: What a nice surprise! Hello Nell, Sophie. I've heard all about your chat room from Gran. I can't stay for long—I was just about to let Aaron know I was on my way up for supper.

<u>Moira</u>: Hello, my sweet girl. It's good to have you here, and a wee bit of a surprise, as well. Nell's fetching spell must have misfired. We were looking for some new witches for our chat. Perhaps one of the students was on your computer earlier.

<u>Elorie</u>: That wouldn't be a surprise. Kevin's fascinated by anything electronic.

<u>Nell</u>: Hang on a minute; I'm looking at the code now. Sorry, Elorie—not sure what went wrong. It's nice to "see" you again, however.

Sophie: Your show's coming up soon, isn't it?

Elorie: It is. I'll be heading out in less than a week now. Nell, do you still have room for me to stay with you?

Nell: We always have room. If you want a little more quiet, though, Jamie and Nat would be happy to have you. Their house is starting to look pretty lived in, but it could use a guest or two to get rid of the new house smell.

Elorie: Either one is fine, and appreciated.

Nell: So, I hate to ask a dumb question, but the code for the fetching spell is getting a clear power reading on your end, Elorie.

Moira: Well, it can't be from Elorie. If she were a witch, we'd have detected it long since.

Elorie: Maybe a student, then?

Nell: No, the spell is specific to an individual, not a computer. And it's an untrained power signature again. Kevin's had enough training that his would look more like the actively practicing witches we've been chatting with lately.

Elorie: I don't understand what that means.

Nell: It means my code is suggesting you're an untrained witch, but that doesn't make any sense.

Sophie: Has anyone run a scan on you lately, Elorie?

Elorie: We both got scanned often enough growing up. You can't possibly believe I've got magic now, Soph.

Sophie: I'm sorry, I wasn't thinking. I know it was hard for you then, and I'm really sorry we've managed to stick our finger in it again somehow.

Elorie: It was a long time ago, and no apologies needed. I'm happy your magic grew, and I stopped crying about the lack of mine a long time ago. And now I really do need to run—there are perogies for dinner, and I'm starving. Good night, all.

Sophie: Ouch.

Moira: Oh, dear.

Nell: I feel like we stepped in something there, and I don't know the whole story. Anyone care to fill me in?

Moira: Elorie has always longed to be a witch, ever since she was a small girl. She hides it very well now, but I don't know that she's ever really grown out of it. I was so certain she would develop power that I wasn't as careful as I might have been in helping her accept the alternatives.

Sophie: Non-witches are as welcome as any witch, Aunt Moira—you've always made sure of that.

Moira: Of course they are, but the magic has always called to her. Normally when a witchling has that kind of attraction to the craft, their powers emerge at some point, but hers never did. And it was doubly hard with her and Sophie being so close. You handle that beautifully with your triplets, Nell—I didn't handle it nearly so well.

Nell: Not to ignore the history, but maybe she should be tested again. It sounds like she hasn't been scanned in a while. I swear, my code says she's a witch. Maybe your instincts weren't wrong.

Sophie: She's around practicing witches and active circle work all the time. It's hard to believe she has stealth witching talents we've all failed to notice.

Nell: Yeah, active power streams usually make any nearby untrained talents pretty obvious.

Moira: It shames me somewhat to say it, but she's been scanned much more recently than she knows. I stopped telling her when I do it, since it saddens her so, but it's been no more than a few months since I last checked.

Sophie: And we've surely saddened her and you again tonight. I'm so sorry, Aunt Moira.

Nell: Crap. I'll debug my code and try not to screw up again. Sorry—with the girls doing most of the work on this, I've obviously missed something. No excuses, but we'll go through it with a fine-toothed comb tomorrow.

<u>Moira:</u> Not to worry. Aaron will tend to her heart; he's a very good man.

Elorie closed the door of her studio and leaned against it, sucking in the brisk ocean air. No, dammit. She was not going to let this get to her. Teenagers got to cry about the powers they wanted and didn't get. Grown women needed to make peace with the life they had.

She had a good one, and right now, it involved a big plate of perogies.

Chapter 2

Elorie figured that at twenty-six, she'd looked at more small rocks than most people would see in three lifetimes. Finding sea glass on the beach was the art of scanning and letting your eye catch the unusual, the bright glimpse of color in a sprawl of gray and brown.

Which would be simpler if ocean pebbles actually were gray and brown. Especially when wet, the stones on the beach were an astonishing variety of colors, with glints of gold and green and occasional glimpses of almost every other color in nature. Add in fragments of pretty shell and unidentified chunks of sea crud, and it wasn't as easy as you might think to spot the hidden bits of tumbled glass.

Elorie had loved hunting for them ever since she was a little girl. Her mother would bring her to the beach, making up stories about the glass and where it had been. She remembered the first time she'd taken a treasure find, suspended it from a black shoelace with dental floss, and presented it as a Mother's Day gift.

It had taken fifteen years and the shoelace breaking to convince Mom to let her put that little piece of purple glass on a proper chain with a handcrafted silver-wire setting. And she was pretty sure her mother still had the shoelace remains tucked away somewhere.

Sentimental, maybe, but now that she was considering a baby of her own, it was a little easier to understand why Mom had worn a shoelace around her neck for a decade and a half.

As she strolled along the beach, Elorie rubbed her belly and pondered what it would be like to grow a baby. Children weren't much of a mystery when you'd grown up surrounded by them, but having a baby inside you was a wonder. Aaron had been dropping hints lately. Maybe after she got back from San Francisco.

A piece of water-blue glass caught her attention, and she reached down to tuck its wet coolness in her pocket. This beach was out of the way enough to have quite a scattering of finds left by the ocean waters. She could afford to ignore the brown and green glass and just seek out the rare and special colors—the blues, reds, and purples that hadn't been made for centuries.

The next piece to catch her attention was perfectly round and a deep cerulean blue. A child's marble from centuries ago, rough now from its ocean voyage. It would make a gorgeous necklace if she could bear to part with it. Her studio and home were littered with small treasures she couldn't resist keeping.

Elorie slid the marble into her cargo pocket and walked over to a sunny rock. Time for lunch and listening to the waves for a while.

The morning mists had burned off, but the air still felt wet—not enough wind today to chase the spray away. Unusual for this stretch of beach. The tide was out, the smells of seaweed and salt all a little riper under the noonday sun.

She was well aware the main purpose of her morning escape hadn't been to increase her sea-glass stash. It was the old hurts in her heart that needed the soothing ritual of the treasure hunt. Another thing she'd learned as a grown woman—doing was often far more soothing than crying.

Even Aaron, fully content as a non-witch, didn't truly understand what it was to know the desire of your childhood would never come to be.

For as long as Elorie could remember, she had assumed she would be a witch. Gran was a witch, and the history and the craft called to her blood. Or at least that's what she'd believed as a young child, waiting for her powers to emerge.

She'd thrown herself into the lessons taken by all young ones in the witching community, and sat for hours listening to Gran talk of witches past.

Then she'd tried to be patient as a teen, as so many around her came into their powers. Watched in an agony of envy as Sophie had grown into her magic. Gran had scanned her regularly, and Elorie knew that she still did, seeking traces of talent in her beloved granddaughter. Nothing had ever appeared.

Walking the beaches in search of sea glass had turned from childhood treasure-seeking into a kind of therapy, and from there, into a purpose and direction for her adult life. She was an artist, a wife, a dancer, a trainer. Not a witch, and she'd come to terms with that.

Most days.

Then there were the days when a fetching spell went wrong and sparked the tinder of hope she couldn't quite eradicate from the hidden corners of her heart. She wasn't a witch, but neither was she entirely free of the desire to be one.

She squeezed her eyes shut against the hurt, just for a moment.

As a thirteen-year-old girl, she'd believed she *needed* to be a witch. When that had failed to come, and with Gran's gentle persistence, she'd found a path for herself, a purpose and a sense of belonging that didn't require magic. Not an easy feat for a non-witch.

And still not quite enough to free her from the wanting.

Sitting on the beach in the quiet morning sun, Elorie could admit to herself one more hard truth. She was afraid that part of the reason she wanted a baby was the hope that power might skip a generation and bloom in her child.

Then she shook her head ruefully. If Gran had taught her nothing, it was that every child needed to find their own way. If she turned into some terrible, hovering mother, Gran would lead the charge to thunk her over the head. In Nova Scotia, you still had a village raising a child, and that was a very good thing.

She pushed away the errant thought that Gran might not be around to watch her children grow. Irish witches usually lived very long lives.

Then there was Aaron—he would make a wonderful father.

One day she would walk these beaches with a toddler of her own, looking for colorful bits of glass. And that would be a magic of its own.

~ ~ ~

Nell shook her head at her triplets. "There must be a bug, girls. We fetched Elorie. You remember her—Moira's granddaughter."

Mia rolled her eyes. "We know, Mama. She was here for our birthday. But we tested our code a lot. It's not wrong, so Elorie must be a witch."

Ah, the arrogance of youth. Her girls were awesome coders, but no programmer was invincible. "Moira has tested Elorie ever since she was a child, just like we keep an eye on all of you. If your code is right, that means you're saying Moira is wrong. Is that really what you mean?"

Three faces frowned and turned back to their respective screens, brains humming louder than the roomful of computers. They were old enough to know that Moira's word was gospel in the witching world, and for good reason—she was rarely wrong.

Ginia finally looked up. "I still don't see anything. Maybe we need to run a test."

Shay, who often wore the pessimist mantle in their trio, shook her head. "We've already done lots of testing on us. You get fetched, Mia and I don't."

"I know," Ginia said. "But right now, the only way to know if someone is a witch is to see if they get fetched or not. That's what Dad calls an indirect consequence. He says it's hard to debug if you only see the end result—you gotta see all the stuff going on in the middle."

Nell hid a smile and tucked that little tidbit away to share with Daniel. It was largely to his credit that Ginia was still prouder of her coding skills than her emerging elemental powers. And that was a good thing, with two non-witch sisters.

"So, how do we do that?" Mia asked, always ready for a new experiment.

Ginia grinned. "We show Mama our other surprise."

What was it about turning nine that had transformed her triplets into giggly secret keepers? Nell raised an eyebrow and waited.

Ginia typed on her laptop for a moment. Because all their monitors were screen sharing, Nell could see her log into an encrypted file labeled "Keep Out—Girl Coders Only." That made her smile, but Ginia's encryption layers on the file made her blink. Her husband must have added beginner hacking to his coding lessons.

Shay went over to the corner cupboard and got out an old computer mouse with princess stickers on it.

Nell raised an eyebrow. "Where'd you find that? That thing's ancient."

"It was in Aervyn's toy box. We tested different ways of doing the scan, and this works best."

Nell was pretty sure she hadn't caught up yet. "What scan?"

Shay set the mouse down in front of her and plugged it into a vacant USB port. "Here, try it. Just hold the mouse like you were going to use it, but don't do anything."

Nell followed instructions and watched her computer screen. In a few moments, a series of tables and chart readings popped up, along with a flashing pink "Yay, You're a Witch!" graphic.

Holy crap. Nell grabbed her cell phone and texted her brother.

Moments later, Jamie materialized in the room. Teleporting was a very convenient talent for quick arrivals. "Hey, my favorite nieces, what's up?"

Ginia gave him a hug. "We built a witch scan!"

Jamie had plenty of practice rolling with surprises. "Cool. What's that?"

Ginia led him over to Nell's chair and handed him the mouse. "Here, hold this."

Jamie looked at the princess stickers in perhaps not entirely fake disgust. "I'd be happy to get you girls a new mouse. This thing's an antique."

Mia laughed. "Don't be silly, Uncle Jamie. No one actually uses a mouse any more. It's our scanning device. Just sit there and hold it."

He followed instructions too, and pretty soon the "Yay, You're a Witch" graphic showed up onscreen again, along with party streamers and glittery stars.

Holy shit, he mindsent to Nell. *Did you help them with this?*

She just shook her head.

"Very glittery. How come I get pink messages—can't it tell I'm a boy witch?"

The triplets looked at each other in consternation. "Maybe we could add that. Does girl-witch power look different than boy-witch power?"

Ha, Nell sent. *You walked right into that one, brother mine.*

"Stop mindspeaking, Mama," said Ginia. "That's rude."

Jamie looked at Ginia in surprise. "You're picking up mindspeech now, kiddo?"

Three sets of eyes rolled. "No," Mia said. "You and Mama both get wrinkles between your eyes when you do it. Aunt Jennie says it's because you don't practice enough."

Jamie belatedly got smart enough to change the subject and turned back to his screen. "So, tell me about all these little graphs and squiggles. You're obviously scanning power signatures, but what's the rest of the data?"

Nell sat back and watched in amused pride as three heads joined his and started pointing to all the bells and whistles they'd built into their new toy.

In a few moments, he leaned back and glanced at Nell. "So, what we have here is a remote scanning device that can detect power traces and give a probability readout on whether the person being scanned is a witch."

Ginia nodded. "It only works for elemental and mind powers. Aunt Jennie said it wasn't a good idea to scan for some of the other kinds of power."

Nell blinked. "Aunt Jennie helped you with coding?"

Mia giggled. "Mama, don't be silly. She helped us with the scanning spell, cuz Ginia didn't know how to do that yet. Then Ginia spellcoded that to hook it up to the rest of what we'd done."

Okay, that made more sense. Aunt Jennie was awesome cool, but a spellcoder she was not.

"So, what do we do with this fancy new toy?" Jamie asked.

"Use it to scan Elorie," said Ginia. "Except we need a little help to make it work with a trackpad if she doesn't use a mouse."

Jamie laughed. "I think they're still using mice in Witch Central East, although maybe not one quite this old."

Ginia paused for a moment, looking suddenly shy. "And we wondered if maybe you could use it in Enchanter's Realm."

You didn't need to be a mama to read the hope gleaming in three sets of eyes. Nell felt her own misting over. She and Jamie had been the primary coding team for their gaming world for almost fifteen years. It looked like they had just gained an assistant staff of three.

Jamie looked over at Nell and grinned. "Oh, I think maybe we could find a use for it." He pointed at the graphics on his screen. "We might have to tweak your design a little, though."

Shay looked at the screen in confusion. "Why? What's wrong with it?"

Nell did the smart mama thing and slipped out to make lunch. Jamie could handle the explanation of why Realm wasn't pink and glittery.

~ ~ ~

Nell: Moira, have you had a chance to talk to Elorie?

Moira: Not today. She disappeared to the beach this morning, looking for more of her sea glass.

Nell: Hmm.

Sophie: What's up?

Nell: Well, I spent the morning digging into the fetching spell with my girls. It's clearly picking up power traces from Elorie, and I can't find any errors in their coding.

Moira: There must be, Nell. I'm not trying to tell you how to spellcode, but I wouldn't have missed a witch who practically lives under my own roof.

Nell: Exactly. Which is very puzzling. The girls have rigged up another nice piece of programming that might help. I was hoping I could run the test on the two of you.

Sophie: I'll be your guinea pig. What kind of test?

Nell: It's a virtual scan. They took a regular scanning spell—Aunt Jennie's, in this case—and twinned it with some snazzy programming code. Let me activate the spellcode, and then all you should need to do is hold onto your mouse.

Sophie: Should I be using power?

Nell: No, not necessary, although I'll have you do that in a minute so I can see how the readings change.

Sophie: It's not easy typing with one hand. Should I be feeling anything?

Nell: I'm done. It shows you have strong earth power, a little water, and an unidentified power source. The girls only have this set up to test for elemental and mind powers right now, so that would be your healing talent.

Sophie: Wow. Think how useful this would have been in the spring with Lauren!

Nell: I'm guessing Jamie's pretty happy he had to go to Chicago, but yeah. It's a pretty cool toy.

Moira: Can you really see Sophie's powers through the Internet, then?

Nell: More or less. It's not all that different from what the fetching spell does—it's just giving us more information.

Moira: I don't want to sound suspicious, but are you sure it isn't just reading your knowledge of Sophie? That's always a risk when we scan in person.

Nell: Do you have a spare witch nearby? We can test them without you telling me who it is.

Moira: In fact, there are witchlings eating cookies in my kitchen. Let me go get one.

Sophie: You so have to put this in Realm.

Nell: Jamie's already on it, with three very willing assistants.

Moira: All right, I have a volunteer. He just needs to hold this wee mousie, then?

Nell: That's all. Give me just a minute... Okay. The scan is picking up fire, water, and air power, with a little mind power as well.

Moira took the mouse back from Kevin and switched to video chat. She was getting pretty comfortable with all this modern gadgetry for an old witch, but some things were much easier done face-to-face. Nell and Sophie's faces showed up on her screen.

Making sure Kevin was fetching her a cookie as she'd asked, she turned back to Nell. "You're sure on the last? The rest is true enough, but we haven't tested young Kevin for the latter in quite some time."

Nell grinned. "That might be worth doing in the next day or two. I'd be very curious to see if our little scanning program is right."

Moira wasn't entirely convinced yet, but she had two other witchlings at her elbows clamoring to be scanned. Lizzie's readings showed her strong water elementals, and hints of something else. That was no surprise—little ones could grow new talents as fast as they grew out of their clothes.

When Sean held the mouse, Nell looked very surprised. "Sean, honey, are you a spellcaster?"

Sean brushed cookie crumbs off his face. "Gran says so, but I've only worked with small circles so far."

Moira hadn't lived this long without knowing some things weren't meant for small ears. She picked up the plate of cookies. "Why don't you three take the cookies into the garden and pick some nice, fresh flowers to brighten my table."

When their voices grew faint, she turned back to Nell. "What are you seeing in our Sean?"

Nell frowned. "I can't be sure of this part of the code—we haven't done enough testing. But Sean has a big spike in the unknown powers category, which could be healing, casting, or something more rare."

"I don't think he's a healer," Sophie said. "I spent some time with Sean last summer, and he didn't show any evidence of healing talent."

Moira nodded. "I agree, and we've seen no signs of astral travel or precognition. He does very well with complex spells for a boy of ten, so we assume he'll be a solid spellcaster."

"His spike is almost as big as Jamie's," said Nell.

Oh, my, Moira thought. Jamie was a talented spellcaster at the peak of his powers. "That's a little more than we thought we were dealing with. We haven't a full circle's worth of witches on hand at the moment, but the next time we do, perhaps we'll test him in a bigger circle."

"Maybe when we all come for witchling training this summer," Sophie said. "With me and Nell, you'll have enough, I think."

"Jamie and Nat are going to stay here," Nell said, "but Lauren would like to come. She's turning into an able trainer—with her mindspeaking, she could guide Sean through the process of hooking into a full circle quite nicely."

Moira's heart warmed at the thought of seeing Lauren again. She'd developed such a fondness for their first "fetched" witch. And it was good to know they had a spellcaster of some considerable talent to train, even if the method of discovery had been a bit unorthodox.

She glanced toward Great Gran's crystal ball, sitting in its usual place in the corner of the room. Perhaps if the darned thing had ever worked, they wouldn't need all these new-fangled witch tools. The old ones could be a tad unreliable.

Ah, well. Witches made do with what they had. "That's quite the pot your little scanning spell has stirred up, Nell. I'll speak with Elorie about what we've discovered—she coordinates training for the young ones."

"Do that." Nell frowned. "And if it turns out the readings are right, we have a bigger mystery to solve."

"And what's that, dear?"

Sophie spoke gently. "The fetching spell said Elorie has power, Aunt Moira. If this new tool of Nell's is accurate, she'll need to be scanned again."

Moira shook her head slowly. Her own power had reached out to Elorie in hope time and time again, but found no magic. It didn't seem possible that a wee gadget could see what she couldn't. "It will cause her pain, just in the asking."

"I know," Sophie said. "So let's not go there just yet, and take one step at a time. Test Kevin first—see if he has mind magic. If he does, then we can think about the next step."

"Aye. That much I can do. I'll contact Marcus myself." Moira turned at the sound of running footsteps down her hallway. "I'll let you know what we find."

"Blessed be, Aunt Moira."

Chapter 3

Elorie shook her head at Kevin. "Nope. My favorite color's not blue."

Kevin scowled. "I think your brain looked a little blue."

Elorie handed him a bowl of blueberries, still wet from a quick rinse after picking. "Maybe you're just hungry. Why don't we wait until Uncle Marcus gets here, and then you can try mindreading with someone who can help you?"

"I read about it all last night, ever since that computer test said I might have mind powers."

There was just no keeping secrets from witchlings. "And how do you know that's what the computer said? Weren't you in the back yard eating cookies?"

Kevin shrugged. "I dunno. I just knew it." Then his eyes got big. "Wait, *I just knew it.* Isn't that a sign of developing mind powers? Picking up things you're not supposed to know? I was just reading about that."

He scrambled into his backpack for a book, but Elorie didn't need a reference guide. Gran had known the results of the computer scan—and as a non-sensitive, she wouldn't have the barriers to keep out an emerging mind witch.

Kevin looked up from the page in his book, one of Gran's old, dusty ones. "It's true, Elorie!" He squinted his eyes and stared at her. "Think of your favorite color again."

Elorie focused as hard as she could on red. Strawberries. Fire engines. Blood. Eww. Back to strawberries.

He stared silently for a moment longer and then shrugged. "Your brain still looks blue. Huh—I wonder what I'm doing wrong."

Probably eating too many blueberries. She closed the book gently before he could dive back in. "Fortunately for you, there's a real mind witch coming over for tea, and you can ask him all the questions you like."

Kevin looked crestfallen. "I can't read the book?"

"Of course you can. You just can't read it all day long. I'll bet you fell asleep reading under the covers again last night, too." She grinned at his look of surprise. It didn't take a mindreader to know that, given the dark circles under his eyes, but she liked to keep her little secrets.

Elorie refilled his glass of milk. "Now remember, Uncle Marcus is a very skilled witch, but he's not used to working with children."

"You mean he doesn't like us."

Close enough, but since he was the strongest mind witch in their little corner of the world, he was the right person to test Kevin. He just lacked a fair amount in the bedside manners department.

"He lives alone, Kev. Some witches like to be very solitary, and Uncle Marcus is one of them. Sometimes that makes it hard to know how to be around people. Just use your best witchling manners, and it will be fine."

And this visit, she wouldn't be leaving the room. The last time Marcus had tested one of her students, he'd left behind a wake of tears and misery. Powerful witch or not, he had no right to make small boys cry.

Elorie tried to clear any acrimonious thoughts out of her head. When the witch in question could mindread, it was better to be thinking about milk and berries when he arrived. Judging from the voices outside, that event was imminent. She patted Kevin's hand and went to the door to greet her guests.

"Hi, Gran. Hello, Uncle Marcus, and welcome to my home."

"Blessed be." Uncle Marcus scowled and peered past her into the house. "Where is this student you want me to test? You can bring him out—I've promised Aunt Moira I won't eat him for afternoon tea."

So much for small talk. However, if Gran had given him a stern talking-to as well, maybe they could get through this testing without tears.

Elorie remembered how scary Uncle Marcus had seemed when she was a little girl and he'd threatened to throw her in his cauldron. Since—unlike most witches she knew—he actually had a cauldron, she'd kept her distance for a very long time. In hindsight, that had probably been his intent.

She stepped into the kitchen and gently closed Kevin's book again. "Uncle Marcus, this is Kevin. He's my nephew, and a big reader, as you can see." The two had actually met before, but Uncle Marcus was awful with names and relationships, even though that was a basic life skill in Nova Scotia.

Marcus sat down at the kitchen table and studied Kevin. Elorie put out a plate of treats and several cups of tea, and tried to be invisible. She didn't want to disrupt the testing, but she had no intention of leaving the kitchen. Since Gran was making herself very comfortable with a cup of tea and a cookie, it looked like Uncle Marcus was just going to have to cope with some observers.

Kevin tended to the quiet side of things, but he wasn't shy. He met Marcus's gaze for several moments, and then asked the important question. "So, do I have mind magic?"

Marcus raised an eyebrow. "What is my favorite color?"

Kevin concentrated.

"No, no, no." Marcus slammed his hand on the table. "You're trying far too hard. You need to relax your mind, not clench it up like a fist."

Elorie rescued her fallen spoon. No one was going to be doing a lot of relaxing if he kept pounding on the table. Well, except for Gran, who was stirring her tea as if nothing had happened. The gentle, calming scent of chamomile wafted over the table. Hmm. Perhaps Gran was doing a little more than just stirring.

Kevin shook his head. "I don't understand."

"Most people have very messy minds. They leave their thoughts hanging out where anyone can see them. Your Aunt Elorie here is worried I'm going to make you cry."

Kevin looked fascinated. "What else can you see?"

Marcus sat silent until Moira raised her eyebrow. Twice. "You're curious about why her mind looks blue today. It likely means you have some empathic talent."

Kevin cocked his head. "Empathic witches see feelings as colors?"

"Isn't that what I just said, youngling?"

"So Elorie's sad, then."

"Obviously." Marcus didn't sound the least bit perturbed about her emotional state, and Elorie was rather dismayed her privacy was that easy to invade.

Moira's spoon clinked in her tea and she spoke pointedly. "Polite mind witches don't read the thoughts or feelings of others without their permission."

Marcus grunted. "I've never been a polite witch."

The sound of a giggle shocked everyone. Kevin seemed mortified to discover it had come from his mouth.

Elorie held her breath as Marcus's scowl deepened, but when he spoke, his tone was relatively civil. "With all these messy minds around, you don't need to work hard to hear what people think. You only need to open your mind a little, and their thoughts will come to you. Unfortunately."

Elorie started walking through the steps to bake oatmeal cookies in her mind. Perhaps that would keep her more embarrassing thoughts quiet.

Kevin considered for a moment. "But your mind isn't messy, so how can I hear your favorite color?"

"You're a thinking witch." Marcus nodded grudgingly. "That's good. You can't hear my mind unless I want you to. Right now, I'm sending that thought out toward you. I want to see if you can open your mind enough to hear it."

"How do I do that?"

"It will require some actual effort on your part. Magic is hard work."

Kevin scowled. "You just told me not to work so hard. Training's hard work, too, and I need your help."

Elorie looked on in shock, wishing she'd ever shown that kind of guts, and Gran hid a smile behind her cup of tea.

Marcus nodded shortly and tapped the book on the table. "Pretend you're reading, where your brain is focused, but ready to learn something new."

Kevin thought for a moment, and then closed his eyes. Moments later, they popped open. "Orange!"

Elorie tried not to let her disappointment show. Marcus never wore anything but black. There was no chance his favorite color was something as bright and cheerful as orange.

"Not bad. Perhaps you'll make a decent witch one day."

Uncle Marcus's favorite color was *orange*?

Marcus picked up a handful of berries. "Now, tell me what else you heard."

Kevin blushed and looked down at the table. "I didn't mean to."

Marcus snorted. "My mind isn't messy. This is a test, my young witchling. A decent mind witch should have picked up more than just a color."

Straightening his shoulders, Kevin answered. "You have an itch on the back of your neck. You wish Elorie put raisins in her cookies." He paused, and then spoke in a voice full of soft sorrow. "And you miss your brother."

Dead silence. Elorie could see Gran's face pale as a very dark moment of family history got yanked into the light.

Marcus's voice was very husky, and probably not as gruff as he thought it was. "Aye. I do. And it's hazelnuts her cookies need, not raisins. You need to practice."

Kevin stood up and wrapped his arms around Marcus's neck. "You're not as mean as they said."

Elorie wondered when she'd landed on the alien planet where Uncle Marcus tolerated hugs from children. Then his deep voice spoke inside her head. *I'm not quite as old and crotchety as you think, my dear. And you keep forgetting the flour in those mental cookies you're making.*

Marcus touched Kevin's back awkwardly. "Enough. Go find someone else to bother." He looked at Moira as Kevin raced out the back door. "He'll need training, and clearly no one else here is competent enough to handle it. Now, tell me about this new scan that found his powers."

Uncle Marcus was going to help with training? Elorie looked around for flying pigs.

Moira sniffled and wiped her cheeks. "It's something Nell did with her fancy spellcoding. I don't pretend to understand it. The children each held my computer mouse, and Nell got a reading on their powers. Most we already knew, but it suggested Kevin might have mind talents."

"It shouldn't have taken a computer to see that."

"And it wouldn't have, if our best mind witch wasn't a hermit." Oooh, Gran was steamed. "When was the last time you bothered to come check the young ones for talent?"

Marcus's face could have been made of stone. "You know where to reach me, and you know how to do a basic scan."

Now it was Elorie's temper bubbling. "It's never any one witch's job to monitor all the young ones." She hurled her next thought—if her mind was as leaky as all that, he should hear it well enough. *I can't, and she's getting old.*

She thought he looked a little pained, at least. "It's good his talent was found, one way or the other. And now we need to test Elorie as well, do we not?"

Gran looked horrified. A sick feeling slid into Elorie's gut. "What do you mean?"

Marcus raised an eyebrow. "Kevin's been mindreading more than you all realize." He looked at Moira. "What in tarnation is going on here?"

Gran picked up Elorie's hands. "I'm sorry, child. I was trying to keep you from getting hurt, and I've truly messed this up. You know that Nell's fetching spell pulled you into Witches' Chat the other day."

Elorie nodded. "Sure, but wasn't there something wrong with Nell's code?"

Marcus snorted. "I doubt it. Nell's a very talented witch."

"How would you know?" Elorie's temper was spiking again. "You've probably only seen her twice in the last five years." *And if you were your usual friendly self, she ran screaming the other way.* She no longer cared if he heard that or not.

I'm not deaf. And you're having a temper tantrum better suited to a witchling. His face was back to imitating a statue. "Nell and Jamie do some impressive spellwork for the witch-only levels of Enchanter's Realm."

Elorie had that alien planet feeling again. "You know about their video game?"

"I'm the third-highest ranked witch in Realm."

Uncle Marcus played video games? He was *good* at video games?

"Yes, quite good, in fact." Marcus raised an eyebrow. "But let's get back to what Nell's little scan said about you, shall we?"

Gran's voice was gentle. "What you picked up from Kevin's mind isn't entirely accurate. We haven't scanned Elorie, but Nell would like to. She and her girls built the scan to give better readings than the fetching spell."

Moira looked down for a moment, and then met Elorie's eyes. "You don't know this, my beloved girl, but I scan you myself quite regularly. I've always hoped you would come into the powers to match your witch's heart."

Elorie reached out to ease the sadness and guilt. "I know that—it always makes your eyes sad when you test me." She took a deep breath, trying to ease the turbulence in her stomach. "I'm not a witch. I don't know what's wrong with Nell's spells, but I can't believe they could see something you can't."

"I'm not as sure of that anymore, child. I missed Kevin's mind powers. Perhaps I missed something in you as well."

The slick in Elorie's gut was almost overwhelming. "What are you saying?"

Gran took her hands. "Let Nell test you, sweet girl."

Elorie would have raged at anyone else who asked. As it was, she struggled to contain the anguished fury of the thirteen-year-old girl who had begged and pleaded with the universe for a shred of power and been denied.

Marcus reached for a cookie. "Alternatively, I'd be happy to do the honors."

Over her dead body. She wasn't a child anymore. If she had to be tested, she could at least choose how. Trying to tamp down her roiling emotions, she looked straight at Gran. "Arrange the test. And when I fail, I want this to be the last. No more scans, and no more sad eyes. I am what I am, and it needs to be enough."

~ ~ ~

Nell slid her chair over to let Ginia fit in beside her. "Remember, kiddo—this is probably going to be hard for Elorie."

"Because Aunt Moira doesn't think she's a witch?"

Murky waters. "Well, none of us really knows the answer to that question right now. We have two ways of knowing that are giving us different answers, and that's a bit tricky."

"Our code's right, Mama."

The trouble was, Nell agreed with her middle triplet. "One step at a time. Let's see what the scan says, and then we'll have more data to work from. Go ahead and spell us into video chat."

Nell had commandeered Jamie and spent all day working with the three girls, refining and testing the scanning code. In addition to mind and elemental powers, it now took a reading on healing and spellcasting talents. They could distinguish between active, trained power and untrained potential, and even get a decent estimate of magical strength.

It was a sweet piece of coding, and they'd tested it on practically every witch in California who owned a computer mouse.

Mia and Shay were at Jamie's place, working to integrate the scans into Enchanter's Realm. Ginia, who had the deepest attachment to Moira, had asked to stay for Elorie's test.

Nell hoped that wasn't a really bad idea.

Ginia bounced on the chair beside her. "Hi, Aunt Moira!"

"Hello, sweetling. And hello to you as well, Nell."

Nell could see Elorie's face. Her eyes were full of sadness and dread.

Her empathetic witchling could see it, too. "Don't be scared, Elorie. The scan is really easy, and we worked hard all day to make it a lot better."

A face Nell recognized, but couldn't name, came onto the screen.

"This is my nephew Marcus," said Moira. "I think you've met him a time or two, Nell, but it's been a while."

Marcus spoke in a kind of arrogant growl. "She'll know me better as Gandalf."

Ginia gasped and stomped her foot. "*Oooohh!* You locked me in a high tower yesterday and gave the key to the evil sorcerer's apprentice!"

Marcus raised an eyebrow. "*You're* Warrior Girl?"

Nell thought he should look a little more impressed. Ginia, having just displaced Sophie, was now the number-four-ranked player in the witch-only levels of Realm, and hot on Gandalf's heels. Her girl had some mad gaming skills.

"Don't worry, Mama," Ginia whispered behind her hand. "He's toast—he just doesn't know it yet. *Nobody* locks me in a tower and gets away with it."

Marcus held up his mouse. "Okay, Warrior Girl—run this scan of yours on me. I want to see how it works."

Nell leaned forward and hit a few keys. "I've sent a screen-share so you can see the readouts we get." She nodded at Ginia to start the test.

The trio of heads on the Nova Scotia end all squinted at the screen. Marcus read aloud. "Mind powers at moderate to strong levels. That's right."

Elorie pointed at the screen. "Strong air elementals, weak in water and earth."

Marcus snorted. "Someone needs to double-check their code. Air and water are correct, but I don't have earth power."

Ginia glared. "You do so, Gandalf."

Nell elbowed her witchling. "This is real life, daughter mine, not the game. No trash talking—show some manners."

Moira chortled. "You might keep that in mind yourself, Marcus."

Still mutinous, Ginia eyed her archnemesis through the screen. "Have Aunt Moira test you, then. I bet you do so have earth power."

The tone of her delivery earned another elbow, but Nell couldn't fault the idea. Marcus raised his eyebrow again. "That's not necessary. I'm a trained witch; I can pull any power sources available to me."

Ginia crossed her arms. "So pull earth power, then."

He gave an arrogant shrug and reached off-screen, coming back with a closed flower bud in his hand. Nell smiled. Moira always had flowers nearby. Marcus closed his eyes for a moment, and then focused on the bud.

Ginia was the only one not the least bit surprised when the flower very slowly bloomed. Moira gave a delighted laugh. "I guess you can teach an old witch some new tricks."

Marcus studied the flower a moment longer. "That's some nice coding you've done, Nell."

Nell grinned. "Wasn't me. Warrior Girl and her two sidekicks did almost all the work."

Marcus scowled. "There are three of you?"

"Yep," Ginia said. "But if you wanna take on all three of us, you have to leave the witch-only levels. Fight us code-to-code. My sisters aren't witches."

He almost cracked a smile. "I think I'll stay where I have magic on my side, little fighter. I have no doubt the three of you could take me down coding with one hand behind your backs."

It took a moment for Nell, caught up in the banter between her daughter and Marcus, to notice Elorie's white face.

Oh, shit. They had more important things to do than schedule a Realm take-down. Time to end the agony of waiting. "Okay, Elorie, you're up next. Grab the mouse, and let's see what we've got."

Elorie sat frozen. Marcus shoved the mouse in her hand with an impatient arrogance that had Nell gritting her teeth.

Ginia ran the test, and the numbers popped up on both screens.

Moira was the first to speak. "I don't understand this."

Nell shook her head. "I don't either. It says Elorie has significant power potential, source unknown."

"Speak English," Marcus growled.

Ginia stepped into the breach. "It means she's a witch, and probably a strong one, but we don't know what kind. It's not any of the types the test can read."

"So, what can't your primitive test read?"

Nell growled. No one insulted her kiddos.

"Chill, Mama. He's just a grumpy old man who wishes he could code half as good as me." Ginia ticked off on her fingers. "It can do elemental, mind, and healing. So that leaves precog and animal magics."

Moira shook her head. "Those talents always develop very young and very hard. We'd hardly have missed Elorie communing with the spirits or flying with the seagulls."

Marcus crossed his arms. "Use of those power sources still leaves traces we should be able to detect. I've scanned Elorie myself. There are no traces."

"The code hasn't been wrong yet," Ginia said firmly. "And it says Elorie's a witch."

Moira's helpless shrug was a perfect reflection of how Nell felt. How could you prove the existence of power only a computer could see?

Marcus was still in arrogant-king-to-peasant mode. "Are you saying my testing is wrong, little girl?"

Ginia laid her hands on the table in full Warrior Girl form. "Maybe Elorie is an extra-special kind of witch we've never seen before."

"Maybe your nine-year-old imagination is overriding your logic."

"Maybe your imagination got drowned in a moat and eaten by crocodiles."

Steam was going to come out of her daughter's head any minute, and Nell wasn't in any mood to stop her. Hell, she was a hairsbreadth away from stepping up and holding her cloak. Pompous old witch.

"Enough." Elorie started to speak, eyes anguished. Then the screen went blank. Ginia dove under the desk to troubleshoot. When she didn't surface quickly, Nell went down to help. Ten minutes later, she called Moira's landline.

No one had any idea what had happened, but Moira's computer was entirely cooked.

Chapter 4

Elorie sat down at the kitchen table, rubbing her tired hands. After a full day of jewelry making, she appreciated both the break and the sublime smells emanating from the stovetop—the unmistakable scent of basil, melting butter, and something else she couldn't identify.

"That smells incredible, sweetie."

Her husband turned around and grinned, his "I Cook for Sex" apron splattered in unidentified green stuff. Aaron was an amazing cook, but not a neat one. "Pesto meatballs and risotto. It'll be just another couple of minutes."

Pesto explained the green goo on the apron. "Whatever you're trying to soften me up for, it's working."

"You're just a lucky bystander. I'm making pesto omelets for breakfast tomorrow, so I blended a fresh batch this afternoon. I figured I could use some of it to liven up our dinner."

"Gran's totally jealous of your basil patch. Even with magic, she can't match it."

Aaron grinned. "We non-witches have our skills."

And he was a constant, solid reminder of that. Elorie got up from the table and laid her head against his back. "I'll miss your cooking while I'm gone. I wish you could come with me."

He turned around and popped a meatball in her mouth. "So do I, but the guests get grumpy when there's no one here to feed them."

While technically they were co-owners of the Sea Trance Bed & Breakfast Inn, Elorie knew she could slip away for a week and hardly cause a ripple in the smooth functioning of the inn.

Aaron, unfortunately, was fairly indispensible, especially since their most experienced staff person was currently out on maternity leave. They'd managed to sneak away the night before to celebrate their anniversary, but a whole week was unthinkable.

He carried two plates to the table and Elorie followed, drooling. As they sat down, he reached for one of her hands and started gently massaging. "Are you all ready for the show?"

Elorie nodded as she spooned in risotto. She'd been feverishly preparing inventory for the San Francisco Art Fair for over two months, ever since her totally unexpected selection as an emerging artist. Her mentor insisted she would need at least ten thousand dollars of wares to sell, double that if her sea glass was popular.

It was mind-boggling to imagine selling that much in a weekend, but Elorie believed in her art. She had almost four hundred pieces ready to take with her to California, and her exhausted hands were evidence of just how hard she had worked.

"I need to go back out tonight and pack up for the plane, but everything is ready to go."

Aaron smiled and switched to rubbing her other hand. "I'll come out and help you with that. Your booth setup should arrive in California tomorrow, and Nell's going to pick you up at the airport."

Elorie tried to find the energy to protest. "She doesn't need to do that. I can catch a cab."

"And when was the last time we let a guest take a cab?"

He had a point. "It will be nice to see everyone again. I made sea-glass pendants for the girls, since they were so enamored with mine when I visited in March."

"They're pretty magical for young girls. I've seen it here, too. Lizzie would happily have a different necklace for every day of the week."

Aaron held out his last meatball. All of hers had magically disappeared. Maybe her super-secret hidden witch talent only worked on meatballs.

He tugged her hair, as if following her jumbled thoughts. "Sorry, I didn't mean to remind you about all that." She'd spent a decent chunk of their night away in tears.

"It wasn't you, it was the meatballs." Her husband, long used to her conversational tangents, waited patiently for her to start making sense. Rather than explain the meatballs, she just told him what he really wanted to know.

"I've already wasted far too much of my life hoping to turn into a witch. I've held on to that dream for so long, what happened with the computer scan was bound to affect me some. But I have a good life, and a really important opportunity coming up, and I don't plan to blow it by worrying about stealth magical powers."

He just smiled. Aaron was always good for a sanity check, and when your world was full of witches and spells, that was a very good thing.

Getting away for their anniversary had helped. Her adult life had always had two important gravitational pulls. Her work for and with the witching community was one, and her life with Aaron and her sea glass was the other. A little time away had helped her find steady footing again, on entirely non-magical ground.

She reached for his hands. "When I get back, maybe we can get started on adding a little Shaw around here."

Aaron scooped her up. He moved fast for an innkeeper. "What's wrong with now?"

That pretty much ended dinner.

~ ~ ~

Jamie scowled at the melted computer parts on the table. Marcus had quietly overnighted him the innards of Moira's cooked computer, but there wasn't much to see besides a mess of mangled metal.

Not that he could see very well with three curly heads all leaning over the table too.

"What do you think?" Ginia asked.

"There's not a lot to work with, girls. I was hoping Elorie had just shorted something out and we could get a read on some of the data, but..."

Mia giggled. "I don't think there's any data left alive in there. She totally fried it."

Jamie nudged Shay, usually the most contemplative of the three. "What do you think?"

Shay tilted her head. "Are we sure Elorie did this?"

Quiet didn't mean slow, Jamie thought. Shay was by far the best debugger of the three because she never skipped any steps, even when the answers seemed obvious.

Mia shrugged. "What else could have done it? Uncle Jamie, have you ever seen anything like this?"

He shook his head. "No, but Shay asked a great question. I suspect Elorie's the culprit, but good coders rule out weird possibilities, too. Elorie wasn't the only person in the room when this happened."

Mia considered the melted mess. "I bet Aervyn could melt a hard drive if he wanted to, and he might not even have to be in the same room."

Three sets of eyes looked up in sudden fascination. Uh, oh. This was the kind of stuff where he was supposed to be the adult. His internal debate didn't last long. He wasn't a father yet, and trying to zap hard drives with magic sounded like serious fun.

Mia grinned and jumped up. "I'll go get Aervyn."

Shay looked at Jamie. "I bet you could do it too, couldn't you?"

Jamie started digging in boxes, looking for old hard drives. They were about to find out.

Aervyn bounced into the room with glee written all over his face. "I get to melt computers, Uncle Jamie? Can I blast 'em, just like Cyclops?"

Jamie jumped in front of his brand-new laptop. "Hold on a minute, hot stuff. Not this computer. And, think Superman, not Cyclops—focused magic. Your mom will be mad at me if we start a big fire in the basement again."

He picked up an old hard drive and sat it next to Moira's melted heap on the table. "First, let me explain what we're trying to do. We think that one of the witches in Nova Scotia managed to turn computer insides like these ones—into this."

Aervyn looked at the cooked hard drive in fascination. "It's pretty hard to melt metal stuff. They must be a pretty good witch."

"Well, that's part of the problem. We're not sure who did it, or how they did it. I thought we could do some experiments and see if we can copy what they did."

Jamie stopped talking and let his nephew think for a minute. He had his own ideas to try, but Aervyn was a highly creative witch. Left to work out his own solution, he might well come up with something none of them had considered.

Aervyn looked up with a grin that gave Jamie just enough warning to throw up a hasty training circle. Nell was pretty lenient, but she drew the line at house fires. A few seconds later, the edges of the hard drive were melted, but it wasn't anywhere close to the puddled goop of Moira's drive.

Aervyn frowned. "It's pretty hard. The metal doesn't want to melt." His eyes brightened. "I could do it with a circle to help."

Jamie shook his head. "Not just yet, hot stuff. We learned something important here. You used fire power, right? If you can't melt it by yourself that way, then that's probably not how this happened. We need to think of a different way to try."

Ginia held up a mouse. "If we believe it was Elorie who did it, then she was using one of these."

Shay spoke up. "And she was on an open Internet connection."

Jamie hardwired the mouse into the hard drive. "Aervyn, do you think you can direct power through this?"

For once, his trainee looked bewildered. "Maybe."

Several tests later, including one where Jamie and Aervyn joined forces, they had managed to do no more than melt the edges of the hard drive, and one small witchling was a tired, hungry boy.

Jamie sent him upstairs for cookies and stared at the failed experiments on the table. He looked up to see Ginia eyeing his laptop with speculation. He'd been a witch trainer long enough to know when trouble was brewing.

"Don't even think it, niece of mine."

She looked so innocent. "Think what?"

"Whatever you were planning to do with my computer."

"Not your computer, exactly. I bet I know how we could do this, but I need a full computer, not just a hard drive."

He hoped it was for a good cause. Jamie concentrated for a moment and teleported one of the old clunkers from his home office. "You can use this one, but use the firewalled port to hook it up to the Net. We don't want to fry anything else by accident."

"I'm not going to fry this one—I just need the screen interface." She nodded to her sisters. "Help me wire the old drive into the USB port."

Jamie sat and watched, and soon the old drive was hanging off one of the clunker's USB ports. They were good, and he was still totally lost. "What are you planning?"

Ginia flexed her fingers in a movement common to master coders everywhere. "I'm going to melt it with spellcode. Go away. I'll tell you when it's ready."

Damn. Why hadn't he thought of that?

He went upstairs to swipe some of Aervyn's cookies. By the time he came back, three faces were grinning with maniacal glee. Mia bounced in a circle. "It's gonna work, Uncle Jamie. Watch!"

Ginia focused, clicked twice with her mouse, and the old hard drive hanging off the side of her computer turned into a puddle. The acrid smell of melted metal underscored her success.

Jamie hugged his excited nieces and tried to think. He was totally impressed. There was only one problem. No one in Nova Scotia could spellcode their way out of a paper bag. Well, Marcus could, but he hadn't been the one sitting at Moira's computer when it fried.

He was pretty sure they hadn't actually learned anything at all, except that Ginia was a freaking awesome spellcoder. Elorie was still a total mystery.

~ ~ ~

Ginia prepared to login to Realm. She had a whole hour, a new strategy, and three new spells. Gandalf was going down. He deserved it, for thinking her coding sucked. If she could spellcode a computer melt, she could take down some old guy who learned to code in the last century.

Well, he was actually a pretty good coder, but his spellcode had some cracks. She'd tried taking him in a duel, and he'd locked her up in a tower. Her friends had busted her out, but he was too strong in a head-on battle. She needed to be sneaky.

She logged in and headed to the pub, pretty sure she'd find him on his usual chair in the corner. She didn't get that—Realm was a lot more fun with friends, but Gandalf always played alone. People had tried—the third-best player in Realm would make a powerful ally—but he was always his usual rude self, and they eventually went away.

Today he was dressed like a monk. Generally, the simpler his disguise, the more dangerous he was. She set a couple of warding spells in place just to be safe.

<u>Warrior Girl:</u> Good evening to ya, Gandalf.

<u>Gandalf:</u> Merry meet, Warrior Girl. I see your friends aided in your escape. Can I buy you a drink?

Warrior Girl: Some of us *have* friends. Cider, please.

Gandalf: Get the girl a cuppa. Make it a small one, since she's being rude today.

Warrior Girl: I have a proposition to make.

Gandalf: Big word for a little girl.

Warrior Girl: I'm big enough.

Gandalf: Really. And what big things have you done lately?

Warrior Girl: I melted a computer this morning.

Gandalf: On purpose?

Warrior Girl: I'm a well-trained witch. I don't do magic by accident.

Gandalf: Ah. Trying to recreate the incident with Aunt Moira's computer, were you?

Warrior Girl: Yup.

Gandalf: Learn anything?

Warrior Girl: Well, it wasn't just power overload. Even Aervyn couldn't melt a hard drive that way, and he tried. Uncle Jamie thinks he could do it with the juice of a circle behind him, but—

Gandalf: If the baddest witchling in the West couldn't do it alone, then it's unlikely that's what happened.

Warrior Girl: Exactly.

Gandalf: So, if Aervyn couldn't do it, then how'd you pull it off?

Warrior Girl: I didn't just use magic; I used coding, too.

Gandalf: You spellcoded a computer melt? Remind me to keep you away from my electronics.

Warrior Girl: It worked, but you're the only spellcoder at Aunt Moira's house.

Gandalf: I didn't cook her computer, little fighter.

Warrior Girl: Could you?

<u>Gandalf:</u> Good question. I don't happen to have a spare one around to test on, however.

<u>Warrior Girl:</u> Uncle Jamie doesn't think Elorie could have spellcoded.

<u>Gandalf:</u> Ha. The girl can hardly answer email.

<u>Warrior Girl:</u> But what if she did it by accident? Not spellcoding, exactly, but something like that.

<u>Gandalf:</u> Hmm. Different process, but same result?

<u>Warrior Girl:</u> Huh?

<u>Gandalf:</u> Never mind. You've got me thinking now, which I'm guessing was your intent.

<u>Warrior Girl:</u> Yup. You might be a crusty old witch, but you're pretty smart.

<u>Gandalf:</u> Be gone with you, brat.

Ginia logged out of Realm and giggled. Mission accomplished. Well, two missions, actually. It probably *was* a good idea for Gandalf to think about Elorie's magic. Maybe he'd figure something out.

More importantly, however, the conversation had distracted him long enough for her to plant her weaving spells. By this time tomorrow, his two most potent spells wouldn't recognize him as caster. They'd belong to his two biggest challengers besides her. She hoped they got the hint and ganged up on him. And while they were doing that, she'd be going on a spell raid.

Warrior Girl was going to rule Realm. It was just a matter of time.

~ ~ ~

"It's so you don't forget about us while you're gone," Lizzie said.

Jeebers, Elorie thought. You'd think she was going away for years instead of a week. Her three students had shown up with a care package of homemade snickerdoodles, some freshly picked blueberries, and a painstakingly drawn and lettered card—clearly Lizzie's handiwork.

"We picked the berries this afternoon," Kevin said. "There were more, but it was hard to stop eating them."

Elorie looked at the gallon bucketful and tried not to giggle. It didn't seem likely they would let her take those on the plane. Aaron would be serving blueberry pancakes to their guests for days. And the snickerdoodles wouldn't make it as far as the plane—their cinnamon-y goodness was already teasing her nose.

She hugged Lizzie. "I'm only going for a few days, so I won't forget you, and I most definitely won't be hungry. Don't get into any trouble while I'm gone, okay?" She looked at Sean as she said the last.

He rolled his eyes. "We don't try to get into trouble. It just kind of finds us."

"Find a better hiding place." She kissed the top of his head, sure to annoy him. "I don't want Gran having to do a lot of spellwork while I'm gone. Remember, she tires more easily than she thinks."

"She won't have to," Kevin said. "Uncle Marcus is staying here while you're gone. He says we need better supervision."

Uncle Marcus? Wow. He only came out of his cave a couple of times a year, and never for more than a day or two.

"He likes people more than you think," Kevin said, and then blushed. "Oops, sorry. I'm not too good at mind-witch manners yet. Uncle Marcus says I need to practice harder, but your mind is really leaky."

Lovely. Just what she needed to hear as she headed off to Witch Central, where there were mind witches practically wall-to-wall. "You can practice while I'm gone. Or maybe if you're hearing things you shouldn't, you could at least help keep Sean out of trouble."

Kevin shook his head. "Nope. His mind isn't leaky at all."

Lizzie talked with her mouth full of blueberries. "Is my brain leaky?"

Sean grinned. "It's gonna be leaking blueberries soon if you don't stop eating them. You're gonna have purple poop, too."

"Eeeewwww, I will not," Lizzie said. She looked at Elorie. "Can poop really turn purple?"

"How many of those have you eaten?"

Lizzie contemplated the blueberry container. "Maybe one whole bucket. Granny Moira said I could eat as many as I wanted. She said blueberries are good for witchlings."

Elorie gave her a hug. "They're very good for you—and that many blueberries will definitely give you purple poop. Did Gran want any blueberries for herself?"

"We left her a bucketful," Kevin said.

"Maybe she'll have purple poop, too." Lizzie seemed to think that was a pretty cool possibility. "And the blueberries made her stop crying."

Elorie's purple-poop induced giggles shut off abruptly. "Gran was crying?"

"Just a little," Sean said. "She wouldn't tell us why. She said that sometimes old witches just get a little teary."

"She was sitting with her scrying bowl," Lizzie said. "I think she was sad because it wouldn't answer her question."

Kevin gave Lizzie a strange look, the kind that triggered Elorie's "uh, oh" radar. "What's going on, Kev?"

He shook his head. "Uncle Marcus said I shouldn't talk about things I pick up accidentally from other people's minds."

Tricky territory. "Mostly you shouldn't, but sometimes it's important to share things about somebody you love. Is Lizzie right about why Gran was sad?"

Kevin nodded. "Yeah, but how did Lizzie hear that? Gran only said it inside her head."

Lizzie grabbed another handful of blueberries. "Maybe I'm a mind witch, too. Or maybe I'm just a good guesser." She seemed entirely unconcerned about a possible new magical power.

Just what we need, Elorie thought—a whole flock of mind witches with questionable manners. It took a moment to recognize the spurt of jealousy in her belly. Why couldn't she have been the child with a growing collection of nice, normal magical talents?

Crazy thoughts like that were a sure sign of just how ridiculous she was getting about what some computer scan said. It was time for nice, normal Elorie Shaw, non-witch, to go to bed.

Chapter 5

Nell sat down at her computer and prepared to get some serious grocery shopping done. Not only did she have her hordes to feed, but poor morning-sick Nat couldn't stand the sight of even online food, so she had two grocery orders to fill.

Aervyn said there was only one baby in Nat's tummy, but Nell had to wonder. Her nausea had been far worse with the triplets.

She'd only made it as far as the virtual cheese aisle when a Witches' Chat alert popped up on her screen.

Nell: Good morning, Moira.

Moira: It's not, actually—it's Marcus. Hang on a minute while I change my user name.

Marcus: There, that's better.

Nell: We can do video chat, if you like.

Marcus: No, I'd prefer this conversation stay private for the time being.

Nell: What can I do for you? How is Elorie doing?

Marcus: You'll know that before I will. She's on a plane heading your direction.

Nell: Yeah, we'll pick her up in a few hours. I don't think we'll be able to entirely avoid talking about what happened, but we'll try to keep it out of the way of her art show.

Marcus: Isn't being a witch more important than any hobby?

Nell: Spoken like an old-school witch. Elorie is a deeply talented artist, and if what I hear is true, she'll likely earn more in the four days of the Art Fair than most people in Nova Scotia earn in six months.

Marcus: I stand corrected. Her bobbles are attractive enough, but they're just beach glass. Decoration.

Nell: This from the guy who has the biggest costume collection in Realm?

Marcus: Those are necessary for my game strategy.

Nell: Dammit, warn me when you're going to be funny. I just spit coffee all over my monitor.

Marcus: Try a simple kitchen spell, dear.

Nell: I'm not a kitchen witch, and only Moira gets to call me dear. If you're not careful, Gandalf, I'll be helping my daughter take you down a notch.

Marcus: She doesn't need your help.

Nell: Oh, really.

Marcus: I'm the biggest challenge she has left, and it's not going to take her much longer to leave me in the dust. She took a good run at it earlier today. The little punk sent a sneaker to try to infiltrate one of my spells. I'm not entirely convinced there was only one. She's a very tricky little witchling.

Nell: Well, I guess you're not a total loss.

Marcus: What I am is the only witch in Nova Scotia who believes your computer scans. Which means, like it or not, I'm in a position to help.

Nell: I don't know that there's much of anything to do until we can figure out what kind of power source Elorie's accessing. The girls and Jamie are huddling over code, trying to figure it out.

Marcus: Warrior Girl got me to thinking this morning, and I have an idea about that.

Nell: All ears.

Marcus: Her power might be connected to the online world in some way. A kind of power we haven't seen before.

Nell: It seems a little hard to believe she has some kind of completely unique magical talent.

Marcus: Exactly. Perhaps she's not unique.

Nell: Now you've lost me.

Marcus: Pay better attention, then.

Nell: Careful, or I'll have Moira drag out her cauldron for you to scrub.

Marcus: I'm in possession of an excellent scrubbing spell. Let me try to explain more simply. Elorie's not the first witch to combine technology and magic.

Nell: Well, there's spellcoding, but that's different.

Marcus: How?

Nell: It's a blend of magical power sources with online code. But the power sources are the traditional ones.

Marcus: Correct. Can every witch spellcode?

Nell: Hell, no.

Marcus: Why not?

Nell: What is this, a test? Because most of them are crappy coders, for one.

Marcus: Agreed. But think about Realm. There are plenty of players in the witch-only levels who are pathetic spellcoders, and it's not always well-correlated to either their coding capabilities or their strength as a witch.

Nell: True... Wait—are you suggesting that spellcoding is a separate talent?

Marcus: Something like that.

Nell: Keep talking.

Marcus: If spellcoding was simply about adding good code together with decent magical strength, then I think the rankings in Realm would be very different. Look at your daughter. She's an innovative little witchling, and a smart coder, but she can't come close to matching my magical power yet. She's been a witch for what, a few months now?

Nell: Huh. Yeah, she's leapfrogged some pretty skilled witches recently. You don't think it's just her coding skills?

Marcus: Your husband Daniel has reason to respect my coding abilities. I'm not quite at his level, but not all that far behind, either. Your daughter would find me more difficult to beat code-to-code.

Nell: That's not the impression you gave her.

Marcus: Contrary to popular opinion, I don't eat young girls for breakfast.

Nell: That's still open for debate. So, you think she has some separate dose of spellcoding talent.

Marcus: I'm wondering if perhaps there is a magical ability we've never really isolated and identified because it tends to come along with other powers.

Nell: Ah. And you think Elorie might possess this talent.

Marcus: Yes. And only that talent.

Nell: But any known talent leaves power traces. Why wouldn't this one?

Marcus: It does. It simply leaves them in a different place.

Nell: ??

Marcus: Online, Nell. That would be why Moira and I can't read it, but your scanner did.

Nell: It leaves virtual power traces?

Marcus: A fascinating thought, no? And one I leave with you to pursue. There are very few computer-competent witches on this coast, but you have access to two groups with deep coding skills and witch power. A good test population, I would think.

<u>Nell</u>: Yeah, the witch-level Realm players would go nuts to help with this. What's the second group?

<u>Marcus</u>: Your family, my dear. If this is a talent that runs in family trees, I'd predict it runs straight through you.

Nell stared at her suddenly blank monitor. Dammit, he'd just called her "dear" again. The man had no social skills and some seriously outdated ideas about women, but he'd jumped to a plausible theory faster than any of the spellcoding geniuses in her household.

She looked at her hands ruefully. Spellcoding came so naturally she'd never really tried to break down how it worked. Leave it to some crusty old hermit witch to ask the obvious.

Time to page the troops. She'd set them loose on Marcus's brainstorm before heading to the airport to fetch Elorie.

~ ~ ~

Nell had a strange moment of déjà vu as she waited with Aervyn in the always-bustling San Francisco airport. Why was it that her fetching spell kept finding these women who were unhappy to be witches? Maybe next time around they could grab some nice person who would say "thank you" and show up for the occasional solstice circle.

Lauren's first days as a witch had been more than a little rocky, and Elorie's didn't look to be any easier—hell, they couldn't even reach consensus that she *was* a witch.

"Mama, do you need a snack?" Aervyn asked. "You feel grumpy."

Nell grinned. He was probably right. He was also angling for one of the cookies she had stashed in her bag. She pulled out the cookie container and handed it to her permanently hungry son.

Aervyn opened the tin and studied the contents for a moment. Then he handed Nell two of the three cookies inside. "Here. I think you need more cookies than I do. I'm only a teeny, tiny bit grumpy."

Punk witchling. She rubbed his head and took the two cookies. Passengers started flooding out the arrivals gate, and Nell tried to spot Elorie.

"I see her, Mama!"

Elorie waved and walked over to meet them, carrying the world's biggest backpack.

"That's a huge bag, girl," Nell said. "How'd you get that on the plane?"

Elorie sighed. "I'm not sure, exactly, but it has most of my work for the show, and I wasn't about to let it out of my sight. Customs was a small hassle, but I'm here now, and grateful."

Aervyn held out half his cookie. "Here, have some of my cookie. It's good for making the grumpies go away."

Elorie smiled, clearly used to questionable witchling manners. "I'm not really grumpy, just tired, but thank you. I feel like I ate breakfast three days ago."

"You didn't eat for three days?" Aervyn's eyes got big. He wiggled his fingers just a little and held out the much larger cookie canister he'd obviously just teleported from the kitchen at home. "Here, have lots of cookies. Mama can make more if we run out."

Nell shook her head and laughed. "Welcome to Witch Central, where life is always a bit crazy. Aervyn, send the cookies back home, please. Elorie already has enough to carry." And the smell of Nutella cookies might cause an airport stampede.

Aervyn contemplated Elorie for a moment, and then wiggled his fingers again. Nell didn't have to wonder what he was up to for long. Elorie squealed and spun around. "My backpack!"

Nell tried to reassure her with a look. "It's okay. Aervyn just ported your bag to our house." The look she gave her son was more pointed. "That bag has some things in it that are really important to Elorie. You scared her when you made it disappear without asking."

She could see his brain twisting that around for a minute. "I'm really sorry, Elorie. I didn't mean to scare you. Do you want me to bring your bag back?"

Elorie shrugged her shoulders. "No, actually. Thanks, it's a lot lighter this way." She reached for the cookie tin Aervyn was still holding and grinned. "Besides, now I have two hands free for cookies."

Phew, thought Nell. Thank God for visitors who could roll with witchling antics. That would make the next few days a lot easier. Normal life at the Walker house tended to register pretty high on the chaos scale.

Aervyn reached for Elorie's hand to lead her out of the airport. "So, how come you don't want to be a witch?"

Didn't I tell you to wait until she was settled before you asked questions like that? Nell sent to her son.

I did, Mama. I gave her cookies, and ported her bag, and everything. Besides, you want to know, too. Everybody does.

Her son might need a refresher on mind-witch manners, but he was right. Nell did want to know.

Elorie met Nell's eyes for a moment, and then she looked down at Aervyn. "When I was little like you, I wanted to be a witch more than anything. But I grew up and found out I'm not a witch. That used to make me a little sad, but now I know it's just who I'm supposed to be."

"Nuh, uh." Aervyn blew off her answer with the confidence of a four-year-old who knew he was right. "You melted a computer, and Uncle Jamie and I can't do that. You must be a witch, just like Superman."

Oh, crap. Nell was pretty sure Elorie's confused face meant no one had actually told her about the melted computer. She linked elbows with their visitor and pulled out the best distraction she could think of. "So, do you think my daughters have found your backpack full of jewelry yet?"

Elorie turned a little pale. Nell reached into the tin and gave her a cookie.

~ ~ ~

Jamie walked up to the door of Nell's house, holding the hand of his lovely wife and wishing he didn't feel like he was about to lose yet another argument. "It just seems like we should be extra careful with our girl in there."

Nat snorted. "Babies are supposed to bounce around a little. That's why they live inside a nice water cushion."

A personal water balloon didn't seem like nearly enough to keep a baby safe. "I just don't see a lot of pregnant women doing handstands." Watching Nat do yoga used to give his hormones a good kick. Now it just scared the crap out of him. He kept expecting her to land in a big belly flop on the floor.

She touched his face. "She's more protected in my belly, even upside-down, than she'll be the whole rest of her life. Relax, Daddy—she'll be fine."

Nell opened the door as Jamie tried to marshal his rebuttal. Maybe *she'd* be on his side. "Hey, sister mine. Did you ever do handstands when you were pregnant?"

"Do you honestly think I'm dumb enough to answer that question? Come on in."

Nat hugged her sister-in-law. "Feel free to tell him the truth."

"I don't do handstands ever, so no. But we were in the middle of a new Realm release when I was four months pregnant with the girls. I coded sixteen hours a day and lived on Doritos and peanut butter. They turned out fine."

Jamie remembered. He'd never been able to eat Doritos again after watching Nell dip handfuls of them straight into the peanut butter jar.

Nat's face brightened. "Hey, do you have any Doritos? Those sound totally yummy."

Nell laughed. "Sorry, no. I can't even look at them anymore."

His wife wanted to eat Doritos? The woman who made him eat vegetables and tofu for dinner? He'd Googled everything he could find on what to expect during pregnancy. When this was all over, he was going to create a new website for expectant fathers—one that told the truth. Nobody warned you about Doritos and handstands.

Both women were looking at him expectantly. He'd clearly missed something. "What?"

Nell shook her head in dismay. "Doritos, brother mine. Your job is to procure whatever weird things the mother of your child wants to eat, at whatever weird time of day she wants to eat them."

He took mental notes for his new website. Fortunately, Doritos were easy. Closing his eyes for a moment, Jamie mentally raided the cupboard in his basement. Nell might not eat them anymore, but her three girls were all Dorito fiends, so he kept a large supply on hand.

Nat dove into the teleported bag like a teenage boy. "Thanks, sweetie."

Drawn by Dorito fumes, several sets of feet came thudding down the stairs. "Uncle Jamie, Auntie Nat!"

A little slower than the triplets, Elorie smiled and waved in welcome.

Oh, crap. Not again. Even as he felt himself being pulled under, Jamie was aware enough to hold onto something other than his pregnant wife. He grabbed his sister instead and felt visions of the future roll over him.

When he snapped back into the present, he was sitting against the wall, Nat crouched at his feet, and way too many sets of eyes peering at him.

Once she'd decided he was okay, Nat smiled and spoke very quietly. "Are you going to have precog episodes every time you see a pretty girl?"

God, he really, really hoped not. Meeting Nat had triggered the mother of all precogs, but this one had been pretty loaded, too. And not one he really wanted to discuss while sitting on the floor surrounded by inquiring minds.

He struggled to his feet and faced Nell's new houseguest. "Hi, Elorie. Welcome to insanity, and sorry about almost passing out on you."

Jamie was just contemplating whether he could skirt the whole issue of his precog episode when Aervyn's voice piped up from the crowd. "See, Elorie—I knowed you were a witch."

Aervyn! Jamie had just enough energy left to halt his nephew before he let anything else out of the bag.

Fortunately, Nell, who was very used to directing chaos, caught the edge of his mental blast. "Aervyn, can you and your sisters go get snacks and drinks for everyone from the kitchen?"

She herded the adults into the living room and raised an eyebrow at her brother. *What the heck's going on?*

In answer, Jamie sent back a snapshot from his precog—Elorie, belly enormous, standing at Ginia's right shoulder in the magical light of a full circle at peak power.

What is up with you and precog and pregnant women?

He shrugged helplessly. *Now what the hell do we do?* No one was better thinking on the fly than his sister.

Nell looked at him for a moment. *Leave it be, for now. Precog isn't a guarantee, so we really don't know anything more than we knew before. One step at a time, brother mine. Let's see if we can learn more about our maybe-witch via some slightly more scientific methods.*

Damn, he hated precog.

~ ~ ~

Moira: Hello, Nell—do you have our Elorie?

Nell: We do. She's settling into her room now, which really means she has my three daughters urging her to pull out every last piece of jewelry and show it off.

Moira: She makes truly splendid things. I have a new pendant she made for me with some lovely blue glass in it.

Nell: I hope she brought enough with her. I think half the witch population of California plans to visit her at the Art Fair.

Moira: I do appreciate that, Nell. She was a little nervous about bringing her designs to such a fancy exhibition. It's a bit different than selling it in a few shops like she does here.

Nell: We support our own, you know that. And witch or not, Elorie is one of our own.

Sophie: Do me a favor and snag me a couple of things if you go, Nell. Something green, maybe.

Moira: And good evening to you, Sophie. I didn't see you come in.

Nell: She's a sneaky witch, our Sophie.

Sophie: Ha. I was brewing a couple of potions on the stove—sorry I'm a little late.

Nell: Can we switch to video chat? I spent a lot of time coding today, and my fingers are tired.

Moira: I'm not entirely sure how to do that on this new computer of mine. It doesn't have one of those wee cameras sitting on top.

Nell: If it's new, it likely has the camera built in—try clicking on the video chat button and see what happens.

    Just like magic, Moira thought as she watched Nell and Sophie come to life on her screen. "Isn't that lovely, now."

    "I'm envious of your new computer," Sophie said. "Mine feels like a clunker, even though it's only two years old."

Nell snickered. "The witchlings in my basement are having fun melting laptop hard drives. If you want to donate yours to the cause, just let me know."

Hard drive. Moira tried to get her creaky brain working. That had been one of the words Marcus used when he tried to explain what had happened to her old computer. "And why would you be melting computers?"

The guilty look on Nell's face was timeless.

"Nell Aria Walker, what kind of trouble are you getting into?"

Sophie burst out laughing. "Aunt Moira, you do that very well, but Nell's a grown woman. I'm guessing it won't be quite as effective on her as it is on witchlings."

Nell rolled her eyes. "It might. That was pretty good—I might have you give me lessons when I bring my crew out this summer."

An old witch could still be embarrassed. "I'm sorry, Nell, forgive me—I've been a wee bit unsettled lately. This has something to do with Elorie, doesn't it? Marcus is convinced she's the one who caused my old computer to stop working."

"It's more than that," Nell said, looking serious. "Someone utterly melted the insides of your laptop. That's no easy feat, even with witch power. Aervyn couldn't do it, even with an assist from Jamie."

It was good to know there were things beyond Aervyn's power just yet. Small boys needed some limits. However, the rest of what Nell was saying seemed like nonsense. "Then why do you believe Elorie was involved? Things don't seem to be very well made these days, so perhaps my little machine just broke."

Nell shook her head. "I've seen pretty much every way a computer can break, and I've never seen anything like this. With three witches in the room when it happened, it's not a big leap to believe power was involved."

It wasn't often she lost her temper, so Moira struggled for calm. "Unless we had a small child under the table, there were only two witches in the room. I'm sorry, Nell, but I just can't take the word of your scanning program over everything I know to be true. Marcus scanned Elorie as well. I even—" she ground to a halt for a moment, ashamed to go on.

There should be no secrets amongst witches. Speaking quietly, she continued. "I asked my scrying bowl to look into her future. It wouldn't speak to me. I even tried Great Gran's crystal ball. If Elorie was a witch, surely the portents would foretell."

Sophie smiled sadly. "You love her so very much, Aunt Moira. And that crystal ball's never worked, you know that."

Tears threatened, and Moira tried to fight them off. "I know it. But I had to try. I'd be the very first in the line of happiness if my beloved girl were a witch, and I know you'd be right behind me. But this isn't right, and we need to stop. It's tearing her apart. Your scan must simply be wrong, Nell."

"It's not just scans now." Nell shrugged helplessly. "This isn't really mine to tell, but Jamie had a flash of precog when he first saw Elorie earlier today."

Moira felt her heart clench. "And what did he see of my girl's future?"

"Remember, precog isn't certain," Nell said, her eyes pleading.

"I know that." Moira reached gently for the screen. "Tell me, Nell. It's better that I know."

"I didn't have time to talk with him, but he mindsent at least part of what he saw. My girl and yours, in the magic light of a working full circle."

Now the tears came, a great well of them. "My Elorie, she does magic?"

"It's only a possibility," Sophie whispered, her face a tangle of emotions.

In her head, Moira knew what Sophie said to be true. In her Irish heart, she felt the agony of hope.

Precognition was an age-old way of witch knowing—unpredictable at times, and fickle at others, like many magics—but her blood heard and trusted, in a way it never could with Nell's gadgets and machines. If Jamie *saw* magic in her girl, then they must seek to unveil it.

"Well, then," she said, her voice a wee bit quavery. "We need to find out, don't we? An untrained witch is a dangerous witch."

Chapter 6

Elorie put her hand on the mouse and watched in confused frustration as once again, the readout she'd dubbed the Power-O-Meter spiked happily. That screen was becoming her own personal definition of hell.

She'd been working with Jamie and Ginia for almost an hour as they tweaked and re-tweaked the scanning code for more precise readings. Even her renowned patience was becoming very thin.

She'd been raised to serve the witching community in any way she could, so when Jamie had asked for an hour, she agreed.

Now it was time for this insanity to end. Elorie Shaw was not a witch, and she was very tired of trying to prove it. "It still says I'm a witch. I don't feel like we're making a whole lot of progress here."

Nell walked into the room with a tray of milk and cookies and a big bowl of strawberries. Elorie's heart tightened in momentary homesickness as she remembered the going-away bucket of blueberries her witchlings had picked. Jamie glanced at her in brief sympathy, a reminder that her brain was clearly still very leaky where mind witches were concerned.

He tapped Ginia's shoulder, and she looked up from her code. "Okay, group huddle. Nell, can you brainstorm with us for a few minutes?"

Elorie got up to leave, but Jamie motioned her back to the table.

"I'm not a coder, Jamie. I don't think I can contribute to this conversation." *And I think it's better you work on this without me.*

He met her eyes for a moment. "You're a thinker, and a student of witch history. Brainstorming works best when there are lots of different ideas at the table."

Elorie tried to fight off a lifetime of good manners, and lost. She sat.

Nell handed her a cookie, the witch fix-all. "So bring me up to speed, daughter mine. What have you tried so far?"

Ginia squared her shoulders. "We know that the computer is reading power traces for Elorie, and Uncle Jamie can't pick them up in a regular scan done at the same time."

"Okay." Nell swiped the cookie Jamie was trying to grab. "And have we checked anyone else for this power source yet?"

Jamie nodded. "Yup. When you passed on Marcus's idea, we headed to Realm and scanned everyone we could find in the witch-only levels. That's why we're trying to refine the scans, to see if we can find a common element in their readings and Elorie's."

Elorie frowned. This was a lot more information than she'd been given up until now. "What idea of Uncle Marcus's?"

"He thinks," Ginia said, "that maybe you aren't the only one with this new kind of power."

Since when had Uncle Marcus stopped being a hermit and started making up wild theories about new kinds of magic?

Nell touched Elorie's hand. "It's only a theory right now, but Marcus thinks you may be accessing a form of power that only registers in Internet space. He also thinks it might not be just you."

Three exhausting days were catching up with Elorie. "Let me get this straight. Uncle Marcus thinks there are a bunch of witches running around the Internet with some kind of invisible magic?"

Nell shrugged. "Okay, it sounds a little hocus-pocus when you put it that way. But it's a good idea. He thinks people like Ginia, who are good at spellcoding, might share your mysterious talent."

Why was it so stinking hard for everyone to believe she wasn't a witch? Elorie shoved in the last of her cookie. They could sit in dark basements and theorize all they wanted. She was done.

Ginia finished her milk as Elorie stood up. "We tried scanning me, but nothing showed up."

Nell was silent for a moment. "What were you doing when you got scanned?"

"Holding the mouse, just like Elorie does..." Ginia slid to a halt, her eyes opening wide.

Jamie snapped his fingers. "Nell, you're brilliant. Elorie, two more minutes. Please."

Elorie stood and watched the sudden flurry of activity in the basement, utterly confused. In moments, there was a new computer setup at the table, and Ginia was typing madly into her keyboard. Elorie could see the graphics for Enchanter's Realm on her screen.

"Keep it simple," Jamie said. "We just need a basic spell to do the test."

Ginia nodded. "I'm coding an easy three-step spell. That way, you'll have three chances to get a reading."

Jamie nodded, watching over her shoulder. "Good thinking, cutie."

If she had to stand here, the least they could do was explain why. Elorie leaned over toward Nell. "I'm so confused. What's going on?"

"We're trying to figure out if Marcus is right, and witches who can spellcode share your talent. You test for it even with passive readings, but it's trickier in witches with multiple magics. We're thinking that if Ginia has what you have, it might be easier to read when she's actively spellcoding."

That much made sense. Active magic was a lot more visible—even she could sense the power flows sometimes when one of her witchlings was doing a more complicated spell.

Ginia looked up, all nine-year-old seriousness. "Ready."

"Ready here, too." Jamie intently watched his screen.

Elorie watched. Absolutely nothing happened.

Suddenly a familiar voice spoke out of Ginia's computer. "You called, Warrior Girl?"

Ginia giggled. "Hi, Gandalf. We're doing a test to see if I have the same power as Elorie. I needed to code a spell to get the reading. I hope you like your new costume."

Nell leaned over to look at the screen and clapped a hand to her mouth, snickering. She motioned Elorie to look.

Marcus's gruff voice boomed out again. "It's not funny, Nell. I'll be the laughingstock of Realm." Elorie moved in and got an eyeful of Marcus dressed in Xena splendor.

Ginia grinned. "Nah. That will happen tomorrow. I wrote this one in a hurry, so it probably won't take you too long to reverse it."

Marcus's eyes narrowed. "What happens tomorrow?"

"I hate to interrupt," Jamie said dryly, "but is anyone interested in the results of the scan while Ginia was spellcoding?"

Every head in the room swiveled, including Marcus's onscreen. Jamie looked around and grinned. "Whatever magic you've got, Elorie—Ginia has it, too. We got a very nice spike of the same unknown power during step two of that spell."

Ginia bounced on her seat. "That's the hardest step, so it should have been the easiest to see." She and Nell both jumped up to look at the readouts on Jamie's monitor. Elorie felt oddly naked, floating on the edges of something she didn't pretend to understand.

Jamie looked up at Elorie, eyes deep with sympathy. "You're a witch, little sister. Welcome."

She felt the breath simply leak out of her.

Ginia came to hold one of her hands, and Nell the other. Elorie looked down at the joining of her very first witch circle, and let the tears come.

~ ~ ~

Moira: Hello, Nell. Is my sweet Elorie there? I was hoping to speak with her.

Nell: Sorry, you just missed her. With the time change, it might be tricky to connect with her in the next couple of days. Jamie, Nat, and the girls took her down to the Art Fair to set up her booth. That's probably way more help than she needs, but everyone is a little excited right now.

Sophie: I just heard the news—I ran into Marcus in Realm.

Nell: Yeah, he's rounding up witch players so we can do more widespread testing.

Moira: Pardon an old woman for a moment. It's true, then—my Elorie is a witch?

Nell: She is. She was just a very well-hidden one.

Sophie: Your girl's a witch, Aunt Moira. We have a new sister.

Moira: It's a little hard to take in just yet. I never imagined we would find out quite like this, with her practically on the other side of the world.

Sophie: Nell, please give her a hug, and all my blessings. We haven't been as close in recent years, but she is the sister of my childhood.

Moira: It was very difficult for her as you grew into power, sweetheart.

Sophie: I know it.

Moira: I also know it's one of the reasons you live so far away.

Sophie: Not the only one, but yes. Her heart is there, and it would ache more often if I lived underfoot.

Moira: Know that mine aches for the choice you made. It wasn't a fair one to ask of you. In my heart, you have always had a home here.

Sophie: I love you, too :-). Power is not always fair, or easy. It won't be for Elorie, either, but this feels right. I'm so very happy for her.

Moira: My heart is full to bursting, but my head is very confused. Nell, please have pity and explain to me exactly what you've discovered. Marcus was talking about spells and coding and such and I admit to not understanding a word of it. My granddaughter is a witch, but that's all I know.

Nell: The important part is that we believe there's a power source we hadn't previously identified, and Elorie is not the only one who can use it.

Sophie: Net power. That is so cool.

Nell: You're a pretty good spellcoder, Sophie—make sure Jamie tests you in the next few days. He and Marcus are just doing some tweaking first to make sure we don't melt any more computers doing the remote scanning.

Moira: Old-lady English, please…

Nell: Sorry, Moira. We're still trying to understand this new power source. You remember back when I was a child, and they were just beginning to understand how shapeshifting and such worked?

Moira: Indeed. It took some of our best minds to figure out the source powering those magics. Harder still because it's a relatively rare talent.

Nell: Well, this is another power source we don't understand much about yet. The good news is, it may not be so rare. Ginia tests for it, and we think that anyone who can spellcode probably has some degree of this talent. Marcus does, as do Jamie and I. Ginia's the strongest we've found so far, though.

Sophie: I repeat, this is so cool.

Nell: Get Jamie to test you, girl.

Moira: And you think my Elorie has this Net power. She will be a spellcoder, then?

Nell: That's where things get confusing again. For most of us, our scan only registers power when we're actively spellcoding. For Elorie, all she has to do is touch a mouse and we get higher readings than we see from anyone else.

Sophie: Meaning what, exactly?

Nell: We're all guessing. Moira, maybe you can help us think this through. There are witchlings who have an unusual affinity for certain power sources, right? Even when they're not actively doing magic?

Moira: Certainly. Your Aervyn was one of them, playing with power threads while he was still in your belly.

Nell: Exactly. And Jamie and Nat's babe plays with fire, although no one but Aervyn can see that yet.

Moira: It's normally a sign of a very strong talent, and one that will emerge early.

Nell: Right. So if Elorie has a natural affinity for Net power, even when she's not doing active magic…

Moira: You're saying she might be particularly strong with this talent.

Sophie: I want her for my partner in Realm.

Nell: Get in line. However, we don't know that spellcoding is the only way for this talent to work. That's how most people use it right now, but really, it's just a power source.

Sophie: Ah. So just like I use my earth magic to heal or make flowers bloom, Elorie may be able to use her power in more than one way.

Nell: Possibly. Most magics have a likeness to their power source—it would be really hard to use earth magic to create a windstorm—so we're guessing she's not a weather witch, but we're not exactly sure what she might be able to do.

<u>Moira:</u> Start at the beginning, then.

<u>Nell:</u> Which is?

<u>Moira:</u> She must learn to call her power reliably and use it in small spells. Once she has that control, you can work out what else she can do.

<u>Nell:</u> Wise words, Moira. Thanks.

<u>Sophie:</u> Does this mean Elorie gets spellcoding lessons?

<u>Nell:</u> I think so.

<u>Moira:</u> The poor girl.

<u>Sophie:</u> I'll take her into Realm. Ginia could use some backup taking Marcus down.

<u>Nell:</u> Careful with that. Next to Ginia, Marcus has the highest Net power reading on our scans so far.

<u>Sophie:</u> That figures.

<u>Moira:</u> It's like a foreign planet, that game of yours.

<u>Nell:</u> You're welcome to come for a visit. Marcus will be over later today to teach you the basics of spellcoding.

<u>Moira:</u> Me? Goodness sakes, why?

<u>Nell:</u> Because most witch talents are hereditary. If your nephew and your granddaughter are both Net witches, there's a decent chance you are, too.

    Nell pushed back from her computer and grinned. She really should have put on video chat—Moira's face would have been priceless. She didn't envy Marcus his task. Moira might just turn him into a frog, or worse.

    Then again, her assignment for the afternoon was to teach Aervyn some basic spellcoding, and that was a fairly risky proposition as well. Mia and Shay were currently unhooking all the most precious electronics in the house from the Internet so Aervyn didn't fry them with an errant line of code or two. Daniel was reinforcing their network firewall so Wonder Boy didn't accidentally fry the computer of anyone else in the neighborhood, either. Life was never boring at Witch Central.

Jamie, Ginia, and Marcus would test the Realm players, and by the end of the day, they'd likely have a pretty good list of Net witches.

Then they just had to figure out what to do with them.

~ ~ ~

Jamie had no idea how he'd gotten roped into setting up a jewelry booth with five giggly girls. Nat and Elorie were no better than the triplets, trying on a gadzillion different necklaces and debating which ones were their favorites. As far as he could tell, the favorites pile was bigger than the discards.

Nat sidled up to him, some creation of copper and sea glass around her neck. "What do you think?"

He was wise in the ways of women. "Don't you have to wait until tomorrow to buy stuff?"

She shook her head in amused dismay. "In six months, you're going to be the most important man in the world to our baby girl. You need to get better at questions like this."

"Don't I get a couple of years of training while she learns how to talk?" He hoped.

His wife gave him one of her brain-melting smiles. "You're a slow learner, so you might want to get started now." She gestured at his three nieces, all festooned in jewelry and giving him the same "so what do you think" look.

He was taking Aervyn to a ball game later. It was a matter of guy survival.

Elorie dug in her bottomless backpack. "Girls, I have something special for you." She pulled out three very similar chains, each with a gorgeous piece of sea glass entwined in silver wire and two smaller pieces of glass, one on each side. Each necklace had the same three colors of glass, but with a different color as the central focus.

Even Jamie, a triplet himself, could see that Elorie had captured the bond of identical, but unique, sisterhood. His nieces were speechless.

He could feel Elorie's joy at the gifting. She had an incredibly open mind, and that wasn't always a good thing, but right now, he appreciated the second-hand glow. It was a nice improvement over the emotional swings she'd been going through since yesterday.

She grinned and reached into her bag once more, this time coming out with a copper pendant holding a blue orb. He would have denied it to his last breath, but he coveted the deep blue. It called to him.

"It's a marble," Elorie said, handing it to Jamie, "tumbled in the sea for years, or maybe centuries. Guessing from the size, it's hand blown, and probably very old."

He rolled the rough sphere between his fingers, sensing that it was a hard piece for her to give up, one of her favorite treasures. Refusing to take it, however, would dim her joy, and that he wasn't willing to do. He'd never bought into the trappings of witchcraft, but as he hung the pendant around his neck, he was very sure it would stay there.

Elorie handed two very similar, but smaller, pendants to Nat. One was a gorgeous pink, and looked like it was born to match the crystal already around her neck. The second was fire red.

Jamie was puzzled, but as four sets of eyes got all gooey, it was obvious he was the only one who was lost.

"Oh," Ginia said softly. "It's for the baby."

Fire red for his little fire witch.

He could feel his eyes getting all gooey, too. Dang.

As Nat linked her fingers with his, a very official-looking man arrived, asking Elorie to come sign some paperwork. With a last worried look at her booth, she followed him off.

"She's a really special person," Nat said. "She's struggling, though."

As always, Jamie was somewhat awed by his non-witch wife's ability to pick up emotional undertones. "I think it threw her to find out she really is a witch."

"Why does that make her sad?" Ginia asked.

Nat helped Ginia clip on her necklace. "I think it's mostly confusing, sweetie."

"But she's always wanted to be a witch. She told me it was her dream. And she's a really cool new kind of witch."

And that, Jamie thought, was the crux of the problem. "Not everyone wants to be something new and different, cutie. It's exciting for you, but where Elorie comes from, witches are pretty traditional. When she dreamed about being a witch, I don't think this is quite what she imagined."

He watched as Ginia, who had been born adaptable, struggled to understand someone who was less open to change. "Maybe she just has to get used to it a little. I can teach her how to spellcode."

He nodded. "That's definitely a good thing to work on, but first she has to be able to access her power. We don't really know how to do that yet, so we need to figure it out before we can train her."

Ginia frowned. "I tried to do it really slow so you could see."

"I know you did. We'll keep trying."

Nat cocked her head. "What are you trying, exactly?"

"Uncle Jamie's trying to watch inside my head while I spellcode, but he can't quite see what I'm doing."

He handed out granola bars from his messenger bag. Nat was looking hungry, and nine-year-old girls were always up for a snack. "One of the advantages of being a mind witch is that I can watch and see how people are using power. Then I can mindshow the steps to someone else."

Nat nodded. "So, you want to see what Ginia's doing, and then use that to teach Elorie."

"Right. Except it's all kind of fuzzy, and it doesn't seem to work like elemental power, so I'm having trouble getting the steps in focus."

"It's cuz he's a feeble mind witch," Gina said, mouth full of granola bar.

"Brat." Jamie wondered if she was too old to hang upside-down in public.

Nat held up her hand to forestall any niece tormenting. "So, if you were a stronger mind witch, you'd be able to see what Ginia does more easily?"

Great, now his wife was calling him feeble.

She kissed his cheek. "Stop thinking like a man and ask for help. Lauren's coming over this afternoon, and I'm sure she'd be happy to play."

Ginia nodded. "That'll work. Lauren's a rockin' mind witch. She can see practically anything."

Duh. He'd totally missed that one. Feeble and slow. Good thing he had a really smart wife.

~ ~ ~

Sophie: What's up, Marcus? I was just about to trip a nice little spell on Warrior Girl when you interrupted.

Marcus: You should thank me. I tried that exact move last week—she has a stealth counterspell in place.

Nell: And at least you could have helped me out of the sorcerer fog when you called.

Marcus: You can blame your daughter for the fog. She's been leaving deception spells like that all over Realm. I think she's preparing something big.

Sophie: She's got mad spellcoding skills. If we can get it figured out, I bet she's one of our strongest Net witches.

Marcus: I might have another candidate. I spent some rather unenjoyable time teaching Aunt Moira to spellcode this afternoon.

Sophie: Aunt Moira's *coding*??

Marcus: Hardly. She threatened to curse my computer—one of those old Irish witch curses you can't get rid of—and I believe she meant it.

Nell: Go, Moira.

Marcus: Wait until it's your laptop she's threatening.

Sophie: So how'd she do?

Marcus: I handled most of the coding, but she has a deft touch blending spell and code.

Nell: Moira's a Net witch—now there's deep irony for you.

Sophie: That is so very hard to imagine.

Marcus: Indeed. Nell, did you manage to get a reading on that boy wonder of yours?

Nell: Nope. We tried, but he's four. He just doesn't have the logic circuits to program yet. It never occurred to me to try doing the coding part for him, though.

Marcus: It stood to reason that the important part was activating the spell, not writing it.

Nell: You'd have saved me a couple of painful hours by mentioning that a little sooner.

Marcus: You have a perfectly good brain of your own.

Nell: Try to avoid being a conceited ass for five more minutes, and then we'll let you go back to getting your butt kicked by my nine-year-old.

Sophie: Keep it up, and I'll help her.

Marcus: As I believe I've said before, she doesn't need help. Have you managed any more work with Elorie?

Nell: Not really. She's fairly shaken, and also very busy with her Art Fair, so right now, we're proceeding without her. Ginia's readings are really strong, and Jamie's mindlinking with her as she spellcodes to try to figure out how the magic actually works.

Marcus: Smart man.

Nell: Smart girl—it was Ginia's idea. Lauren's coming in tomorrow to help as well. I don't think you've met her yet, Marcus. She's our newest resident mind witch.

Marcus: We hear things even in the boonies of Nova Scotia.

Nell: Cranky old man.

Marcus: No one would argue with you.

Sophie: I need to head to bed, you two. Blessed be.

Nell: It seems I need to go chase Warrior Girl to bed as well.

Marcus: Do that. Perhaps the rest of us can catch up while she sleeps.

Chapter 7

Jamie lounged on the grass in his new back yard, a pint of ice cream in his hand. Lauren had vetoed working in the coding cave in the basement. Feeling the warm sun and the light touch of a breeze on his face, he conceded that maybe she had a point.

No need to let her know that, though. "So we're outside, catching some sun, and we've fortified ourselves with chocolate ice cream. Are we finally ready to begin actual work?"

Lauren rolled her eyes at Ginia. "Girls work better on chocolate. So, what is it I'm supposed to be looking for, exactly? And please tell me it doesn't involve learning how to code."

God, he hoped not. "In theory, Net power is just like any other power source. You need to access it, and then apply it. Spellcoding is one application, but there may be others. First, we need to know how Ginia accesses Net power."

"Okay, makes sense," Lauren said. "Jennie did something similar when she worked out how I powered Cat Woman with Aervyn."

That had been the first magic trick where they'd gotten some clue as to the strength of Lauren's talent. As the guy who'd been on the receiving end of their illusion spell, Jamie resisted the temptation to reach up and make sure he wasn't wearing fuzzy ears again. "I've been trying to link with Ginia and watch, but I'm not getting a good read. All I see is a burst of light, and that's not very helpful. We figured you'd get better results."

Ginia giggled. "Auntie Nat figured. Uncle Jamie and I were dopes, and we didn't think of it."

Lauren poked Ginia with her spoon. "That's probably because I'm not a supreme awesome coder like you, hot stuff. Show me what you can do, and I'll try to watch."

Ginia picked up her laptop, which already had several simple spellcoding sequences set up. Lauren closed her eyes and dropped quickly into mindlink. Jamie wondered if she had any idea how skilled a mind witch she was becoming.

I do now, said Lauren's amused voice in his head. *Want to watch? I think I can pipe you a channel, too.*

The easy strength of her mind powers was obvious the instant she linked him in. His view of Ginia's brain via mindlink had been murky and distorted; hers was crystal clear.

He watched as Ginia pulled earth power to weave the initial spell. Then she reached for her computer keyboard, and small fireworks of light exploded everywhere.

He could feel Lauren's shock. *What the heck was that?*

I assume it's Net power in action, sent Jamie dryly. *That's the first time I've seen it that clearly. Any idea what she did?*

Not really. Most power use comes from a single focal point, so I wasn't expecting anything like this. There was no focus—it's like it was all over her brain.

Try it again please, Ginia, Lauren sent. *As slowly as you can.*

They had Ginia loop through the spellcoding routine five or six more times before Lauren dropped them all out of mindlink. Jamie's brain hurt just from watching.

"So," said Ginia, picking up her ice cream, "did you figure out how I'm doing it?"

Lauren looked at Jamie. "Maybe. It's a bit similar to mind power, actually. It behaves like an internal energy source, rather than an external one like earth or fire power."

He wasn't trying to be disagreeable, but that didn't make any sense. "Well, since you have to be hooked up to a computer to use it, it's obviously not an internal source."

Lauren shrugged, and swiped Ginia's ice cream. "Okay, but if we skip that little technicality, once it activates, it looks like an internal power source. If it looks like mind power, maybe it trains like mind power."

Ginia frowned. "I don't get it."

He didn't get it either. Jamie reached out with his spoon, since his pint was mysteriously empty.

"When I use mind power," Lauren said, "it's just kind of there, but I have to turn it on. From the inside, not like elemental power where you reach externally."

Jamie nodded. His mind-witch powers were a little clunky, but definitely different from his other talents. "Kind of like flipping a mental switch."

"Close enough. You get readings on Elorie even though she isn't actively using power, right? What if Net power is just kind of there, at least when you're online, but you need to turn it on?"

And Elorie's switch was stuck partway on. That made an odd kind of sense.

"Okay," said Ginia, always the adaptable witchling. "How do I turn on my switch?"

Lauren grinned. "We're going to experiment. I'm going to pretend you have mind power and walk you through turning it on. You keep your hand on the mouse."

Jamie mentally groaned. Powers weren't interchangeable like that. They needed to figure out how Net power worked before anyone was going to be able to just flip a switch.

You're such a guy, Lauren sent, rolling her eyes at him. "You don't have water power, and yet you teach witchlings how to use it. How do you do that?"

He was getting backed into a corner here, he could just tell. "It doesn't really matter which elemental power it is—you tap into them more or less the same way. But those are both elemental energies. Net power isn't mind power."

Lauren shrugged. "We don't have any idea what Net power is, and it looks like mind power." She pulled them both into mind connection one more time.

Jamie watched in skeptical silence as Lauren walked Ginia through the most basic steps of accessing mind power. Zilch. Nothing.

Lauren mentally elbowed him. *Do all your witchlings get it on the first try?*

Ouch. She could be loud when she wanted to be.

She very patiently walked Ginia through the exercise several more times. Jamie yawned, and then sat up in shock as the mental lights went on. Holy crap.

He dropped partway out of mindlink and grabbed his laptop. *Have her do it again*, he sent to Lauren. *I want to get some readings.* Jamie watched his screen as Ginia caused three spikes in a row. The last one was as big as anything they'd seen when she was spellcoding.

He looked up just in time to catch his niece in mid-leap. "I did it, Uncle Jamie!"

"You sure did, cutie. You know, this makes you famous."

"Why?"

"First person to ever intentionally activate Net power. You'll be in the witch history books."

"Cool!" No one missed what she didn't say. *Just like Aervyn.*

Damn. The next logical person to teach was her baby brother, but Ginia deserved her day in the sun before being eclipsed. Especially if she was having one of those rare days when being big sister to the world's most powerful witchling was a little touchy.

Give her some time, Lauren sent. *And don't make assumptions. Maybe Super Boy won't be the most powerful Net witch in the land.*

Jamie had lost too many times recently to make any more bets with the women in his life, but he was unconvinced. There were very, very few things where Aervyn wasn't the strongest.

~ ~ ~

The Art Fair was crammed full of people who loved handmade items and things of beauty. It buzzed with the sounds of thousands on a mission, mixed with the occasional cry of a baby or the squawk of a loudspeaker.

Elorie's reticence had melted away in the first ten minutes, and now she was having a glorious time sharing her wares with all the fascinating people flowing into her booth.

She was also starting to get a little worried that she might run out of things to sell, which was flabbergasting. She was an artist first, but a businesswoman second. At the rate her bits of glass were selling, she was going to clear over twenty thousand dollars in four days.

A small girl caught her attention. She was managing to twirl in the crowded booth space, holding one of Elorie's favorite pieces—a simple chain with four small droplets of glass.

Elorie smiled at the woman with the little girl and crouched down. "That's a very special necklace. I call it the Mermaids' Tears."

The child's eyes got big. "Are you a mermaid?"

"Well, my feet are a little sore in these shoes, but no, I'm just an ordinary girl. What about you—are you a mermaid?"

The girl looked at her shoes very seriously for a minute. "Not today. It's hard to walk around with a tail, so today I put my legs on."

Elorie smothered a smile. "I'm glad you did, so you could come see me and try on a pretty necklace." She lifted the child's soft hair, draped the chain around her neck, and led her to a small mirror.

"How do you make all the pretty colors? Is it a magic necklace?"

"Perhaps," Elorie said. She liked to believe there was magic in the ocean waters, and maybe even a mermaid or two. "The colors are pieces of glass that live in the ocean for a long time. All I do is walk along the beaches and collect them. I like to think maybe the mermaids send them to me so I can make beautiful things."

The child looked skeptical. "I've never seen any tears on my beaches."

Elorie skipped her usual explanation of ocean currents. "Well, maybe mermaids don't swim near your beaches. I'll have to go walking on one myself later today and see what I can find."

"They come and play," the girl said. "But they don't cry, because I sing to them a lot. They like singing."

The girl fingered the bits of glass on her chest, and Elorie knew this was one of those times when one of her creations simply belonged to someone. "Well, that must be why they sent me these tears."

The child looked puzzled. "Why?"

"The mermaids must really love your singing and want to say thank you. I believe that every necklace I make has a true owner, and this one must be yours." The girl beamed, and Elorie shook her head as the woman dug out her purse. "It's a gift from the mermaids. No charge for those."

It was so easy to make a small child happy.

Elorie realized a little belatedly that she'd been ignoring everyone else in her booth. As she turned to help them out, she heard the lilting and slightly off-key notes of a little girl's song float into the air.

She wasn't sure if it was the song or the adorable girl modeling her treasure that caused the general flood of goodwill into her booth, but she sold out of Mermaids' Tears necklaces in the next hour.

~ ~ ~

Lauren laughed at Jamie's look of disgust.

"I don't get it," he said. "I can see what you're telling me to do, but it just doesn't turn on the same way as mind power for me."

They'd been trying to replicate Ginia's success activating her Net power. As both mind witch and talented spellcoder, Jamie had seemed like a good candidate, but so far he was getting exactly nowhere.

"Maybe we should try with someone else," Ginia said. "Mama's a wicked spellcoder, or we could get Aervyn. He's a good mind witch, so maybe he can figure this out."

She's right, sent Lauren, as Jamie spluttered in protest. "Sounds like a plan. Why don't you go fetch them?"

"We're already here," Nell said, walking out into the back yard with a pizza box, Aervyn skipping at her heels. "I came to trade Ginia for food, but there's enough here for everyone. What do you need?"

As they all settled on the grass, lulled by gloriously cheesy pizza, Lauren explained what they were working on.

Aervyn spoke with his mouth full. "So it's just like mind power, but we hafta hold the mouse when we turn it on?"

Jamie rolled his eyes and grabbed another slice. "I hope it's that easy for you, short stuff."

"Let's give your mama a try first," Lauren said. She looked at Nell. "We assume it will be easier for people who already know how to spellcode. I'll pull you into mindlink so you can watch Ginia, and then I'll walk you through it more slowly."

Nell nodded and hooked easily into mind connection. After watching Ginia access Net power several times, she backed out. "Got it. It's kind of like gathering energy for spellcasting."

"Uh, huh," Jamie said. "But it's a lot harder than it looks."

Nell smirked. "Watch and learn, brother mine."

Big witches were sometimes no more mature than the witchlings, Lauren thought. When Ginia was ready to track the scanner readings, Nell closed her eyes, and Lauren dropped into monitoring to watch.

After several tries, they knew two things. One, Nell was indeed better than her brother. And two, that wasn't saying much. She'd managed to get a couple of tiny bursts of light to fire, but that was about it. The power levels had been no more than a blip on Ginia's screen.

Lauren hoped Aervyn wouldn't squish the growing sense of pride she could sense in Ginia.

Go ahead, Jamie sent. *Let Aervyn show us creaky old witches how it's done.*

She'll be okay, sent Nell, with a small nod toward Ginia. *I think. And if she's not, we'll deal.*

Lauren wiped the tomato sauce off Super Boy Wonder Witch's face. "Aervyn, why don't you mindlink with me, and we can watch what Ginia does. Then I'll walk you through it slowly."

"Okay." He finished wiping his mouth on his sleeve, causing Nell to roll her eyes.

Lauren dropped quickly into their very familiar connection, and together they watched the mental fireworks of Ginia accessing Net power.

I can do that, Aervyn sent.

Oh, boy. Let's go through it a few more times, buddy. I know it moves kind of fast.

Nuh, uh, I can do it. Aervyn dropped out of mindlink long enough to take the mouse from his sister. Lauren watched in bemused awe as he set off his own mental fireworks seconds later.

Nell looked at her grinning son and shook her head. "I take it he can do it, too."

"Yeah." Lauren shook her head. "Sorry, I didn't even have time to clip you in to watch."

Ginia looked at the computer readouts and waved at Jamie to take over. "Hey, Aervyn, can you do it again? This time turn on all the power, 'kay?"

Aervyn tried again. And a third time. He was consistent and fast, and Ginia was a very good coach. In a few minutes, they were all convinced he was accessing his full power. But Lauren, with a mind channel hooked into Jamie, could read his surprise. Aervyn's spikes weren't nearly as high as Ginia's.

Well, damn, Jamie sent on a very narrow band. *He's got decent power, but Ginia's far stronger.*

Nell nodded in approval as she watched her two witchlings work together. *Good.*

Elorie walked into the back yard, sniffing. "Please tell me that's food. I'm hungrier than a herd of seals."

Nell shook her head and laughed. "Witches are always hungry. Glad you got my text to come here. Aervyn, honey, there are two more pizza boxes on the counter. Can you get them?"

Jamie pouted in protest. "There's more, and you were hiding it?"

Two boxes thunked onto the ground at Elorie's feet, causing her to jump. Aervyn giggled. "Sorry, I didn't mean to get your toes."

She rubbed his head. "I forgot you can teleport, sweetie. We don't have any witchlings in Nova Scotia who can do that. It's kind of handy when I'm this hungry, though—thanks!"

Jamie's voice spoke in Lauren's head. *Do we hit her with this now?*

We don't have a lot of choice. She leaves the day after tomorrow.

Elorie looked around at all the computer equipment strewn in the grass and sobered. "Are you still doing readings on that new power?"

"Sort of," Jamie said. "We're trying to figure out how to train it."

Lauren could feel mixed emotions streaming out of their new arrival. Jamie was right—Elorie's brain was really leaky. She tightened up her mental barriers.

"It's okay," Aervyn said, obviously reading the emotional storm as easily as Lauren. He took Elorie's hand. "It's really easy to use. I can show you."

Lauren started to interrupt, and then reconsidered. Elorie might well respond better to coaching from a pint-sized teacher—she seemed to have a real fondness for kids. *Go ahead, Super Boy*, she sent to Aervyn. *But go SLOW. Remember, she's a brand-new witch.*

Jamie's mental voice was highly amused. *If he goes as slow as he did when you were new, he'll scare her silly.*

Lauren remembered all too well the totally overwhelmed feelings of her first week at witch boot camp. She hooked into Aervyn's mental connection with Elorie, ready to put on the brakes if necessary. Hearing Jamie's mental knock, she patched him in as well.

Aervyn, taking his trainer responsibilities very seriously, helped Elorie watch as Ginia accessed Net power. Then, in a very nifty move, he replayed it in slow motion for her.

Well, heck, Lauren muttered. *Why didn't I think of that?*

That'd be why he's Super Boy, and we're just old and creaky, Nell sent dryly. *Although, even seeing it in slow motion, I don't think I could do it any better. We'll see how our newest witch does.*

After watching the replay several times, Elorie's emotions had settled. *Good*, Lauren thought as Ginia handed over the mouse. *And very interesting.* Unlike everyone else, her brain showed a low level of Net power activity even when she wasn't trying to pull power.

That's why we were getting readings on the scanner, Jamie sent. *She's got a really strong affinity for Net power.*

So, what does that mean, exactly?

Damned if I know.

Aervyn very patiently walked Elorie through her first attempts at accessing Net power, and like most newbie witches, her initial efforts got nowhere.

By now, Lauren had patched in Nell and Ginia as well, and they let out a collective mental sigh at each failed try.

Lauren thought she could see the problem. At the key point of engaging more active power, Elorie balked.

She's not the first, Jamie sent. *I remember a certain mind witch who didn't step up and claim her power happily, either.*

Lauren stuck out her mental tongue at him. Then she paused. Aervyn was setting his student up for another attempt, and she had the distinct feeling he had something up his sleeve.

As Elorie hit the sticking point, Aervyn moved like mental lightning. Giggles reverberated in all their heads as he launched a sneak tickle attack.

A moment of shock and laughter—and then fireworks exploded in Elorie's head.

Lauren could feel the awe of every witch present, including Aervyn. *Oh crap*, Jamie sent. *Now we're in the big leagues.*

Yup, said Nell. *With a newbie at bat and a four-year-old manager.*

Ahem, came from Ginia.

Well, I guess you're a little better than a four-year-old in charge, Jamie teased as Ginia spluttered.

Who's going to tell Elorie she's the baddest Net witch in the West? Lauren asked—and was promptly reminded that when push came to shove, the Walker clan voted as a bloc, and Jamie was all too happy to join them. Terrific.

~ ~ ~

Elorie took off her shoes and enjoyed the feel of sand between her toes. Most Nova Scotia beaches had more pebbles than sand, so this was a strange, but lovely, feeling.

The crisp night air was a welcome change from the smells of stale popcorn and slightly burned hot dogs she'd been breathing in her booth.

She could feel her very soul exhaling as she began to meander down the moonlit beach. Jamie had dropped her off and then gone for a late-night ride, promising to return for her in an hour. She had a blessed sixty minutes to herself.

The motorcycle ride had been exhilarating, but what she really craved was silence. Or what passed for silence on an ocean beach, with the sounds of waves crashing and occasional birds overhead. Night spray blew against her face as she dipped her toes into the receding water.

She didn't think of herself as a solitary creature, but three days in a row of people-packed art show, and she was ready to drop.

She sighed. And that was what Gran would call utter hogwash. The Art Fair was an amazing experience, with so many people loving her handcrafted glass trinkets. As an artist, she was riding a wave of euphoria. As a witch—well, that was the proverbial whale on the beach.

Truly, it was hard to think of herself as a witch just yet. And even harder to think of herself as a witch with a weird new power, especially when that new power didn't seem much good for anything.

Oh, it had been an amazing rush to feel the whoosh inside her head as she activated her talent purposefully for the first time. It shamed her a little to admit it, but it had also been nice to see witches looking at her with magical respect for once.

But growing up with Gran had instilled strong values, and the first of those was that witches didn't *have* magic—witches *did* magic, for the greater good of the witching community and the planet.

So when the lights had gone on inside her head, she'd asked the question any witch raised with Gran would ask. "What can I do with it?"

Aervyn's answer had left her empty. "I don't know, but it's really pretty!"

If she wanted something pretty, she'd make a necklace. Power was meant to work, to do, to give. If hers couldn't do anything, then she was a fairly useless witch.

Elorie realized she was now marching down the beach like a two-year-old having a tantrum. She paused, wrapping her arms around her waist.

She knew what she needed. Home.

She'd caught Aaron on her cell phone as she left the Art Fair, but she really needed Gran's wisdom right about now. Gran had offered via the grapevine to stay up late for a video chat, but Elorie had reached her limits with computers. She just wanted to be home.

She realized her eyes were casting around the beach. Silly girl, looking for sea glass on the wrong side of the world. She was a fish out of water here. She wasn't a coder, or a modern witch. She was Elorie Shaw—artist, organizer, wife.

One more day as Elorie Shaw, art-fair sensation, and then she would go home.

Chapter 8

Moira: Good morning, Nell. How is my girl doing?

Nell: She's having a wonderful time at the Art Fair. I've been hearing reports from friends stopping by. It's sounds like she's one of the stars of the show, and she's already been invited back for next year.

Sophie: I'm so happy for her.

Lauren: It's no surprise—her stuff is gorgeous, and I say that as someone who doesn't usually get all gooey over jewelry.

Nell: Ha. She made a pendant for the baby. Even Jamie got all gooey.

Moira: She's got a gift, and I'm delighted to see her using it so well. And how is it with her new powers?

Nell: It's a bit more rocky there. She's had a lot thrown at her all at once.

Lauren: I so remember how that feels.

Moira: I was hoping to video chat with her, but I think perhaps she's avoiding me.

Lauren: More likely she's avoiding the computer, Moira. They're not her favorite objects right now.

Moira: Well, I can understand that—they're devilish little devices.

Lauren: They hold the mysterious thing that has upended her life. It's a lot to deal with all at once. She very much wants to see you—that much I couldn't avoid picking up from her. Her mental place of safety and security is rooted at your kitchen table.

Moira: That seems a lot to be reading from her mind, my dear.

Lauren: It's not intentional. Her mind is more open than anyone I've ever met. I have to completely barrier to avoid her thoughts, and I can't do that during training and monitoring.

Moira: That's odd. Marcus hasn't said anything, and he's a solid mind witch. Our witchlings have picked up some of her stray thoughts, but they lack training yet.

Lauren: Now that I think of it, I don't remember noticing it when the two of you visited in the spring, although I had a lot on my mind then.

Sophie: Perhaps her new magics are opening her mind channels. Didn't you say Net power looked a lot like mind power?

Lauren: Duh. I bet you're right, Sophie. If accessing her power is blowing open her channels like it did mine...

Moira: Can you train her in some barriers?

Lauren: I'll give it a try. I only have one chance tonight; she heads home in the morning.

Moira: See if you can get her started. Ten-year-old boys don't have the best of mental manners. Are you still planning to come out with Nell and her brood, Lauren? Perhaps you could help us out with Sean and Kevin. Marcus is not the most ideal person to be training them—he can be a bit gruff.

Sophie: Making witchlings cry again, is he?

Moira: Not so far, but it seems prudent to avoid that if we can.

Lauren: I'd be happy to, and I'll do what I can with Elorie before we send her home.

Nell: I talked with my husband last night, Moira. Given where Elorie is at, and that my two witchlings seem to share her power, we were thinking of coming sooner rather than later. Can you handle us all in a few days?

Moira: And won't that be delightful? Come anytime, Nell. My home is always open.

Nell: Sophie, Lauren—can you manage that?

Lauren: I remember the days when my career took priority in my life :-). That should be fine. Half my clientele these days is witches, so I'll just hang a *Gone to Witching School* sign on my door.

Moira: Witches need new homes, too, my dear. I'm glad they're keeping you busy.

Lauren: Busy doesn't begin to describe it. I almost believe some of them are moving just to have an excuse to drop by for a visit. Sophie, can you get away? I was hoping to see both you and Moira on this trip.

Sophie: I never need much of an excuse to come east. I'll be there.

Nell: Elorie's thinking to avoid all this by heading home, I think. We should let her know we'll be following close behind.

Lauren: What, give a newbie witch warning and a say in her life? Why on earth would you do that? :-)

Nell: We're not bossy all the time. Just mostly.

Moira: I'm sure Elorie will welcome you with open arms. Her heart is a hospitable one.

Nell: I've already tentatively booked rooms for most of us at their inn. Aaron said they had a big party cancel, so assuming I can find flights, we'll be there on Wednesday. He says he's ready to be overrun by witches.

Sophie: Yum, Aaron's breakfasts are stupendous. Lots of chocolate.

Lauren: I'm there. My sense is that Elorie will do better on her home turf, so if we have to ambush her, this is probably the best way to do it.

Nell: We'll bring you over to the dark side yet, Lauren...

Lauren snorted as she closed her computer. It truly wasn't that long ago that she would have protested more loudly on Elorie's behalf. However, they could hardly leave her running around with a leaky brain and totally untrained magic. And wow, she was starting to sound like Moira.

It was amazing how quickly your perspective could change. Six months ago, she didn't think witches existed.

Now she was leaving her real-estate practice during one of the busiest times of the year to go hang out with a couple of witches she missed dearly. She'd have fun helping with the witchling training— but really, she wanted to see Moira's comforting face again and giggle with Sophie late into the night.

She'd turned twenty-eight as downtown Chicago's youngest elite realtor. Next week, she'd turn twenty-nine while teaching magical manners to young mind witches in some tiny village in the middle of nowhere, Nova Scotia.

She could hardly wait.

~ ~ ~

Ginia grinned at her computer monitor. She had a fiendish plan for total Realm domination, and she was about to start training her secret weapon. Gandalf would never know what hit him.

"So remember, Aunt Moira, it has to be a total secret."

Moira chortled from video chat. "I don't think anyone's going to guess it's me, dear one."

She hoped not. It had taken some serious convincing to talk her new trainee into this. She'd had to pull out that whole "an untrained witch is a dangerous witch" line. Which had been pretty smart, since Aunt Moira was like its inventor, or something.

Ginia looked at the other side of her split screen at the costume she'd rigged for Realm's newest avatar. She thought it was highly suitable for Warrior Girl's sidekick, kind of a cross between Cat Woman and Princess Leia. "How do you like your character?"

"She's lovely, but maybe I need a few more clothes?"

"Nuh, uh. Clothes get in the way for fighting."

Moira looked a little distressed. "Witches try not to fight, dear."

Ginia grinned. "If you look like you'll win a fight, then you don't have to fight very often. That's why my name is Warrior Girl. No one messes with warriors."

"Ah. You're a very sneaky witch, sweet girl. So what shall my name be?"

"That's up to you." Ginia screwed up her face into an evil menace. "It should be something that sounds powerful and maybe a little scary."

Moira giggled and thought for a moment. "Ah, I have just the thing. How about Hecate?"

That didn't sound very scary. "Who's Hecate?"

"Your witch history is lacking, child. We'll have to fix that when you come visit."

Ginia had no idea how they'd gone from Realm avatars to witch history, but she was pretty sure it wasn't a good direction to keep heading. "We want something really scary, Aunt Moira. Gandalf isn't gonna be easy to scare."

"Ha!" Moira laughed. "Marcus knows who Hecate is. He'll be plenty scared, I promise you. She's the Greek goddess of magic and witchcraft, and a fierce warrior. She has a great big dog as her familiar—can you perhaps make me one of those, and some wee arrows?"

Ginia grinned. Oh, yeah. She most certainly could. Game on.

"Okay, Aunt Moira. Let's teach you how to move your avatar around now."

~ ~ ~

Elorie looked at Lauren, Ginia, and the big bowl of soup waiting for her and grinned ruefully. "What is this, ambush witch lessons?"

She wasn't all that excited about more of those, but she'd sold out of jewelry, and she was heading home in the morning. Nothing could dim her good mood.

Ginia held out a basket of garlic bread. "I made this from garlic I grew—it's really good. We're gonna have a lesson, but you can eat first."

Be grateful for small gifts, Elorie thought, amused. She bit into the garlic bread, and butter oozed over her tongue. To heck with lessons. The garlic bread rivaled Gran's.

Lauren grinned and snagged another piece before handing the basket back to Elorie. "You probably don't realize it, but your mind is really open right now. We need to help you barrier a little, so you can keep your privacy."

She blinked. They were reading her mind?

Lauren shook her head. "Not most of us, just the mind witches in the group, and we're all trying pretty hard to stay out."

Her inner thoughts were flapping in the wind? Cripes. It had been that way with Uncle Marcus, but she'd just thought he had bad manners. "Have I always been this way?" That didn't even bear thinking about.

"I don't think so. No one remembers this from the last time you visited. We're thinking that maybe working with your magic a little is opening your channels. That happened when Jamie first started helping me with my mind powers."

It had happened with some of their Nova Scotia trainees as well, but it was very different to be the one with the leaky head. Uncle Marcus had very little patience with undisciplined minds. Oh, God. And the twins. She looked at Lauren, trying not to panic. "Please tell me how to fix this."

Lauren squeezed her hand. "Basic barriers are pretty easy. In your case, you just need to block outgoing thoughts, and that's easier still. Don't worry. We're not going to send you back to the evil Marcus with a naked brain."

Ginia giggled, and Elorie felt her cheeks fire up. She focused on her soup, trying to refuel for the work ahead. She was not leaving this room until she could keep her thoughts to herself.

An hour later, she was almost ready to rethink that promise. Lauren was a thorough and patient instructor, but they were making exactly zero progress. She had a strainer for a brain, and she couldn't plug any of the holes. So far, being a witch sucked.

The three of them leaned back against the couch. "Take a short break," Lauren said, "and then we'll try again."

Ginia twiddled with an errant curl. "What if we're doing this all wrong?"

Elorie couldn't stop her groan. Good grief, she was beginning to sound like her students, complaining about a little hard work.

"What do you mean?" Lauren handed out cookies, which seemed to be in constant supply at Nell's house.

"Well, what if Net power is a little like mind power, but not all the way? It turned on the same, but maybe other stuff works different."

"Okay..." Lauren considered, and then shrugged. "So, what do you think we should try?"

The gears spinning in Ginia's head were almost audible. "I think she should try it connected to the computer."

Dead silence, as everyone contemplated what was suddenly a blindingly obvious idea. Ginia got up and went to get her laptop and mouse.

Elorie sighed. She was beginning to intensely dislike computer mice. Taking it in her hand, she braced for more failed efforts. "Now what?"

Lauren looked shocked, but very pleased. "Your mind just went totally quiet."

Ginia grinned. "Awesome!"

Elorie dropped the mouse in horror. So very far away from awesome. Maybe it was just a fluke.

Lauren shook her head and spoke gently. "When you're in contact with Net power, your mind is shielded. As soon as you let go of that mouse, I could hear your thoughts again."

Grabbing the mouse, Elorie fought down her panic. "I can't have one of these with me everywhere I go."

"Maybe you can." Ginia turned to Lauren. "Remember Uncle Jamie's iPod gizmo? The one that gave you barriers? I bet we could tweak that to work for her. Kind of a Net shield."

"That's brilliant." Lauren nodded. "Why don't you run over now and see if you can get him to help you? That'd be the easiest way to send Elorie home with a private head."

Ginia flew out of the room.

"It's just an iPod you can put in your pocket," Lauren said, and came to sit by Elorie. "Trust me, I know it feels like betrayal when your own head doesn't seem to work properly. It will get better."

It felt like standing in an ocean-side storm waiting for the next rogue wave to knock you over again. "I'm sorry. I've seen enough witches come into their powers—you'd think I'd know better than to believe it was easy."

Lauren wrapped an arm around her shoulder. "You didn't exactly get a smooth road, but I think it will be less bumpy once you're home. Think of Jamie's gizmo as your shiny red Dorothy shoes—it will let you go home, and that's all that really matters."

Elorie had awful visions of being hooked up to electronics for the rest of her life. So many people would think that was totally awesome. Unfortunately, she just wasn't one of them.

She didn't live entirely in the Dark Ages. Laptops were tools, and she used hers competently. But having one with her always? It was like some new and awful form of witch captivity.

Elorie Shaw, prisoner. Just lovely.

~ ~ ~

Nell collapsed on the couch and waved a hand in Jamie's direction. "Can you port me some root beer and a banana, or something? It's been a long day."

Her brother rolled his eyes and complied. The bananas arrived as a clump of six, and the root beer was warm, but she wasn't going to complain. Some days, being chief organizer and bottle washer at Witch Central was a big job, especially when you were trying to get everything ready for imminent departure.

Jamie helped himself to one of the spare bananas. "So, when are you leaving again?"

"Two days. Elorie goes to the airport tomorrow morning, and we leave Wednesday morning."

"It's going to be strange for the girls to be separated."

Nell nodded. She'd given that particular issue some serious thought. "I think it will be better for them, though. Ginia's going to be pretty busy with witchy things in Nova Scotia. I don't want Mia and Shay to feel left out, and they're really excited to stay with you and Nat and work on coding the Realm surprise for summer solstice. That was a pretty clever idea, brother mine."

Jamie shrugged. "If I handle this right, I'll do very little work and get all the glory. We should have tried this child-labor thing sooner."

Nell threw a mental banana at him. She didn't have enough energy to throw a real one. "Nat's really okay with the invasion? I know she's tired from all the morning sickness right now."

"You really think two girls ready to fulfill her every wish are going to be a burden?"

He had a point. All her triplets thought Auntie Nat should sit with her feet up and eat bonbons until the baby arrived. She had no idea where they'd picked up such a silly idea, but it was cute, and probably not too terrible for Nat.

"Relax," Jamie said. "Nathan's at summer camp, your girls are farmed out into servitude, and we promise to feed Daniel occasionally. You'll have the two most likely troublemakers with you."

Another good point. "Hopefully Moira will spoil them silly, and they won't have any time to find trouble."

He snorted. "Good luck with that. I seem to remember a few witchlings native to that coast who will welcome new blood with open arms."

Nell remembered some of the antics of summers past and opened one eye. "Maybe they've matured."

"Twin ten-year-old boys? Yeah, that's likely."

"I'll keep them busy. I'm supposed to be teaching them how to spellcode. Marcus refuses to give any more coding lessons after his less-than-enjoyable afternoon with Moira."

"Marcus is an old grump. He has a soft spot for Ginia, though."

Nell grinned. "That's because she's about to wipe the floor with him in Realm. Have you been watching?"

"Yeah. Those cloaking spells the other day were seriously good. She's up to something else now, though—she made a new sidekick avatar."

That got her attention. "She's partnered up?" You didn't let a nine-year-old gamer online without keeping very close tabs on who she was playing with. The witch-only levels of Realm were a pretty small community, but still.

Jamie's grin got bigger. "Yup. And so you know, she told me who it is, but asked me to lock down admin access to the new player's identity. I'll tell you if you really want to know, but trust me, it will be a lot funnier if you don't ask."

Nell's curiosity almost got the better of her, but if Jamie had vetted the new player, Ginia was hardly in danger. "Are they any good?"

"Not yet." Jamie smirked. "But give Ginia time, and they will be."

Must be one of the other witchlings. She'd have to have one eye online while they were in Nova Scotia.

"In other news," Jamie said, "we tested an awful lot of people today, and no one else can do any better than you can in activating Net power."

Nell frowned. The greater San Francisco area had a pretty high density of spellcoding witches, and most of them had probably come running when Jamie put out the call. "How many people stopped by?"

"Enough to go through three giant pots of spaghetti."

Even by witch standards for food portions, that would have been at least a dozen people. "Did you get the best of the spellcoders? Caro and Govin, or maybe Mike?"

Jamie grinned. "Mike's visiting Sophie again. The other two both showed up. I thought Caro might get somewhere, being a mind witch, but nothing. Govin got a few sparks, and he's one of the very few who did."

Huh. "Maybe we're doing something wrong."

"Maybe." Jamie shrugged. "But your two kiddos and Elorie all light up like Christmas trees. It's as if people who are good at spellcoding can't shift gears to use Net power differently, or something. So far, Ginia's the lone exception."

"Hmm," Nell mused. It was second nature to think out loud with Jamie after years of troubleshooting code together. "Ginia's good, but she hasn't been spellcoding for very long. Coding, yeah, but adding magic is still pretty new for her."

He slapped the table. "Bingo. I didn't think about it that way, but yeah—everyone who stopped by today has been spellcoding for years." He paused for a minute. "How the heck do we find witches with Net power who haven't already learned how to spellcode?"

She was on a roll. Two good answers in one night. "We go some place where not every witchling learns to use a computer."

"Nova Scotia." Jamie laughed. "Moira has no idea she's about to be invaded by the minions of technology. Good luck with that."

Nell winced. They'd gotten Moira as far as using video chat, but her brother was right. Nova Scotia witches were far more traditional in their craft, and Moira was their matriarch.

A new witch power with technology at its very core? Not exactly traditional. It was going to be an interesting trip.

Chapter 9

Elorie stepped off the plane in Halifax and breathed in. She loved the old-fashioned feel of the Halifax airport, where they still unloaded passengers onto the tarmac. The air smelled of the sea in California too, but it wasn't her sea. She was home.

She looked toward the airport building and spied three faces pressed against the glass. Aaron stood in the shadows just behind them.

Quickly she made her way across the tarmac and inside the doors. Agile Lizzie got to her first, squeezing through a couple of DO NOT ENTER HERE signs. Elorie figured you probably got a pass if you weren't old enough to read.

"You're back! You were gone almost forever."

In that moment, it almost felt true. Elorie crouched to hug her and looked up at Sean and Kevin, drinking in their familiar faces. If they weren't ten now, she'd have smothered them in kisses just like she was doing with Lizzie.

"Eww!" Sean said. "No baby kisses. That's gross."

Kevin frowned. "It's not nice to read her mind, Sean."

And just like that, a crack ran through her homecoming. Elorie fought off a wave of sadness as she dug in her bag for Jamie's gizmo and turned on her own personal force field. She hadn't greeted her husband yet, and darned if she was going to do it with two ten-year-old boys listening in.

Aaron stood back, the only one who had been even slightly daunted by the Do Not Enter signs. She soaked in his steady presence and the love in his eyes.

Closing the last few steps, she reached to touch his face. "Hi."

His grin chased the remnants of sadness away. "Hi, yourself. Welcome home."

Home was the place where four words could make you feel right again. Visually rounding up her witchlings, she reached for his hand. "Feed me—I'm starving."

Aaron grabbed Lizzie's hand as well. "I have a picnic in the car. I thought we could stop along the way, let the kids play on the beach for a while."

The children would enjoy the beach, but Elorie was pretty sure the stop was meant for her, a chance to root her soul in the ocean breezes. Her husband understood her very well.

"Can we help look for sea glass?" Lizzie asked. "I want to find a pretty pink piece."

Elorie grinned. "Those are hard to find, sweetpea."

"I'll find one. And when I do, maybe you can help me put it on a chain. I want to give it to Momma for her birthday. I want to use the hole-maker whizzer."

Elorie tried not to wince at the thought of her beloved Dremel tool in the hands of a six-year-old. "I'm sure we can come up with something spectacular. Let's see what you find on the beach first. A good artist needs to be flexible."

She looked over at Sean and Kevin. "You guys want to help with the sea-glass hunt, too?"

They both looked horrified. "Nah," Sean said. "I can practice my pitching, though. Coach says throwing rocks into the ocean is great practice."

Aaron looked fairly interested in that idea. Elorie hid her grin. He wasn't the biggest fan of trawling the beach for glass, and goodness knows she'd made him do enough of it. He could throw rocks with Sean and try to keep him dry. She couldn't recall a beach trip where at least one witchling hadn't come home wet.

Kevin would have a book to keep himself busy, she didn't even have to ask—but she might have something he would enjoy even better.

Tugging Aaron to a halt, Elorie reached into her shoulder bag and pulled out three wrapped presents. She had one for her husband as well, but he was going to have to wait for a more private moment.

Lizzie was into hers first and waved her rainbow-silk streamer in delight. When Elorie had seen them at the Art Fair, she'd pictured Lizzie dashing down the beach trailing ribbons of color behind her. It was the perfect gift for a child who loved bright beauty and never stopped running.

For Sean, she had a baseball. This one she was less sure about, but Jamie had assured her that a ball signed by last year's World Series winning team would be an instant hit. From the look on Sean's face, Jamie knew what he was talking about.

Kevin had opened his small, flat package more slowly. He was absolutely quiet when he realized what it contained, but his look of delight took Elorie's breath away. He touched the Kindle with reverent fingers. She showed him how it turned on, and the list of books already loaded, thanks to some helpful hands in California.

Sean looked over in interest. "What's that?"

"It's to read books," Kevin said softly. "All the books in the world."

Sean rolled his eyes in disgust. "Books."

Kevin, well used to his twin's literary disdain, just hugged the Kindle to his chest.

Aaron grinned as they started walking again. "Nice going. What'd you bring me?"

Elorie winked at him and said nothing, which increased the size of her husband's grin. She was pretty sure the handmade baby booties in her bag weren't his first guess.

~ ~ ~

Jamie set down grilled-cheese sandwiches in front of his two trainees. "Okay, kiddos, we have a job to do."

Aervyn ate the grape eyes off his sandwich. "Do we get to melt stuff again?"

Not on purpose, Jamie thought, but made a mental note to keep his new laptop well away from the training circle. "Nope. We have a mystery to solve."

"I thought we already did that," Ginia said. "We figured out how to turn on Net power."

"You did. Now we need to figure out what we can do with it."

His lunch guests scrunched up their faces in identical quizzical lines. "Don't you know?" Aervyn asked.

Jamie shook his head. "I don't. Usually when witches are learning something new, someone who already knows how to do it teaches them."

"Like you teach me, except sometimes I surprise you."

He certainly did. "Just like that, kiddo. But sometimes a new kind of magic or a new kind of spell comes along—not very often, but when it does, witches have to work together to figure out what to do with it."

Ginia tilted her head to one side, deep in thought. "Well, we know you can use Net power to spellcode."

"Right, but that might not be the only use. All we know for sure is that it's a power source, and most power sources can be used to create lots of different kinds of magic."

Aervyn bounced on his seat. "We get to make up stuff?"

Jamie hoped he wasn't digging himself way in over his head. Nothing like letting the world's most powerful witchling loose with a new magic source and no rules. "It's more like being detectives. We need to do some small tests and see what kinds of magic we can maybe do."

Aervyn's face fell comically. "If we can get the small magic to work, can we try big magic?"

"Absolutely." Jamie closed his eyes for a moment and ported a box of training props from the basement. He started to lift a candle out of the box, and then changed his mind; he wanted Ginia to have first crack at this. Pulling out a closed rosebud, he handed it to his niece.

She looked confused for a moment, and then nodded, clearly having figured out what he wanted.

He dropped into light monitoring contact to watch her work. Reaching for the mouse, she had fireworks going off in her mind almost instantly. Jamie was impressed—someone had been practicing.

Pretty fast there, Warrior Girl. Now let's see if you can get that bud to bloom. Net power only; don't use your earth powers.

He watched several tries and could see her problem. Her mind knew how to pull earth energies for this kind of magic, and she couldn't keep them entirely turned off.

Hmm. Let's try something you can't do with elemental powers.

Jamie poured water into a glass and added a tall straw. *Can you get the water to move up the straw?* Ginia had strong earth power and a little fire as well, but she had no water talent.

It was apparent in a few minutes that she wasn't going to get the job done with Net power, either. Ginia opened her eyes and scowled. "This isn't going to work."

"That didn't, but let's give Aervyn a try, and then we'll move on to something else."

She shook her head, an undersized woman on a mission. "It doesn't make any sense. Net power is new—why would it work to do old magic? Water power works to move water around, so maybe Net power moves... I don't know, 'Net' around."

Aervyn's eyes went big. "What's that?"

Ginia giggled. "Maybe it's like an invisible superpower. So it works best to do stuff that's invisible."

Invisible stuff... light bulbs went off in Jamie's head. "When you spellcode, Ginia, the Net power readings are strongest when you join the programming code to the spell."

"Sure. That's the trickiest step."

"Right." Jamie tried to bring focus to his very fuzzy idea. "But think about what you're actually doing at that moment—you're joining two things together. Maybe Net power is good for joining kinds of magic."

"Like the Internet." Ginia sucked in her breath. "The Net joins people, and ideas, and..." her words trickled off in wordless excitement.

Right. Magic had affinities. Water power worked best with water and other things that flowed. Fire power was most effective at creating heat and light. Maybe Net power was meant to be used to form connections and links.

He put together a picture in his mind of what he wanted to try and pushed it out to his trainees. He picked up a candle out of the box for himself and handed the closed rosebud to Aervyn. Ginia held the mouse and nodded. Ready.

Jamie used fire power to light the candle as Aervyn gently trickled earth magic to open the flower. He could see the fierce concentration on Ginia's face and the building light in her mind.

For a moment, nothing happened. Then flame danced from the petals of the open flower in Aervyn's hand. Ginia had done it. She'd joined their spells.

There were few moments Jamie loved more than watching a witchling own their power for the first time. Her sun-bright joy was contagious, and he felt his magic surge in response.

Unfortunately, the other person who got swept up in the excitement had fire in his hands and a fairly unlimited power supply. A few very busy seconds later, Jamie looked up at the scorch marks on his ceiling and sighed. You'd think by now he would have learned to play with fire outside.

Aervyn looked slightly worried. "Sorry, Uncle Jamie. I didn't mean to."

"I know it, short stuff." He looked over at Ginia, whose delight hadn't been dampened at all by the accidental fire. She was radiant.

He was blindsided by the force of his sudden yearning. Maybe one day, he'd be lucky enough to be there when his baby girl owned her magic for the first time.

He'd paint over all the scorch marks in the world for that chance.

~ ~ ~

Moira sat at her kitchen table, the warm comfort of a cup of tea in her hands, and tried to be patient. It wasn't easy. Her heart needed to set eyes on her granddaughter.

A journey to the other side of the continent was big enough, but Elorie had also walked the path from woman to witch. A sizable part of Moira's heart hurt that she hadn't been there to see it.

No matter. She'd soon see her sweet girl and know for herself how things sat. Being a witch wasn't always sunshine and roses, and if Marcus spoke true, Elorie was having a bit of a difficult time.

She got to her feet at the sound of footsteps coming up the garden path. At last.

"Gran." Elorie took the few steps from the door into Moira's arms.

"Welcome home, my beautiful granddaughter. Let me look at you." It was obvious at a glance that Marcus had indeed been right. All was not well with her girl. "Let's take a walk in the garden, shall we? I could use some fresh flowers, and your young legs could save mine a bit of bending."

"Nice try." Elorie smiled as she reached for the kitchen shears. "Those flowers on the table look cut this morning, and I'm sure your old legs were up to the job."

There we go; that was a bit more like her granddaughter. Moira hid her satisfaction. "Then we'll send flowers home with you. Aaron always has room for another vase or two."

Moira trusted that the gardens would work their magic of soothing and opening. They almost always did. And if that didn't work, there was always good old-fashioned prying. The Irish were masters at sticking their noses in where it mattered.

Elorie cut a few flowers and laid them in the gathering basket. Then she looked up and spoke softly. "It's not at all what I imagined, Gran."

Moira's heart squeezed. "Sometimes it isn't, sweetling. Tell me about what it is like, then."

"There's power—I felt it turn on inside me. But there's no magic." She held up a flower. "I always dreamed that one day I would sit in your garden and watch a flower bloom in my hands, or light a candle."

"I know, my sweet girl." Moira laid her hand gently on her granddaughter's shoulder. Elorie wasn't the only one who had held that dream tightly and needed to let it go now. "But we must live with what is. One day, you'll sit in my garden and we'll work magic together—that I can promise you. For now, your job is to learn about your gifts and what they can do."

Elorie broke away, agitated. "My gift is to put my hand on a computer part and set off some nice readings on a screen. What use is that?" She kicked at a rock. "I'm a freak, not a witch."

Moira hesitated a moment, unsure how best to comfort. "You're not alone."

Elorie took a deep breath. "I know, and I'm sorry. I don't mean to sound like Lizzie when she needs a snack. Ginia is delighted with this new power, but she has a way to use it. The last thing I want to learn is how to play some online game."

"Well, then, we'll just have to find some other purpose for this magic of yours, won't we? We can't have a useless witch in our midst." Moira picked up the basket of flowers. "Come, let's have some tea."

Elorie stood frozen on the path. "I'm not useless!"

Moira swallowed a smile and pinned her granddaughter with a very serious look. "Indeed, you're not. You're simply a witch on a journey to find her true purpose. That's a very important difference, my girl, and you've a lot of people to help you."

"I have a purpose."

"Aye, and one you've fought hard for, child. You stand at the very heart of this community, and you do wonderful work. We're richer because of who you are. All the computer parts in the world won't change that."

She saw that idea land in her granddaughter's heart and deeply hoped it would be true. Sometimes magic rooted in what was already there and added to the beauty. Sometimes it turned the whole garden upside down, and you had to start from scratch. For now, they'd try the easier way. It was a rare witch that took the easier path, but they could surely try.

Her eyes misted as Elorie's arms wrapped around her neck. "Thank you, Gran. It's good to be home."

~ ~ ~

Jamie sat down at his computer and logged into the admin panel for Realm. His niece and Marcus were both online, so he watched the action for a few minutes. She was laying some kind of spell trail, but even with his all-access eyes, he couldn't figure out exactly what she was doing. Tricky little witch.

He laughed as moments later, everything in Realm turned pink and glittery. Trust a nine-year-old girl to waste that many game points redecorating. Feeling some sympathy for crusty old Marcus, he sent out an administrator instant message.

Marcus: Is Warrior Girl putting you up to this?

Jamie: Huh?

Marcus: You all keep grabbing me into chat as she skulks around and prepares whatever nefarious tricks she's going to throw out next.

Jamie: Got you on the ropes, has she? That glitter's definitely scary stuff—I can see why you're worried.

Marcus: She's the mistress of multi-layer spells. I'd bet half my weapons stash that while everyone in Realm is pointing at the pink clouds and glittery castles, she's poisoning our water supply or something. It's embarrassing. She's nine, for crying out loud.

Jamie: Yeah. Be glad her two sisters don't have magic. They code just as well as she does.

Marcus: Someone's keeping them on the straight and narrow, right? They'd make marvelous hackers.

Jamie: Fortunately, that job is up to Daniel. But that's not why I paged you. Let me fill you in on what's happened with our Net power experiments.

Marcus: I've been hearing rumbles in Realm. Sounds like you haven't found any Net witches old enough to drive yet.

Jamie: Well, we have people who can use Net power to spellcode, but the only ones who can take it further than that so far are Ginia, Aervyn, and Elorie. It's like anyone who has done significant spellcoding has hardwired their magical paths, or something.

Marcus: Fascinating theory.

Jamie: I'm not in love with it, since my brain is one of the ones that are apparently too old to adapt. If I'm right, yours is too.

Marcus: Well, we shall see. I trust that one of your crew can walk me through the basics and see if I can break the mold.

Jamie: Aervyn should be able to show you. With your mind powers, you'll be useful monitoring the testing of others, as well.

Marcus: You're thinking that we electronically challenged witches on this coast won't have so many hardwired brains.

Jamie: Let's just say I'm guessing you'll find more raw talent to work with. And if Elorie's potential is any indication, the genes may run stronger in your branches of the family tree.

Marcus: Ah, the irony.

Jamie: Tell me about it. However, you might be interested in the new piece we've worked out. Let's go find Warrior Girl.

Jamie dropped out of chat and flexed his administrator muscles again, pulling Ginia and Marcus into an empty Realm level. He activated three-way video chat, a brand-new addition courtesy of Shay and Mia.

Marcus looked around in approval. "Nice. Not quite so pink."

Ginia waved. "Hey, Uncle Jamie. Did you like my redecorating job?"

"You realize I'm going to have to send your sisters to clean it up, right?"

Ginia raised an eyebrow. "Tell them good luck with that. It's booby-trapped."

Punk witchling. He'd taught her well. "Want to show Marcus your new trick?"

She nodded, always ready for something new. "Sure. Which one?"

"The one where you use Net power to join two spells. I'm thinking we could try that in virtual space."

Marcus leaned forward, suddenly intent, but said nothing. Ginia's eyes got big. "Oh. Because it's kind of a virtual power, right? You think we can do magic in Realm without spellcoding?"

Jamie grinned and headed his Realm avatar over to a nearby virtual flower garden. "I think maybe *you* can. Marcus and I probably aren't so lucky. Let's do some really simple magics first. Marcus, do you have a firelighting spell in your bag of tricks?"

"Of course. And a light globe, if that would be preferable."

It might be. He didn't really want to scorch Realm if it wasn't absolutely necessary. Mia and Shay already had enough cleanup to do. Not all coding work was glamorous.

Jamie realized he was going to have to code a flower-opening spell. No self-respecting witch warrior had anything that soft in their stash. Or maybe one did. "Hey, Ginia, you got a blooming spell already coded that I can borrow?"

His message box pinged almost instantly. *Warrior Girl has gifted you a spell.*

"Cool. Thanks, cutie."

Marcus raised an eyebrow. "Look it over carefully. It's probably got a couple of mercenary fighters hidden inside."

Ginia giggled. "No way. I sent Uncle Jamie the safe one."

And this was the girl who had Realm trembling. Hopefully it kept her out of bigger trouble, at least. "So, Marcus, this is pretty straightforward for us. Trigger your spell and hold the power flow as steady as you can. I'll do the same, and we'll see if Ginia can join our magics."

Onscreen, Marcus's avatar walked over to the garden and lit a fire-globe on his palm. Jamie grabbed a random flower bud, and then triggered the blooming spell. Ginia stood between them in warrior stance, a look of fierce concentration on her face.

And then she held out her own hand, and a blooming ball of light slowly took form.

"Wow," said Marcus reverently. "She's going to wipe the ground with all of us, isn't she?"

Jamie looked at Warrior Girl, power shining in her hands and glee on her face. "I suggest you find some Net witches, dude. You need allies, and fast."

Marcus just put his head on his keyboard and groaned.

Chapter 10

Sophie: Aunt Moira, since I'm packing, do you need any more chamomile lotion? Crystals, anything? I have some new floral tea you might like, too.

Moira: Tea would be lovely, and another jar of your lotion. And perhaps you have something that would make a gift for my Elorie? It's her birthday next week.

Nell: Glad you mentioned that. Do you have any ideas for what she might like?

Moira: I wish there were something we could give her to replace Jamie's force-field gizmo. It's an ingenious little device, but my poor granddaughter is not pleased about having to use it.

Nell: Maybe getting your mind witchlings fully trained is the long-term answer. I'm sure Lauren would be happy to help with that.

Moira: I'm sure Marcus will appreciate her assistance.

Nell: I'll warn her :-).

Moira: My nephew is a bit brusque, but keep an open mind. I think your daughter is having an interesting effect on him.

Sophie: She's about to kick his butt in Realm.

Moira: Sometimes men need to be taken down a peg or two before they can pay attention. Marcus is a bit old-fashioned, but he's coming around.

Nell: I'll believe it when I see it.

Sophie: I have some crystals that might help Elorie a little, but it sounds like she needs barrier training, no?

Nell: Lauren tried, but it seems like Net power has some important differences from mind magic. We're in unknown territory. I assume we'll figure something out eventually, but until then, Jamie's gizmo is better than streaming out your every though to Marcus, a couple of ten-year-olds, and any other mind witch who happens to be nearby.

Sophie: Ouch. Amen to that. I need to go finish getting ready. I can't wait to see both of you tomorrow. Blessed be.

Sophie put down her laptop, looked around the disarray of her bedroom, and sighed. Packing was one of her least favorite things. She wondered how the healers of old managed to travel with a rucksack of herbs and potions, and little else. They probably didn't have five pairs of shoes to take.

She had a fragrant pile of salves, teas, and assorted goodies from her store. Other piles contained a stack of books to return to Aunt Moira, a small fraction of her shoe collection, and enough clothes to survive a week of beaches, witchlings, and potions brewing.

Cripes. She could really use a butler, or an apprentice, or whoever it was that used to pack your bags for you.

"Need some help?" asked a voice from the doorway.

Sophie whirled. "Mike! What are you doing here?"

He held out his arms and grinned. "Looking for more of a greeting than that."

She stepped toward him, shock fading as delight blossomed.

Mike swung her up and kissed her thoroughly. Like most earth witches, he knew how to sink into a moment in time. By the time he was finished, Sophie's brain was gibbering mush.

He cuddled her in tight, and then looked over her shoulder and laughed. "I guess somebody's happy to see me."

Sophie followed his gaze. The flowerpot sitting in her bedroom window was a riot of flowers and blooms. They were practically dancing. Wow. She hadn't lost control of her magic that badly since… well, since the last time Mike had visited, but it had taken a lot more than a kiss then.

Her poor plant was getting a lot of exercise lately.

She *was* really happy to see him. However, they had a small logistics issue. "I'm packing to head to Fisher's Cove. I'm so sorry—I obviously forgot to tell you. The trip got moved up kind of last minute."

He kissed the top of her head. "So Jamie said. I haven't been to witch school in a while, so I thought I might tag along for the ride."

He was coming to Nova Scotia? With her? Sophie gulped. That was serious. She tipped up her head to look at him, a question in her eyes.

The answer in his was clear. Yes, this was a big deal—and he knew it.

~ ~ ~

Elorie grabbed the vase just before it tumbled off the table. "Sean James O'Reilly, since when does dusting involve knocking things on the ground?"

"It's okay," Lizzie said, popping up the last two stairs. "He's getting pretty good at repair spells. I bet he could fix it just like new if it broke."

"That's no excuse," Elorie said, trying not to grin. She whacked Sean on the head with a pillow and winced as she barely missed the vase herself. It was hard to model good housecleaning behavior when she really just wanted to goof off too. It was her first full day back home, and vacuuming hadn't been in her plans.

However, the witch deluge was descending tomorrow, and Aaron would accept no less than perfection in each and every guestroom. Not that she disagreed with him. She just wasn't thrilled about leading the commandeered cleaning crew.

"Have you finished fluffing all the pillows, Lizzie?"

"Uh, huh. And Kevin is bringing some nice books over for everybody. Aaron only has books for old people, so we're sharing some of our kid books."

True—with Ginia and Aervyn coming, the inn would likely end up full of kids. Elorie shrugged and picked up the flower vase. They might as well start witchling-proofing now.

Aaron came up the steps with a fresh set of linens. "Small change of plans, troops. We're going to need one more room set up—apparently Sophie is bringing a guest, so they'll be staying with us, too."

Usually Sophie stayed in Gran's tiny guestroom, but that wasn't what attracted Elorie's attention. "Sophie's bringing someone?"

Aaron winked. "Some guy named Mike."

"Sophie's bringing a *guy*?" That was hard to imagine. There had been no end of matchmaking efforts over the years, but Sophie had always been far more interested in her plants and potions. "Does Gran know?" Gran's sense of propriety was a little old-fashioned, and she loved Sophie dearly.

"She does." Aaron grinned. "She says to make sure they have a bottle of her special cider waiting."

Elorie felt her jaw hit the floor. Gran made only a few bottles of her bespelled sparkling cider each year, and it was a major occasion when one got opened. Not only did she know of Sophie's guest, but clearly she approved.

Fascinating.

Elorie took the linens from her husband as Kevin arrived with an armful of books. "We'll take care of this. Sheets are hard to break." She signaled to her witchlings. Time for a magic lesson.

"Okay, you three. I want you to put the new linens on this bed." She waited a beat, just long enough to see Sean's scowl forming. "No hands. Show me how your circle work is coming."

Sean grinned. "Easy, peasy."

Elorie doubted it, but one of the first rules of being a witch trainer was to lay down the rules and then get out of the way. "No spellcasting, either. I want you to do this as a team. Spell out loud so I can tell what you're doing, but no other talking."

She watched as they called power and linked together with ease. That much, she expected. It was the next part she thought might challenge their teamwork.

Judging from their configuration, Kevin and Lizzie had automatically defaulted power to Sean. That alone would probably dig them into trouble. Sean sailed into his first spell:

"I call on Air of wind and breeze
Lift this sheet, free of fleas
Hold it high over my head
Then drop it down onto the bed.
Perfect sheets for all to see,
As I will, so mote it be."

Elorie tried not to giggle. It was a good thing Aaron hadn't been around to hear the "free of fleas" part. Making up rhyming spells on the fly could be tricky for the younger ones, but Gran insisted on it. Not all witches needed rhymes, but for most, they were a nice power boost. And for Gran, they were a matter of tradition and discipline as well.

She watched her team at work and sighed. Picking Sean as leader had been the first problem—the second appeared to be that he didn't make a whole lot of beds. The sheet was upside-down and sideways. Lizzie glared at him and tried a spell to flip the sheet over.

Tension rose as Sean kept trying new spells to get the sheet to settle back down on the bed, and Lizzie kept trying to turn it over. The result was a really impressive sheet tangle and two frustrated witchlings. Kevin just leaned against the wall and watched. Which was probably smart, but not particularly helpful.

Elorie intervened just before Lizzie exploded. "Stop and freeze." She'd learned the hard way not to intervene in a working circle. The three dropped their circle connection and retreated to their respective corners.

"One at a time, I want you to tell me the biggest problem in what just happened. Just one, and no name-calling."

Lizzie was fastest off the mark. "Sean doesn't know how to make a bed."

That was a good start. Elorie looked at Sean, who was red-faced and mad. "No one was helping me. Lizzie was doing something stupid, and Kevin wasn't doing anything at all."

That came precious close to name-calling, but she'd let it slide for now. It was more insightful than Sean usually managed. "Kevin?"

"We picked the wrong leader."

There we go. Now to dig one step deeper. "A good start. Now tell me one thing you did that wasn't helpful for your team."

Sean looked blank. "I didn't tell Lizzie to stop?"

Elorie sighed. Why were all the mind witches in her part of the world so dense? "Lizzie, any ideas?"

She crossed her arms in an excellent unconscious imitation of Gran. "I could have said no to working in such a disorganized circle."

Youch, but not entirely incorrect. "Kevin?"

He looked down at his shoes. "I could have mindsent a plan to Sean. Lizzie knows how to make a bed, and we kinda don't. I could have made him listen."

Ah, now they were getting somewhere. "And why didn't you?"

Kevin looked up, oozing frustration from every pore. "Why does Sean always get to be the leader? Even when he doesn't know what to do, and his magic isn't always the best for the job?"

She touched his shoulder gently to drive her point home. "Because you always let him."

Sean looked flabbergasted. "You want to lead the magic, Kevin?"

"Sometimes." Elorie hurt for Kevin as he tangled with his inner demons. "But Lizzie is the smartest person for this one. She knows how to make beds, and she has the strongest water power. Sheets are kind of flowy like water. So she should lead, and you and I should mindread and follow what she wants us to do."

That was a lot of growing up in thirty seconds. Elorie squeezed his shoulder in approval.

Lizzie stepped up to the bed, all business. Kevin and Sean moved to where she pointed, with Sean still looking utterly confused. Poor boy. With his spellcasting talents, they'd spent too much time training him to take the lead, and not enough time on being a supporting circle member.

After assessing the tangled mess on the bed for a moment, Lizzie closed her eyes. Given the look of concentration on the twins' faces, she was visualizing the process for them.

Kevin cast a spell to lift the sheet into the air, and Sean fluttered a small wind to untangle it. It didn't go entirely smoothly, but within a few minutes, they had a basically untangled sheet. Ironically, it was still sideways and upside-down.

Lizzie did something nifty with the air to push on the sheet in waves, eventually getting it oriented in the right direction. Then she closed her eyes, clearly sending guidance, and called her element one more time.

"I call on Water of ebb and flow,
Put this sheet where it should go.
On waves of air, lay it straight,
Corners ready where we wait.
Neatly done by we three,
As I will, so mote it be."

Lizzie could rhyme like nobody's business.

The sheet floated gently toward Kevin and settled an edge down around the first mattress corner. They got the next two corners on in quick succession, but the last one was tricky. After a couple of attempts, Lizzie abandoned ship and switched focus to the duvet.

Swift teamwork settled the cover on the bed over the errant sheet corner, and added two pillows.

Lizzie opened her eyes and grinned. "There, we did it!"

Elorie laughed. By six-year-old standards, that was probably an acceptable solution. She'd fix the last corner later.

Aaron arrived in the doorway. "There are scones and milk in the kitchen, if anybody's hungry." He got out of the way of the stampede, grinning at his wife.

"There's got to be a joke in here somewhere about how many witches it takes to change the sheets on a bed."

Elorie laughed and held up the corner of the cover so he could see Lizzie's shortcut. "Don't hire them just yet."

Aaron chuckled. "Not a problem. Aervyn's sleeping in that bed, and he's only three feet tall. He'll never notice."

Elorie fixed the sheet anyhow.

~ ~ ~

Sophie sat down in front of her laptop and let out a long sigh. Packing was finally done, her house was back in order, and her system was settling down after the lovely shock of Mike's arrival.

He'd found excellent use for her zinging hormones and then gone off for a run while she finished packing. Running was serious business for Mike—she didn't expect him back for at least another hour.

She had plans for that hour. A nine-year-old was aiming for Realm domination, and Gandalf wasn't the only witch who could take her down. Sophie'd been planning a sneak spell-raid for almost two weeks now, and her pushed-up travel plans meant she needed to spring the attack tonight.

Warrior Girl was online and on the prowl. Perfect. And odd. She was wandering around in one of the easiest witch-only levels, and she had company. Huh. Normally the top players stayed in the higher levels. It wasn't any fun squishing newbies, and complex spells didn't work as well in the beginners' zone.

Sophie dropped into the level-one world to investigate. Maybe Warrior Girl would be more vulnerable without her fancier spellcoding tricks.

At first, Sophie thought one of the lower-rated players had made the eternally dumb mistake of launching a magic attack on Realm's number-four-ranked player. Watching from the forest, however, it soon became clear that Warrior Girl wasn't fighting—she was training. Which was fascinating on a bunch of levels, not the least of which being that her companion had a very strange mix of glaring weaknesses and nifty magical tricks. Sophie looked up the username. Hecate. Hmm.

She didn't know what gave her presence away, but suddenly Hecate fired a very tricky freeze spell in her direction. Sophie reacted instinctively, pulling a reversing spell out of her bag in the nick of time.

Nothing like being completely unprepared. Ugh. Sophie squared off with Hecate and tried to keep an eye on Warrior Girl.

Hecate had some nice magical moves, and she used them. Sophie dodged where she could, retaliated when she had to, and wondered how the heck she was going to get out of this with even a fraction of her spell stockpile intact.

Just when she was getting somewhere, Warrior Girl tossed in an illusion spell to make things interesting. Sophie would have appreciated her sense of fair play more if Hecate didn't appear to have six arms now.

There was only one way she could see to end this, and she'd better take it before Warrior Girl got more seriously involved. Hecate had snazzy magic tricks, but she had really weak physical fighting skills. Sophie waited for an opening and moved in. One conk on the head with the butt end of her sword, and Hecate dropped to the ground like a stone, out cold.

Ginia flew to the side of her fallen trainee. "Aunt Moira!"

Sophie's brain slowed to molasses. "Aunt Moira?"

Ginia looked up, a very pained look on her face. "Ssshh. Keep it down. She's my secret weapon, but it won't do me much good if everyone figures out who she is."

Oh, God. She'd conked Aunt Moira on the head. In an online game. Either of those events was insane. Both must mean the world was coming to an end.

She bent down beside Ginia. "What do we do?"

Ginia looked up. "I don't know. I don't have any safe zones in this level."

Sophie sighed and drew a cloaking spell out of her bag. This was going to cost her mucho game points. She initiated the spell and a dome slapped into place around them. "It only lasts for fifteen minutes, so think fast."

"I didn't know you could do that." Ginia looked moderately impressed.

She should be. Only four Realm players had cloaking capabilities, and Sophie had managed to keep hers secret until now. "So how do we fix the conk on her head?"

Ginia shrugged. "I could make her a new avatar, but I think Aunt Moira likes this one. I don't have any healing spells, though." She raised her eyebrows. "*Somebody* hasn't been sharing lately."

Spellcoding only worked with magic you possessed in real life, so Sophie was one of the very few Realm players who could create healing spells for the game. Once upon a time she'd done a brisk business trading those spells for other useful things, but in the last few weeks, she'd been hording them. Healing your competition just wasn't all that smart in the long run.

Besides, no decent healing spell worked in this level. Witches were restricted in the spells they could use in level one, mostly for safety reasons. "None of my spells are basic enough to work here—they'd all trigger the spellcode lock."

Ginia frowned down at the still-unconscious Hecate. Then she looked up at Sophie, eyes full of mischief. "The lock only works on spellcode. Maybe we can try something different."

Uh, oh. "Like what?"

Ginia looked around furtively. "Is your cloaking spell soundproof?"

Just barely, but no point letting Warrior Girl know that. "Do I look like an incompetent witch?"

Rolling her eyes, Ginia pulled one of her trademark spellcubes out of her bag. They were remote-triggered, and everyone in Realm had learned to be very careful when they spotted one. She set it gently on the ground. "*Now* we're soundproof for sure."

Yeesh, what was this—a secret spy convention? "What are we doing, kiddo, waking the dead?"

"Close." Ginia's eyes twinkled. "I want you to do a healing spell on Hecate."

"I can't heal in-game, you know that. We need spellcode to do that, and we'll trigger the lock if we try. Maybe we can take Hecate to one of the higher levels."

Ginia shook her head. "Nope. She's almost ready to pass to level two, but not quite. I can't seem to teach her to keep her sword hand high."

Since that was how Sophie had gotten around Aunt Moira's guard, she wasn't about to argue. "So what are you suggesting we do?" Ginia was plenty creative—maybe she'd figured out a way around the lock.

"I'm going to use Net power."

"I thought that just worked for spellcoding."

"Nope. It works to join things. Spellcoding joins magic with programming code, but I can join other stuff, too. I tried it yesterday with Uncle Jamie and Gandalf, and we joined two spells here in Realm."

Splendid. Just what they needed in the game—Warrior Girl with magic no one else could match.

Ginia looked down at Hecate. "So I bet that if you try to heal her, I can use Net power to join your in-real-life healing magic with what happens here in Realm."

Real magic in Realm?

Sophie was pretty sure she'd just heard the final clink in Ginia's quest for Realm domination, but she couldn't resist the lure of a new magic trick. Crouching down, she laid her hands on Hecate's head and chest. "Let me know when you're ready."

When Ginia nodded, Sophie reached for power and tried to pretend she felt Aunt Moira under her hands, rather than her computer keyboard. It was a very strange sensation.

Strangeness vanished when Hecate coughed and tried to sit up. She looked up at Sophie, eyes scolding. "Sophie Ellen Delaney, what on earth were you thinking, conking me over the head like that?"

Oh, yes, definitely Aunt Moira. "How does your head feel?"

"Just fine, but Hecate here will probably have a bit of a bump."

Sophie laughed at herself. It had been a dumb question to ask, but she wasn't used to virtual healing.

Virtual healing. Or rather, real healing magic, done in-game. They'd brought real magic into Realm. Sophie looked over at Ginia, the weight of what they'd accomplished suddenly sinking in. Ginia met her eyes with a very sober, very adult look.

Two things hit loud and clear. One, Net power was a new world, and Ginia was leading the scouting party. Witch school was going to be very interesting. And two, Warrior Girl was about to turn Realm upside-down. With Aunt Moira at her side.

First things first. Sophie grinned, warrior to warrior. "So, how about a girl-power alliance? I might even be able to help you train this one to keep her guard arm up."

They shook hands over Hecate's spluttering laughter.

Chapter 11

Nell heaved a sigh of relief as she climbed out of Aaron's van. Here in the middle of nowhere, she could finally stand down from high alert. Four-year-olds and airplanes were a fun mix for about an hour. Unfortunately, it took a lot longer than that to get from California to Nova Scotia.

And she'd had to clamp a silence spell on Aervyn going through customs. The nice border agent didn't really need to know what an unhappy witchling thought he could do to make planes go a little faster.

"Try not to lose your brother before dinner, Ginia," she called out to her daughter, already halfway across the lawn happily greeting Lizzie, with Aervyn not far behind.

Kevin waved. "Don't worry, Aunt Nell. We'll make sure he doesn't fall in the ocean."

It was hard to take that promise seriously from a boy whose pants were wet up to the knees. "Just make sure you all come back for dinner."

In moments, all five children were around the end of the house and gone.

"It will do them good to run for a bit," Aaron said, grabbing some of her luggage.

Nell grinned. "You just don't want them burning it off inside your inn."

"That, too. Although Elorie assures me it's been witchling-proofed."

"Nothing is Aervyn-proof."

Aaron chuckled. "Remind me to triple your damage deposit, then." He picked up a bag. "What the heck is in here—rocks?"

"That would be Ginia's collection of potions. She wanted to show Sophie and Moira some of her latest creations. Unfortunately, potions are heavy, and not all that easy to get through customs."

Aaron eyed the bag with sensible caution. "I can imagine. Will any of them turn me into a frog or cause me to express my undying love to the wrong woman?"

"Don't worry. I'll make sure you're pointed at your wife if you drink that one." Aaron laughed, and they began lugging bags into the house. Nell decided she approved of Elorie's guy.

A sense of humor was an important quality if you were married to a witch, particularly if there were witchling babies on the horizon. Nell knew a case of baby fever when she saw one. Elorie's eyes had strayed to every baby on the West Coast during her visit. She'd be shocked if there weren't a little Shaw in at least the planning stages.

Moira was waiting in the inn's parlor. "How very lovely to see you." She hugged Nell and gestured to the table. "Come, sit. I've tea already poured. I assume your children ran away with our ruffians."

Nell breathed deeply and downshifted to rural Nova Scotia speed. "They did, but Ginia can hardly wait to sit down with you and Sophie. She's been practicing her potions and threatening to turn our entire back yard into a garden."

Moira beamed. "She's most welcome in my garden. My flowers could use some tending by young hands. They feel a bit neglected these days."

"None of your witchlings have earth magic?"

"Our Sean has a wee bit, but his talents are mostly with the rocks and land. He's not at all interested in the plants, and I don't think he's got the patience to sit and tend to flowers."

"That's women's work," Marcus said from the doorway, nodding at Nell. She wasn't entirely sure he was kidding.

Moira looked heavenward. "Nell, you'd do me the most wonderful favor if you could tinker with my nephew's thinking while you're here. Some of his brain appears to be stuck in the Middle Ages."

Marcus poured himself a cup of tea. "I've never denied it. Welcome to our corner of the world, Nell. I won't ask about your trip—I assume that with two witchlings in tow, it was less than pleasant."

Nell could feel a hiss of protest coming on, even though Marcus was exactly right. He just rubbed her the wrong way.

"Marcus, behave," Moira said, an amused look on her face. "So, Lauren didn't travel with you then, Nell?"

"No, she didn't. There was some last-minute deal she had to wrap up this morning, so she took a different airline and routed through Colorado. She and Sophie will be coming in together in a couple of hours."

Marcus sat and offered Nell a bowl of berries. "Perhaps she reassessed the wisdom of spending hours on an airplane with a four-year-old."

Nell just raised an eyebrow. She knew how to handle bullies. Her pithy reply, however, got cut off by Aervyn's flying entrance. "Blueberries!"

He made a beeline for the bowl in Marcus's hand, and then caught and ported it to safety when it went crashing toward the floor. Everyone froze as a flood of love and pain hammered into every mind in the room. Marcus's face was pasty white and a study in anguish.

"Evan." His harsh whisper as he stared at Aervyn's face cut through Nell's soul.

Her son reached out gently and laid his hands on Marcus's cheeks. "I'm not your Evan, but you can love me. That would be just fine with me." He climbed into Marcus's lap and nestled.

Nell watched the crotchety old bachelor hold her son like he was spun glass, a haunted sadness on his face.

Aervyn ported over the blueberries and held them up. "Here, have some berries. They're my favorites. Did Evan like blueberries, too?"

"Yes," whispered Marcus, kissing the top of Aervyn's head. "Yes, he did."

"Was he your brother, or your little boy?" Aervyn asked. "Your mind is kind of jumbly."

"He was my twin. He died when he was just a little older than you."

Aervyn looked up solemnly. "It makes you really sad."

"Yes."

Aervyn tucked his head into Marcus's chest. "It wasn't your fault. Even really strong witches can't fix everything. You were just little, like me."

Moira sucked in a wavery breath. "You've blamed yourself all this time, Marcus? My sweet boy, it was never your fault. If anything, it was mine."

She looked over at Nell. "Evan's magic emerged young and hard. He was a fire mage, and a strong one. In the midst of putting out fires every night, we somehow missed that he was also an astral traveler." Her voice dropped to almost nothing. "One night he left his body and didn't make it back. He wasn't quite six yet."

Nell's heart bled with all the sadness and guilt in the room. She had always wondered at Moira's strict devotion to training. Magic that killed was the worst nightmare of every witchling's parents.

"I couldn't call him back," Marcus said softly. "I could feel him, but I couldn't bring him back."

Aervyn tilted his head. "You still feel him."

Marcus leaned down and kissed his head again. "Yes, my boy. I still do."

~ ~ ~

Elorie finished her last bite of salmon and looked down the dinner table in satisfaction. Kitchens were the heart of any Nova Scotia home, and while she loved intimate dinners for two, it was also wonderful to have a table full of visitors and laughter. With all their guests now arrived, the table was definitely full.

The seating configuration was very strange, however. She leaned over toward Sophie and Nell. "Since when is Uncle Marcus a kid magnet?" He had Aervyn on one side, Lizzie on the other. Normally he and children gravitated to opposite ends of the table.

Nell spoke quietly. "Since this afternoon—with Aervyn, at least. Apparently my son looks a lot like Evan."

Sophie sucked in a breath and exchanged looks with Elorie. Evan had always been the one subject no one talked about.

And I'd appreciate if it remained that way, Marcus sent.

Elorie felt her cheeks getting red, and the eyes of more than one child turned her way. There were far too many mind witches at the table. She checked surreptitiously to make sure her gizmo was still turned on.

Your brain may not be leaking anymore, niece, but your face is as expressive as usual.

So find something else to talk about, you old fart, Elorie thought, and then blushed even more furiously when Marcus began to laugh. Dammit, how was he hearing her thoughts?

I don't need to hear them. It's not the first dirty look I've received in fifty-two years.

Elorie put her mental foot down. Enough. This was her turf. Her home, her dinner table. She picked the most sympathetic face at the table. "Ginia, I hear you've brought a suitcase of potions to share with us."

The girl's face brightened. "I practiced everything Aunt Moira showed me on video chat."

"Excellent," Sophie said. "I think a potions class tomorrow morning would be a great way to get witch school started. Ginia, perhaps you could help me teach the others some of what Aunt Moira showed you."

Elorie pushed down the small spurt of jealousy. It was only right that Sophie help organize witch school. This might be her turf, but she could surely share it.

Sean groaned. "Potions are boring."

Elorie elbowed him. "That's because yours never work. Perhaps if you pay attention and actually mix things correctly, your potions would be a little more exciting."

"Who wants to make stuff for aches and pains, anyhow?" His brain finally caught up with his mouth, and he glanced at Moira with concern. "Sorry, Gran. I know that stuff works good for you."

"Healing hurts is a great gift," Sophie said, "and not one to be taken lightly." Her eyes twinkled. "But I have a little recipe that says it will help a baseball pitcher's arm recover faster."

Sean looked interested in spite of himself. If anyone could make him sit through potions without grumbling, it would be Sophie. And Elorie had a sneaking suspicion that the pitcher's potion had a lot in common with the one Gran used for her aches and pains.

Aaron and Mike returned from the pantry, bearing pies. "Anyone have room for blueberry pie?"

If anyone didn't, they got drowned out under the avalanche of noise from people who did. However, as Aaron started slicing pieces and plating them, there was a sudden drop in volume—the kind that got any trainer's attention very quickly. Four witchlings were very quiet and all looking at Ginia.

"What are they up to?" Nell asked under her breath.

Elorie shook her head. "No idea."

"They've pulled together a circle of sorts," Sophie whispered. Nell nodded in agreement.

Elorie watched with interest as one of the dessert plates of blueberry pie levitated, and then disappeared. It reappeared teetering on the very edge of the table in front of Marcus.

He scowled and nudged it to safety. "Aim more carefully, young ones. Who's doing what?"

Aervyn looked up quizzically. "Can't you see?"

Marcus shook his head. "Not all of it. I can see you've each called some elemental power."

Aervyn grinned. "That's cuz Net power is invisible. It's like a special superpower no one can see."

Marcus nodded at Ginia in approval. "No mean feat, blending four working spells like that. It looks like you did more this afternoon than accidentally fall in the ocean."

Ginia giggled. The five witchlings had come in for dinner dripping wet and proclaiming innocence. "We practiced with rocks. Good thing we didn't start with plates. We kind of dropped a few at first."

Elorie felt her world tilt. They'd done actual magic with Net power? On the beach?

Nell frowned. "What were you using for a power source, girl of mine?"

Ginia reached into her pocket and pulled out an iPhone, looking sheepish. "I borrowed your phone and tweaked it, Mama. The touch screen works just like the mouse does."

Nell rolled her eyes. "Remind me to have a chat with you about roaming charges, kiddo. How long did you have it on for?"

"Just a couple of hours, Aunt Nell." Sean, obviously trying to be helpful, dug Ginia in deeper.

Marcus stepped in. "Since you've already spent a fortune, a little more won't matter. Do that trick with the plates again. I want to watch."

"Wait." Elorie was astonished to hear her own voice almost shouting. She was not going to be sidelined yet again by witches doing magic she couldn't understand. Her home, her table, *her power*. "Ginia—this is the same magic I have, right?"

Ginia nodded.

Elorie looked at Aervyn. "Can you mindlink with me the way you did in California? I want to see what you're doing."

He grinned. "Sure. Can you turn off Uncle Jamie's gizmo, though? It's a lot of work to hook into your brain when that's on."

And put her mind on display for half the table?

"Not to worry," Marcus said dryly. He gestured to Sean and Kevin. "These two will be plenty busy with their part of the spell, and Lauren and I have better manners than you think. Aervyn is right—he needs the gizmo off if you want to see." He crossed his arms, almost a dare.

She wanted to see.

Elorie laid Jamie's gizmo on the table, focused as hard as she could on blueberry pie, and turned the device off.

Aervyn's mindlink clicked into place moments later. *You can relax now. I can make sure your brain isn't leaky.*

She didn't much care anymore. Mindlinking had brought her a gift beyond measure. For the first time in her life, Elorie could *see* power at work. For someone who had watched thousands of spells from the outside, it was sheer joy to finally see the power in which she so deeply believed.

She could see the five witchlings, each calling a power source. The only one she recognized was the network of fireworks—that would be Ginia's Net power. She concentrated, trying to identify the others. The sinuously flowing lines must be Lizzie's water energy, and the crackling light would be Kevin's fire. Aervyn held earth magic, and that left Sean calling air.

Elorie's heart danced with the beauty of it. The four streams of energy touched and twisted as each witchling created a spell. Lizzie's and Sean's looked fairly simple, but whatever Kevin and Aervyn were doing was complex and convoluted. She yearned to understand.

It's not difficult, girl. Lizzie and Sean are working together to lift the plate, Marcus sent. Elorie jumped. She hadn't realized anyone else was watching.

We're all watching, child, came Gran's soothing voice. *Marcus and Lauren have patched us all in. Kevin calls fire, but he's acting as channeler, helping to blend all the energies and keep them balanced. It's very delicate work he's handling, and well done.*

Aervyn's readying a teleporting spell, Nell said. *But I don't think he's the one that actually uses it. Watch.*

Elorie watched in fascination as Ginia's fireworks suddenly got brighter. The four spells glistened for a moment, and then melded.

It was the most beautiful thing she'd ever seen.

Damn it! Marcus cursed. *They missed!*

Elorie felt Aervyn's giggles beginning as they all thudded out of mindlink. She opened her eyes to find Uncle Marcus looking at the blueberry pie in his lap with disgust, and everyone else at the table in various stages of mirth.

Her own sense of humor kicked in as she realized they probably hadn't missed at all.

You think I don't know that, girl?

Elorie managed to turn Jamie's gizmo back on before she collapsed on the table, laughing.

Gran leaned over and patted Marcus's hand. "It might be a good time to practice those cleaning spells you so disdain, nephew."

Marcus just growled.

~ ~ ~

"The moon's gorgeous tonight." It wasn't often Elorie could convince her husband to take a midnight walk on the beach, so she was pleased the night sky had decided to show off a little.

Of course, it wouldn't be her who had to get up at the crack of dawn to cook breakfast for an inn full of witches.

Aaron wrapped an arm around her shoulders. "So, what exactly happened at dinner tonight?"

"The magic, you mean?"

"Is that how Marcus ended up with my pie in his lap?"

Elorie stopped dead in the sand as realization hit. He'd been the only non-witch in the room. "Oh, honey. I'm so sorry. I should have told you what was going on." Heaven knows she'd been shut out of the magic often enough to know what it felt like.

He kissed her forehead. "So, tell me now."

"I think the children practiced together this afternoon, and they did a nice little demonstration with your pie. Each of the children cast a spell, and then Ginia blended them together to do one big spell."

"Dumping pie on Marcus is a big spell?"

Elorie giggled. "I'm not sure whether they meant to do that part or not."

"And Aervyn made it so that you could see what was happening."

"Right. Uncle Marcus and Lauren patched in everyone else so we could all watch." She winced even as she said it. "All the witches, at least. I am sorry, Aaron. That was horribly rude of us."

He grinned. "Nah. I got to watch the look on Marcus's face as the pie landed. The rest of you missed that."

He stopped for a minute, bending over to pick up a shiny moon opal, and held it out to her. "I also got to see the look on your face. You were happy, Elorie. Really happy."

The joy of that moment still echoed in her heart. "I've never been able to see the magic before, see power being used. It was amazing."

"What Ginia did, blending the spells together—is that what you'll be able to do?"

Elorie's legs simply melted. She sat down hard, staggered by sheer shock. In the magic, and in all the laughter, she had somehow missed that one essential point. "Oh, my God. That was Net magic Ginia did."

He nodded, clearly confused.

She could feel the tears coming. "I can learn to do what she did. I'm not going to be a useless witch."

DEBORA GEARY

Chapter 12

Nell looked around Moira's back yard and grinned. It looked like a tornado had swept through and dumped off random heaps of computer parts. Clustered around them were some excited, but very confused, witches.

Moira had put out the call—everyone should come to be tested. Clearly the witch population of Nova Scotia had taken that literally. There were almost a hundred people in the back yard, with only a handful competent enough to test for Net power. And one of those was four and in need of a nap.

To make matters worse, most of the new arrivals seemed to believe they needed some sort of computer part to activate their Net power. Which was true, but Nell was pretty sure most of the parts littered in Moira's yard pre-dated the Internet. Ginia had been shocked to discover floppy disks actually still existed.

Nell waded through the crowd, dispensing cookies and blueberries as she went. Yup, Ginia was looking a little frazzled. Time for a rescue. "Hey, sweetie. How's it going?"

"It's a little crazy, Mama. I'm trying to get everyone scanned, but most of them can't spellcode, so I have to teach them how to do that first."

Since Ginia's current audience was all over sixty, Nell guessed that wasn't going overly well.

And no way did she plan to spend the entire week teaching the witch population of Nova Scotia to code. Time for Plan B.

"Go find Lauren and your brother, sweetie. I have an idea."

Ginia dashed off, looking relieved. Nell clapped her hands and spell-projected her voice. "Good morning, everybody! Can I get you all to take a seat and face this direction?"

Lauren made her way over with a grumpy Aervyn in tow. Nell handed him a cookie. Chocolate chips could work miracles on four-year-old moods.

"I hope you have a plan," Lauren said. "This is nuts."

"I do. I think we need to teach them how to activate Net power without spellcoding. Just like you did with Aervyn and Elorie, but we'll give them a group demonstration first."

She turned back to the now-seated and mostly quiet group. "We weren't expecting such a crowd this morning, so thanks for your patience. As many of you have obviously heard, one way of using Net power is online, with spellcoding. But it can also be activated much like mind power, and we think that might be an easier way to test most of you."

"Thank goodness," said a voice at the back. Judging from the laughter, a lot of people agreed with him.

Nell grinned. It didn't look like Realm was going to pick up a flood of new players from the east. "What we're going to do first is a quick demonstration, with Ginia activating her Net power. Lauren and Aervyn will mindlink and broadcast so all of you can see."

Marcus stood up on her left. "I'll help with that. This is a sizable crowd."

Nell was pretty sure Aervyn could have handled the job on his own, but she wasn't about to argue with the local talent.

Ginia pulled out her commandeered iPhone, which got plenty of murmurs all on its own. Marcus leaned over toward Nell. "You're going to have to raise the rates for Realm if she keeps using that up here."

Nell snorted. Her girl was smarter than that. "She and Jamie hunkered down last night and hooked up a wireless bubble on her laptop. They juiced the range, so it should work from here."

"Interesting." Marcus pulled an iPhone out of his pocket.

Wait just a minute. "You've had that all this time?" While she'd been paying a gadzillion dollars a minute in roaming charges?

Marcus raised an eyebrow. "Just how many Net witches do you think we have sitting here, and how many iPhones? I'd never get it back."

That grated on Nell's last nerve. Selfish old man. Okay, maybe she was a little cranky too, but witches shared. It was an unspoken rule.

Nell felt Lauren's incoming mindlink and realized the demonstration was ready to begin. Time to stop squabbling with Marcus.

Very slowly, Ginia walked through the exercise of activating her Net power, with Lauren providing mental commentary. When they'd done it several times, Aervyn ran the slow-motion replay. No one in the audience so much as blinked until he was finished.

Then bedlam broke out. Marcus raised a hand. QUIET.

Lauren winced. *Warn me the next time you plan to mind-yell, please.*

My apologies. I wasn't aware you were so sensitive.

Nell grabbed Lauren before she whacked Marcus with a mental two-by-four. *Later, girl. Right now, we have a herd of witches to train, and we need him. Play nicely, and I'll help you get even later.*

She'd never heard Lauren growl before. Trust Marcus to bring out the best in all the women around him.

Are you two done yet? Marcus asked dryly. *I suggest you pick a volunteer to test.*

Nell looked at the waiting audience and tried to figure out the best way to proceed. Ginia tugged on her arm. "Start with the kids, Mama. I'm pretty sure Kevin is a Net witch."

It wasn't a bad idea, but they definitely didn't need several dozen witches watching. "Can I get anyone under twelve to come up here, please? And can I ask the rest of you to collect into groups of five or six and practice? We'll come around to you and help as we're able."

The back yard settled into the relative order of witches hard at work.

After a few minutes with the dozen or so Nova Scotia witchlings, a couple of things were clear. One, the children with Net power caught on fast. Aervyn had figured out a way to piggyback onto their channels, kind of like a pair of guiding hands, and it got results very quickly.

And two, while Net power was evidently quite common, most of them were like Nell—a spark or two, but nothing more. The exception was Kevin. His initial, Aervyn-assisted fireworks were almost as bright as Ginia's—and then he repeated it on his own seconds later.

His quiet grin snagged Nell's heart. She looked over at Elorie, who had been watching with silent pride. "Looks like you have a training buddy."

Elorie pulled Kevin in for a hug. "I guess I do."

~ ~ ~

Preparing tea for her guests, Moira smiled in satisfaction. Apparently you could teach an old witch new tricks. She was a Net witch—imagine that!—and a strong one, if Ginia and Lauren were to be believed.

What an irony that would be. Her entire life, she'd been the witch with a little bit of a lot of magics, but never a big dose of anything. It had made her a good trainer, and she had thought that her life's purpose. Now, it appeared she would be joining her granddaughter in the history books as part of the first wave of witches with an entirely new form of power.

She felt positively giddy.

"Don't rub it in," said Marcus, coming into her kitchen. Nell was right behind him, not trying to hide her grin at all.

"I'm hardly doing that," Moira said. "You've been a powerful witch since you were three years old. Surely you don't begrudge others a little power of their own."

Marcus picked up mugs of tea to carry to the table. She was pleased; hospitality was not one of her nephew's stronger traits.

"I don't," he said. "It just seems rather unfair that those of us who have used our Net power the most are actually the most restricted in what we can do with it."

"Tell me about it," Nell said. "I have an entire crew of seriously unhappy Realm players."

Moira sat down at the table and gestured for them to join her. "So explain this to me—I haven't really understood it just yet. Why is it that some of us are so different? That would be the wee bit I'm not understanding."

"None of us do," Nell said. "But it looks like those of us with a lot of spellcoding experience are limited in how we can use Net power. Marcus gets powerful readings on our scans when he's spellcoding, but he can only access a tiny fraction of that in the way we tried today."

Marcus scowled. "It's as if our brains have gotten hardwired."

"It's not the only kind of magic where that happens." Moira stirred her tea contemplatively. "It works that way with astral travel as well. Mediums and travelers are fueled by the same power source, but generally witches with that talent can only do one or the other, unless they're carefully trained in both while their talents are first emerging."

Marcus raised an eyebrow. "That's interesting. So if both are trained early, then a witchling retains both abilities?"

"That's what our histories say." She reached out to touch her nephew's hand and hoped he might accept a small bit of comfort. "As you know, it's a great sadness that we lose most of our astral travelers far too young."

He said nothing, but she noticed he didn't take his hand away, either. Her healer's heart was gladdened by the small victory.

Marcus looked over at Nell. "If Aunt Moira's correct, we need to think carefully about how we proceed with training."

"Yup." Nell topped up everyone's tea. "We'll need to teach all our Net witches to work with their power offline and online." She grinned at Moira. "We need to teach you to spellcode."

Ginia had been teaching her for several days now, but old witches knew how to keep secrets. "I think you'll have better luck with young Kevin. His mind likes new challenges."

"She has a point," Marcus said. "We have seven Net witches with decent strength of the non-spellcoding variety. We clearly don't want to be teaching everyone at once."

This was a problem Moira could solve. "We shouldn't try. We'll train those from this village first, with Nell's help, and then once we've figured things out here, you can help me with our more far-flung witches."

She could see Marcus fighting with himself. A solitary witch, he had never enjoyed the communal aspects of witchcraft, but no one was more aware of the dangers of power left untended. He finally nodded, just once. "It's a good plan."

"So who do we have from here, then?" Nell asked. "It was a bit crazy, so I'm not sure I caught all the results."

Marcus started counting off on his fingers. "Young Kevin, and Elorie, of course. Aunt Moira, and then your Ginia and Aervyn. I think that's all in the first group to train. Sophie and I can't do the mental fireworks, but we can help teach spellcoding."

Nell nodded. "As can Ginia and I."

Witches to train. Moira could feel the gladness in her heart. "You and Sophie will be busy. We've other witchlings and other magics to train as well."

Marcus grunted. "There are plenty of hands to help. Lauren with the mind-witch lessons, and Mike would be an excellent choice to teach Sean the finer points of his earth magics."

"Aye. It would be good if the ground rumbled a little less around here." Sean's earth talents were not of the gentler sort that worked with plants and growing things, but rather the hard magics of rock and land.

Nell grinned. "Aervyn has some skill in that direction as well, but I'm not sure you want to put him and Sean in the same training group."

Sometimes it was handy to be the wise elder witch. "It will be good for Mike to earn his breakfast. I'm sure he can handle two small boys." And if not, she'd always had a soft spot for witchling mischief, particularly if she wasn't in charge of cleanup afterward.

~ ~ ~

Elorie looked around at her fellow students and leaned toward Moira. "I feel a little old for this class, Gran."

Moira chortled. "How do you think I feel, especially with sweet Ginia about to be our teacher?"

Lauren, Marcus, and Ginia had their heads together in one corner of the room; Kevin and Aervyn were tucked in another corner with a bowl of blueberries. Elorie felt a bit useless. Organizing training had been her job just a week ago.

Sophie sat quietly in the corner, reading one of Gran's herbals. For some reason Elorie didn't want to explore, her presence grated. "Why is Sophie here? I thought her Net power was only the spellcoding kind."

"She's never been a threat to who you are, granddaughter mine." Gran's eyes were quiet and sad. "Do you truly not know why she's here?"

Elorie squirmed. She felt like she was ten years old again, caught napping in witch history class. And she was disappointing Gran—that much was obvious. She just wasn't sure why.

Their three teachers turned around, interrupting her puzzlement. Marcus called the two boys over. "Lets see if we can figure out what to do with this Net power of yours, shall we?"

So like Uncle Marcus. No preliminaries, just straight to the point. Not that she really minded today. Everything in her yearned to finally *do* magic.

Lauren smiled, as if she had read Elorie's thoughts. With her gizmo off, it was entirely possible. Nothing like four mind witches in the room to decimate your privacy.

Well, hopefully action would keep their brains focused on something other than her leaky thoughts. Elorie roused herself and caught Ginia's eye. "Show me what you did yesterday, blending spells together. I want to try that."

Moira spoke just as Ginia nodded yes. "Slow down, my sweet girls. We need a plan." She held up a hand before the protests could begin. "I felt this Net power, and I'd like nothing better to play with it. But we must learn with caution."

She paused and looked around the room with great seriousness. "We are the first, the pioneers. Magic can be dangerous, and we play with unknown magic here. Care and caution will keep us safe."

Elorie had spoken variations of that last sentence a hundred times in her life. And now, with memories of the rush of power strong in her mind, she finally understood why very few witchlings ever paid attention.

Moira leaned over and spoke quietly. "I know it calls you, child, but you must learn control first."

"I know. I had no idea it could feel this way, though."

"Neither did I." Wonder crossed Gran's face. "It's more power than I've ever known. Such magic, waiting for us..."

"Then let's get started, shall we?" Marcus nodded at Ginia. "Let's have you do your joining trick. Aervyn and I will give you two simple spells to work with."

He looked at the rest of the group. "Lauren will mindcast what Ginia does so you can all see. Once you think you've understood, let Lauren know."

Elorie frowned. She was no mindspeaker.

Marcus rolled his eyes. *Trust me, niece—she won't miss anything you're thinking.*

She and Uncle Marcus were going to have a conversation about privacy. Soon.

Until then, she'd better start paying attention. Ginia was already pulling Net power. Much like the day before, Elorie watched from the mind-window Lauren provided as dancing power streams formed into intricate spell shapes, and then melded. Some of it had made sense, but she wanted to watch one more time.

One more time didn't happen, however. Lauren dropped them out of mindlink, and Kevin nodded solemnly. "I can do it, I think."

Marcus raised an eyebrow. "Are you sure you don't want to see it again?"

Kevin met his gaze straight on. "Yes. I want to try." Elorie mentally cheered at his self-confidence. Generally Sean was the twin rushing headlong into magic, with Kevin trailing quietly behind.

Aervyn and Marcus began their spellwork again, and this time Elorie watched with her eyes. Marcus created a globe of dancing color on his palm, and Aervyn whipped up a very small whirlwind. Kevin focused, a look of deep concentration on his face.

The globe disappeared for a moment, and color briefly danced around the room. Then all signs of magic vanished. Elorie's breath caught.

Kevin never wavered. "Again, please."

One more time, Marcus and Aervyn created their spells and Kevin focused. One more time, the globe wavered. Everyone in the room held their breath.

And then light blew around the room, a shimmering stream of dancing color.

The fierce pride in Kevin's eyes nearly brought Elorie to tears.

Then it was Moira's turn, and she repeated the trick with quiet confidence and not the slightest wobble, childlike joy on her face. Kevin looked at her in awe. "Wow, Gran, that was great."

Moira ruffled his head. "I've been practicing spellwork for seventy years, darling boy. Now I know why."

Jeebers. Her turn next, and she had a grand total of about two minutes of spellwork practice.

Globe of light waiting on his palm, Marcus raised an eyebrow. It was time.

Elorie closed her eyes—and realized she had a big problem. By the time she'd opened her eyes, it was clear every mind witch in the room knew as well.

"That's rather an issue," Marcus said.

"What is?" Ginia asked.

Lauren explained. "Unlike the rest of you, Elorie doesn't have elemental power, so she can't see the power streams or shapes for the two spells."

Terrific. She wasn't a useless witch now, just a defective one.

Aervyn looked puzzled. "What's a 'defective' witch? Can you solve mysteries?"

Ginia giggled. "That's a detective, goofy boy."

Lauren shot Elorie a warning look, but she'd already gotten the message loud and clear. No pity parties while the witchlings were listening. Good grief, she wasn't usually this much of a wimp.

She cleared her throat. "So how do we fix this? I could see the power streams when you were patching me in, Lauren—can you do that for me again?"

"Nope." Lauren shook her head and winked. "Welcome to the exclusive and sometimes inconvenient club of witches with no elemental powers. You could see them before because Marcus and I were working together, and he can visualize the elemental energies. I can't."

Elorie tried really, really hard to block the next thought that came to her mind. What on earth had she done in her life to deserve having to partner with Uncle Marcus if she wanted to do any magic?

Given Marcus's snort, she hadn't blocked hard enough. "You'll notice I haven't yet volunteered."

"You're not the only witch on this coast," Moira said crisply.

Kevin rode to the rescue, all valiant four-and-a-half feet of him. "I can do it. I can help you see, Elorie."

Marcus looked skeptical. "You've had mind powers for all of a week, my boy, and they're not that strong. Broadcasting takes a steady hand. If you falter, Elorie's spell could easily go awry."

Kevin gave him a pointed look. "Then you'd better cast a training circle. Gran will be mad if we scorch her furniture."

Elorie bit back a giggle, and then shoved any doubts out of her mind. If Kevin was willing to try, she would do everything she could to make it work. The alternative didn't bear considering.

Marcus and Aervyn readied their spells. She looked at Kevin and felt his mindlink click into place. It wasn't as fast or as steady as Lauren's, but she could see the spellshapes.

She paused for a moment and reviewed the steps Ginia had gone through, then laid her hand on the mouse and reached for power, just as she'd been practicing. Energy stormed through her, and it took every ounce of will she had not to reach out and grab the waiting spells. *Slowly, girl. You've waited your whole life to do this. Get it right.*

Attempting to copy Ginia's delicate control, she gently wrapped power around the two spells, gliding them closer together. Even she could tell her power was far more wobbly than anyone else's, but she pressed on—it took practice to be a better witch. Once the spells were fairly close together, she looked for the points where they needed to connect. When she'd watched Ginia, the spellshapes had pulsed light at those points, but they weren't doing it now.

As she stared at the shapes in consternation, Elorie could feel her power tugging. Not demanding, this time, but asking permission. It had an odd similarity to the tug she sometimes felt sitting in her studio, when a collection of sea glass and silver wire seemed to know what it needed to be. She had long practice trusting that tug; it produced some of her best work.

Very slowly, she let a finger of power go toward Aervyn's spell. Little fireworks of Net power slid into his spellshape. She sent another very small flow toward Marcus's spell. As Net power melded into the second spell, she could suddenly *see*—see them as they were, and as they were meant to be. Now they were her spells, and she knew what to do with them.

With sure hands, she moved the streams of spellpower around, weaving and turning them until they were perfectly aligned. It was exactly like fitting together silver wire and sea glass. So many ways they could go together, but only one way calling to her.

And then everything was ready. Tendrils of Net power reached out from both spells, seeking connection. She breathed deeply, and just as Ginia had done, released the tight hold on her power.

The spells shimmered for a moment, then melded. Power danced and whirled in the beauty of magic completed. Elorie could feel Kevin's delight—and an instant later, his panic and a resounding thunk as his mindlink vanished.

She opened her eyes to a sea of shock and grabbed Kevin as he swayed in his seat. "What happened?"

Aervyn pointed at the ceiling, eyes big. Elorie gazed in disbelief at the large, scorched circle over her head. "I did that?"

Marcus nodded. "Indeed you did. You and that sidekick of yours broke my circle. I'll cast a stronger one next time." He looked at Kevin. "Not bad. Don't drop her at the end next time, but you did quite well. That was some serious power she kicked at you."

Horror crawled through Elorie's gut. She'd pushed magic at Kevin? He was just a child.

He's an able witch, came Lauren's gentle reply. *And your partner. That was very nice work you did together.* She winked at Kevin. "Later today I'll show you some extra-special mind-witch protection for when you're working with Elorie. We didn't know she was going to have magic quite that strong."

Ginia waved her mouse. "First you have to teach me how you did that. That was awesome cool." She looked up. "Maybe we should go outside, though."

Elorie looked at the ceiling again, still distraught at what she'd managed to do with her first act of real magic. She'd preached "do no harm" often enough she ought to have been able to remember it. She turned at a hand on her shoulder, and Gran's delighted chortle. "You're not the first person to leave scorch marks in my house, child, and I doubt you'll be the last."

Then Gran's voice wavered, and she laid a hand on Elorie's cheek. "My sweet girl. Your first magic. I've waited so long for this."

She reached her other hand toward Sophie, still sitting quietly in the corner, herbal in her hand and joy on her face. "And so has she."

DEBORA GEARY

Chapter 13

"Ah, and isn't it nice to chat in person for once," Moira said, setting out a plate of finger foods Aaron had delivered. He was such a thoughtful young man.

Sophie pointed at the ceiling. "If you go have dinner with Elorie tonight, we'll take care of that. Mike's gone to fetch some paint from Lizzie's house."

"Thank you, dear. There was a time I could have fixed it myself, but I'm a wee bit past that age now."

"There are plenty of hands here to take care of things like that for you. Use them." The stern look on Sophie's face was one Moira had seen many times in her own mirror. It worked very well on witchlings, but she hadn't been one of those for a very long time.

"And use them I do, but I'm not an invalid yet, either. In fact, I believe Kevin is off having himself a little post-training nap, and Elorie was threatening to join him." And the old witch was still standing. Well, sitting, but that was a far sight from napping.

Nell grinned and reached for one of Aaron's tasty nibbles. "Full of energy, are you? Aervyn's climbing apple trees, if you'd like to go join him."

"I feel like I could. Handling that much power has left me positively zinging." Moira patted Sophie's hand. "I wish you'd been able to experience it, too. Perhaps then you and Mike would move a wee bit faster on making me some grandbabies." Oh, she *was* feeling feisty today.

Sophie choked on her cake, laughing. "You have plenty of those already, and Mike doesn't need any help in that department." Her eyes softened. "And today was not my day to do magic."

Aye, thought Moira. Sophie had been there as sister, not as witch, even if Elorie didn't fully realize it yet.

Lauren was looking at Moira in fascination. "You still get that kind of buzz from working magic?" Then she clapped a hand over her mouth, as her cheeks flamed red. "Oops, sorry. That came out totally wrong."

"Aye." Moira leaned forward, feeling entirely mischievous. "There's a saying in Ireland, that it's the luckiest of men who is married to an old witch."

Sophie giggled. "You're totally making that up."

"I'm not at all. And the more power you touch, the more true it is." She looked over at Lauren again. "Did no one tell you, lass? If you haven't found yourself a man to share your bed, you might consider it. He'll likely think himself very fortunate. Of course, it's always best when you share love as well."

Now Lauren's cheeks were the color of fresh-picked strawberries. "I can't believe we're having this conversation."

"Sorry." Nell chuckled. "Someone should have warned you that the ladylike and polite Moira you chat with online is not quite what you get at her kitchen table."

"Now you tell me."

Moira laid her hand on Lauren's red cheek. "There's ice cream in the freezer, dear. That will help cool you off."

Ah, it was like being a young witch again. Three wonderful women in her kitchen, full of laughter and magic, and the next generation playing out back.

Nell grinned as Lauren got up from the table. "If you bring two spoons, I'll change the subject for you."

"Deal," said Lauren, rummaging in the drawers.

Nell looked over at Moira. "So, back to the official purpose for this meeting. Besides Net power, what kind of training do we need to be doing with the witchlings?"

"We should confirm with Elorie—she handles most of the training for our young ones now. I do know that we'd like to test our Sean as spellcaster for a full circle. With all of you, we easily have the numbers to do that."

Nell nodded. "I'd be happy to do a little prep work with him, if you like."

"That would be lovely. Perhaps you might impress upon him the importance of discipline in a full circle. He's a wee bit full of himself yet."

Nell rolled her eyes. "I'm not green enough to agree to the impossible. I'll do what I can, but that's a lesson that comes with time, as you know all too well. Do you have a channeler in mind for him?"

"We're hoping his twin might have some channeling talent. Lauren, perhaps you could do a bit of work with Kevin and evaluate his potential. We've not many channelers here, and a young one to train would be very good news."

Lauren set down four spoons and a pint of ice cream. "I think we already know that much. Elorie didn't scorch your ceiling alone—Kevin gave her a pretty big assist."

Oh, my. She hadn't seen anything of the sort, but then again, she'd been swept up in the momentous occasion of her granddaughter's first magic.

Nell nodded in agreement. "Yeah, I thought that, too. Blending spells with Net power is a little like spellcasting. When Ginia does it, she pulls power directly from those who cast the initial spells, but Kevin handled that for Elorie."

"Exactly," Lauren said. "He also helped hold everything steady as she organized the power streams. It was quite a nice piece of work, and very similar to channeling for a traditional circle."

Now, wasn't *that* interesting. "Well, then. It sounds like this would be a very good week for a gathering. Sunday's a full moon, so that would be auspicious timing. Three circles, I think—we've lots of witches that could use the extra training. We'll make sure Sean and Kevin get their chances."

"What's a gathering?" Lauren asked.

Sophie grinned. "Prepare for an invasion, Nova Scotia-style. I'll go have the witchlings start spreading the word."

~ ~ ~

"Put me down, Aervyn Walker!"

Sophie spun around at Lizzie's furious words and spied her young charge floating four feet up in the air. "What's going on, kiddos?"

"He started it!" Lizzie was an only child and getting a crash course in having a younger munchkin around. It wasn't all going smoothly.

Aervyn, well used to holding his own as the youngest of five, just tried to look as innocent as possible. Since he was soaking wet and Lizzie was their best water witch, Sophie was pretty sure he wasn't the only guilty party.

Mike appeared around the corner of the house, grabbed Lizzie's ankle, and pulled her to the ground. "Aaron's looking for some help picking strawberries. Anyone interested?"

Lizzie's mad vanished. She grabbed Aervyn's hand and towed him toward the inn. "Come on. I'm a really good picker, and Aaron always lets us eat as many as we want."

Sophie laid her head on Mike's shoulder, feeling his arm wrap around her. "Saved by the berries. Thanks."

"Still think you want a couple of your own one day?"

"Ssh!" Sophie giggled even as she hushed him. "If Aunt Moira hears you talking like that, she'll be knitting baby blankets by this afternoon."

Mike's eyes were suddenly intent. "Would that be such a bad thing?"

Sometimes, life's moments of decision snuck up on you. Standing in Moira's garden, mouth half open in shock, Sophie met the gaze of the man she loved and did as he asked—opened herself to possibility.

She felt her heart bloom. Decision made.

Glowing with certainty, she reached for his free hand, palm to palm. Letting her power flow, here in this place of her childhood roots, she made him a promise, silent and strong. Time had often stopped for her in Moira's garden. Now it stopped for them both. And Sophie knew, whatever the future brought, it would be for the two of them together.

"Uncle Mike, we hafta go!" They looked up at Lizzie's yell from the street, where Aaron's van awaited.

"Sorry, I'm on strawberry-picking detail." He bent over and plucked three flowers for her. "I'll try to save some for you."

As he jogged off, Sophie looked at the blooms in her hands. A daffodil, a dahlia, and a daisy. In the language of flowers, a message of new beginnings, joy, and forever love. A promise.

Elorie walked over with two glasses of lemonade. Her eyes widened as she looked at the flowers. Anyone raised around Moira knew the language and lore of blooms. "Interesting bouquet."

"They're from Mike."

"Oh, *really*. Does he know what they mean?"

Sophie stroked the daffodil's soft petals. "He does."

She looked up to see tears glistening in the eyes of her childhood friend. "I'm really happy for you, Sophie. He seems like a wonderful man."

Ah, this was the sister she had missed. So very much. Words disappeared into feeling. She hugged her friend, held her flowers, and sniffled, entirely happy.

After a moment of quiet bliss, Elorie grinned. "Did you warn him that Gran will expect grandbabies?"

"He's on her side on that one."

"Well, I guess he knows what he's getting into. He seems really balanced, and he's clearly got a good dose of courage, going strawberry picking with the young ones."

Sophie laughed. "I'm grateful. I think those two have had about as much witch school as they can take for one day."

"Not everyone finds plants and herbs fascinating."

Sophie nodded over to where Ginia and Moira had their heads together. "Some do, and that's all we need—just one or two to pass on the lore. Aunt Moira knows so much—I feel like I can't possibly hold it all. Ginia's drinking it up, but the two little ones were done."

"They're not the only ones. Nell was a tough taskmistress for Net power training this morning." Elorie yawned. "Kevin's fallen asleep on the couch, and I'm thinking about joining him."

"That sounds tempting. How is it going, being on the trainee end of things?"

"I have a lot more empathy for how hard it is now. I used to wonder why an hour of training usually had my witchlings racing for the nearest exit."

Sophie grinned, delighting in the comfortable rekindling of sisterhood. "At least you don't have to take witch history."

"Don't tell Gran," whispered Elorie, "but I hope I make it at least a little more exciting than she used to. Not that Sean would agree, but he's never had to sit through the lectures we used to get."

Sean. Uh, oh. Sophie scanned the garden.

Elorie obviously recognized the look. "Lost one, did you? Try the beach—that's usually where I find him when he's gone AWOL."

Sophie frowned. "He's supposed to be doing mind-witch practice with Marcus this afternoon. Maybe they're working together."

"I don't think so. Uncle Marcus is asleep in the hammock behind the inn."

"What is this, siesta time?" Sophie finished her lemonade. Time to go on a witchling hunt. "Ginia, Aunt Moira—have you seen Sean lately?"

"Check the beach, dear," Moira said without looking up.

Elorie hooked her arm through Sophie's. "They're in plant-magic stupor; they're not going to be any use. I'll help you look."

They wandered over to the back yard of the inn. Sure enough, Marcus was snoring in the hammock. It brought back sharp memories of an afternoon, long ago, and a rather memorable witchling prank. Sophie grinned at Elorie. "Do you think we can pull it off twice?"

Elorie's eyes gleamed. "If you let me go get Gran's computer and Lauren, I bet we can pull off something even more glamorous this time."

The giggles struck as Sophie waited. It was like being ten again and finding cranky old Marcus napping on the back porch.

Elorie came back out, computer in hand.

Lauren trailed just behind her. "It's usually Aervyn getting me in trouble."

Sophie winked. "It's only trouble if we get caught." Corrupting innocent witchlings was a tried-and-true witch school tradition. Time they got Lauren caught up on a little more of what she'd missed growing up a non-witch.

Well, that might not be entirely accurate. Elorie had grown up a non-witch, and she'd been involved in plenty of witchling antics.

"So what's the plan?" Lauren asked. "I owe Marcus one."

He did have a gift for rubbing people the wrong way. "Well, last time we did this, we cast a princess illusion spell and left him holding a bouquet of flowers. We need to step it up for a repeat performance, though."

Lauren snickered. "I can make him *think* he's a princess—will that do? And I can visualize your mind for Elorie so she can work with whatever nefarious spellwork you have in mind."

Now they were getting somewhere. Sophie grinned. "I can grow him a bed of flowers that would make Sleeping Beauty proud."

Elorie started to speak, and then stopped. "Huh. I don't know what I can do. You guys don't need me for your spells."

Newbie witch, thought Sophie fondly. She looked at the computer in Elorie's hands. "Oh, I think we can come up with something." She grabbed the laptop and logged quickly into her private Realm costume stash. "Here. Princess gear. Can you pull that out here and dress our dear Uncle Marcus? If you meld that together with Lauren's mind magic, and my floral décor, he'll look and feel rather convincingly royal. And girly."

Sophie knew it was a heck of a challenge. Only Ginia had tried blending more than two spells at once, and one of these was in virtual reality.

Elorie looked at the screen and considered. "Have you got a prince in there?"

Damn. Sophie eyed her with serious respect. "That would be a tricky piece of magic, sister mine. Are you ready to try something that fancy?"

Elorie's eyes twinkled, but there was steel behind the humor. "There's only one way to find out."

Some quick cut-and-paste coding, and Sophie had a full set of princess gear and a handsome prince avatar all ready to be ported to real life. From Lauren's state of concentration, she was readying whatever mind magic was needed to convince grumpy old Marcus that he really was Sleeping Beauty.

Facing Elorie, Sophie pulled earth power, activated the spellcode, and nodded. Ready. Today she would do magic with her sister.

Elorie took a deep breath and laid her hand on the mouse, focusing. Sophie could see nothing but her blooming spell.

Sorry about that, Lauren sent. *This is a little tricky. Let me patch you in, too.*

In moments, Sophie could see the challenge Elorie faced. Three swirling spellshapes—and wow, mind magics looked complicated. How the heck was she going to get all of those to meld together? Real remorse hit. This was supposed to be a joke, not a big ding to the confidence of a new witch.

Have faith, girl. I think she can do this. We were all new, once.

Sophie shoveled her doubts aside as power sparked and spells began to move. Elorie had the spellcode and earth magic aligned with impressive speed, but adding the mind magic looked like one of those impossible puzzle games. Maybe some kinds of magic just weren't made to fit together.

Suddenly Elorie pushed the simpler spellshapes away and pulled the mind magic shape to the center. Sophie had no idea what was going on, but Lauren's mind felt highly impressed.

Watch. She's brilliant.

As Sophie gazed in fascination, Elorie created a mirror shape from Net power, and then overlaid it on Lauren's spell. The two flared, and then merged, and then flared again as she began manipulating the flow of the merged power streams.

Fascination turned to awe as Elorie formed a final shape with two connection points obviously meant to interlock the other spells. It was creative, precise, and unbelievably beautiful—the magic of an artist.

Hold steady, Lauren cautioned. *She's about to release it.* Light danced, and then the bright joy of power unfurled.

Wow. Just. Wow.

Sophie let her dazzled delight loose as she opened her eyes to the friend of her childhood. Her new sister in magic. And then their shared awe dissolved in helpless mirth as Marcus roared.

"Sean James O'Reilly, what foul magic is this?" Marcus sprang from the hammock and pushed the prince furiously away. Sophie held her ribs and tried to laugh quietly. Apparently he didn't appreciate being awakened by a gentle kiss of love. That figured.

Sean came running over the lawn. "Whoa, Uncle Marcus. Did you do that?" Then he skidded to a halt, hand over his mouth. "Never mind, that was a really dumb question."

Marcus looked down at the princess gown he was wearing. "Indeed. However, my accusing you was equally dumb. You'd need a circle to pull this off, and clearly you don't have one."

"Nope. Wasn't me." Sean shook his head with glee and looked around for the culprit.

His eyes got huge as he noticed the three of them sitting on the porch. Uh, oh, Sophie thought. Busted. She avoided looking at her companions in crime and tried to look innocent. That was hard to do when you had a case of the uncontrollable giggles.

"Elorie Shaw," growled Marcus, "undo this spell right now."

His niece looked rather pained, in between giggles. "I'm not sure I know how to do that yet."

Sean snickered. "It often takes more power to undo a spell than to cast it in the first place. Best you be remembering that." He was an excellent mimic—Sophie could almost hear Aunt Moira talking.

Elorie blushed. "You're exactly right." Then she looked at Marcus and fell over laughing again. "But it was so worth it."

Oh, boy, Sophie thought, watching the glee on Sean's face. This was going to throw a bit of a wrench into witchling discipline.

~ ~ ~

There were few things better than chocolate in bed, Elorie thought. Well, maybe one thing. She dunked a strawberry in chocolate and fed it to Aaron, then leaned back to enjoy the tangy summer breezes on her skin and the distant sound of ocean waves. Their sleeping porch was one of her favorite places.

He snuggled her in a little closer. "Are we finally done blowing off all that extra steam of yours?"

She blushed. "I think so. Sorry, I'm not usually quite so demanding." Obviously the rumors about some of the side effects of magic were all too true.

He laughed. "Guy manual, page one. You never, ever have to be sorry for that. Save your apologies for Marcus—I think you're going to need them."

"He'll live. At least we picked on someone our size." It wasn't lost on her that her first big act of magic had been one more suited to witchling troublemakers. She didn't care. It had felt... magnificent.

"I hardly expected you to start torturing small children," Aaron said dryly. "Although Lizzie would probably think so if you dressed her up as a princess."

"By rights, I should have done it to Sean, to make up for that pirate stunt he pulled."

Aaron stroked her hair. "I never did get to see that. Maybe I can bribe him into a repeat performance."

She elbowed him, mostly in jest. "He doesn't need any more encouragement. After today's escapades, the witchlings are going to be on the rampage."

"Yes, they are. I've set up the picnic tables so we can eat outside tomorrow."

"Trying to keep them out of the inn, are you?" Her husband was a smart man. Witchling practical jokes could be really messy.

"Darn straight. And I expect some folks will start arriving for the gathering, so that way it's easier to feed whoever shows up."

"You know it's not your job to feed everyone, right?"

"It's my pleasure; you know that." He grinned and fed her a strawberry. It was luscious—dripping goodness with a chaser of chocolate. "Besides, the fridge downstairs is stuffed full of food people have been dropping by all day, and Lizzie's parents are going to do a lobster bake on the beach tomorrow night. It's not all on me; there's plenty of help."

"Good." Elorie yawned. As her magic-induced high slowly wore off, she was sinking into the serious exhaustion underneath.

Aaron kissed her head. "Big day. You should get some sleep. The weekend's going to be busy."

No kidding. Throngs of people, never-ending food, and the shared joy of magic. It was the kind of busy she loved most.

Her husband settled a hand on her belly. "If we made a baby with all that energy, I bet she'll be one very active little girl."

A baby. In the aftermath of their magical escapades, she'd forgotten to tell Aaron something important. "We're not the only ones. I think Sophie and Mike are getting really serious. He gave her a daffodil."

Aaron tugged her hair. "Translate, please. That's not covered in the guy manual."

She giggled. "It means we may not be the only ones trying to make a baby tonight."

His chest rumbled with laughter under her ear. "Moira will be thrilled."

As she slid into sleep, Elorie made a mental note to ask Sophie about magic and babies. She couldn't ask Gran—she'd never hear the end of it.

Chapter 14

Elorie looked around. In an attempt to reassert her responsible-adult persona, she'd called an all-hands logistics meeting. Aaron had the weekend's food and guests under control, but they needed a plan for the magical part of the program.

Moira sipped her morning tea. "I think we should have three circles, dear."

Three? Elorie frowned. That was a lot of circles for one day. "Why so many?"

"Well, we've a lot of new witches for the inner circle, and a request to help with the algae blooms again."

Elorie nodded. Algae blooms along the shore disrupted the lobster beds, one of the main livelihoods of the village. They were often asked to give a little magical push to the ocean's natural cleansing systems. It was one of the many reasons the village of Fisher's Cove embraced their local witches.

"The best time for that work is early morning. We can put some of our witchlings in that one, but we'll need an experienced caster—that's tricky work."

Sophie refilled teacups. "Mike's happy to do that, if you'd like. He's a solid spellcaster."

Nell snorted. "He's a lot better than solid."

"He'll do nicely, I think," Moira said. "Let's test him today with our local channelers, see who might be the best fit. Dealing with the algae involves a lot of water and air power, so we need to make sure those circle trios are strong."

Elorie thought for a moment. "Lizzie's ready, and she'd be a very nice addition to our full circles for water."

She was pleased when Gran nodded. "Aye, she's a mighty water witch for such a little thing. Summer is an auspicious time for her first full circle."

"If you could use help on air," Nell said, "I have another pint-sized witch to suggest."

That would work. Aervyn was a powerhouse. "He does well with Uncle Marcus, so that's a good choice."

"So," Moira started counting off on her fingers. "Marcus on air point, Sophie for earth. Nell, you'll handle fire for us, please?"

Nell nodded. "Who's trio leader on water?"

Moira sighed. "That will still be me, but with Lizzie's power, it will be a much easier job than usual."

"Aervyn can handle point for a trio, if you want." Nell reached for a scone. "Jamie's been working with him on that. He has water talents, but I don't think you want both him and Lizzie in the same trio."

Elorie shook her head, remembering their squabbles of the day before. "No, and that would leave Sean on air with Uncle Marcus, which isn't the smoothest of fits either, especially first thing in the morning."

"Indeed," Moira said. "And young Sean needs to watch this first circle, not participate. We'll want him to pay close attention to Mike's spellcasting."

"So that takes care of all our trio leaders," Sophie said. "We could add Ginia on earth, too—has she done a full circle yet, Nell?"

"No, but she's ready, and she loves working with you."

It was coming together well. Elorie loved this part of readying for a gathering, all the behind-the-scenes work of effective witchcraft. "Kevin can join you on fire, Nell. He and Sean have done a couple of full circles, and he's very steady."

Moira beamed. "So many young ones in the circle. What a lovely thing that is."

Sophie nodded. "Add Lauren as monitor, and I think we have everyone covered."

Elorie debated a second scone as she ran through the trios one more time in her mind. "Aaron has a big breakfast planned, so I'll let him know to give us time for that initial circle first. What did you have in mind for the other two, Gran?"

"One for Kevin and Sean to work as channeler and caster. Nell, if you'd act as Sean's backup, and we can get Lauren to support Kevin."

Elorie nodded. It was always smart to have experienced witches ready to step in and help if things got hairy. "We should be able to leave most everyone else in their same roles from the morning. Sean's best at night, so perhaps his should be the final circle of the day."

"We'll need to make sure some witchlings get naps," Nell said. "I have two that will get grumpy otherwise. That leaves your circle for the afternoon, Elorie."

Her brain slid to a halt. "I'm going to be in a circle?"

Moira smiled. "Of course you are."

And how exactly were they going to pull that off? Laptop cords didn't extend to the beach.

Gran must have read her face. "I have an idea, my girl. But I need Lauren's thinking. Does anyone know if she's up yet?"

Lauren stumbled into the kitchen. "Just barely. Coffee. Begging."

Elorie got up to pour a cup, her mind whirling. Forget the issue of Internet on the beach. Circles were at the core of witch tradition, and every circle began with a call to the four elements. Net power wasn't one of them. What on earth did Gran have in mind?

She wasn't the only one who was curious. "Why don't you fill us in," Nell said. "We can always run back over it when Lauren's brain wakes up."

"Well, I wouldn't normally rush a new witch into a full circle this quickly, but I'd like to do it while we have so many Net witches present. It's new ground we'll be breaking, and more heads will make that lighter work."

Gran was calling for change in one of the core traditions of witchcraft? Elorie frowned, feeling very unsettled.

Lauren grinned in sympathy. *A little strange, isn't it?*

Elorie slapped her hand down onto her computer mouse. Not that Lauren was an impolite intruder, but jeebers, she was tired of having people breezily comment on the thoughts in her head.

She realized Nell and Gran were having a conversation, and she'd missed a good chunk of it. Sophie seemed to approve, whatever the idea was.

"My brain's moving forward now," Lauren said. "Can someone give me the short version?"

Moira set down her tea. Elorie hid a smile. Gran wasn't particularly good at summaries—they went against her Irish instincts. "Well, just like we used mind witches in each trio for your first circle, Lauren, we're going to use Net witches at each element for Elorie's circle."

Lauren nodded. "So they can blend elemental power with Net power, right? Makes sense, and it worked well for me."

Elorie remembered that Lauren's first full circle had been groundbreaking in its own right. Which should have been comforting, but it wasn't. California witches were more... adventurous. Gran had always kept the Nova Scotia witching community firmly traditional. It was a heritage Elorie loved and was deeply committed to preserving.

She had no idea why Gran sat there nodding happily as the very foundations of circle work were undermined.

"So for Net witches, we'd have Ginia on earth, Moira on water, Kevin on fire, and that would leave Aervyn on air?" Sophie ground to a halt. "Wait, we need Kevin channeling. What am I missing?"

"Well," Nell said, "we're hoping it will work to include those of us who have the spellcoding variety of Net power. So you, Marcus, and I will play, too."

Sophie nodded. "Makes sense. That's a lot of computers we're going to need."

"Marcus and Ginia are on that." Nell grinned. "There's a shortage of modern laptops here, so expect yours and Mike's to be commandeered."

"No." Elorie stood and spoke firmly. It was time to stop this madness.

Moira looked confused. "What's wrong, my dear?"

Elorie struggled for the words. "Circles are tradition. They're the core of who we are. This isn't right. What am I going to do, sit in a trio and wave my mouse when we call to earth or water?"

Passion poured out of her. "I don't deny this new power of mine, and we'll figure out how to use it. But it doesn't belong in a circle." She appealed directly to Gran. Certainly, of everyone, it would be she who would understand. "Our traditions matter, our connection to generations of witches past. I won't have it weakened because you love me, because you want me to belong."

She watched in utter astonishment as Gran's fury blazed. "Elorie Shaw, you listen, and you listen well. You have belonged to me, and to this community of witches, since the day you were born. I won't have you cast that aside because of your doubts."

Her spluttered protests died as Gran stormed on. "There is no one who values the traditions of witchcraft more than I do, no one who holds to the past with more joy. But fear is the wrong reason to resist change."

Gran's voice softened, and she reached for Elorie's hand. "Your magic is one of connection and joining, sweetling. Can you think of a talent that is more suited to a full circle? You were born to this. We just need to figure out how to make it work."

Irish temper fully blown, her smile was one of gentle compassion. "To join in community is the very oldest of witch traditions, my darling girl. It's yours by right. Don't push it away."

Elorie stared in stupefied silence, her gut a churning mix of defiance, confusion, and yearning.

Witches gathered under the stars and repeated the words of centuries. How could a power that was ten minutes old be part of that? Everything she'd ever known, ever believed in, screamed "no."

And yet Gran believed.

She jumped as Sophie touched her other hand, eyes laden with compassion. "It's all too easy to walk away from what you want most, to hide in what's comfortable." She swallowed audibly. "I should know."

Elorie shook her head, not understanding, but feeling her sister's pain.

Sophie's grin was a little wavery. "And Gran doesn't raise scaredy-witches."

She dug for something to say. Anything at all. And then pushed by love and the gentle dare of her oldest friend, grasped at hope. "Which trio will I be in, then?"

Gran smiled in approval. "You'll be spellcasting, child. Where else would you be?"

Her brain absolutely ground to a halt again. Spellcasting? Leading the circle? Everyone had gone stark raving mad. She'd been a witch for all of a week.

Panic clawed its way up her ribs.

"Don't worry so, darling girl. After that stunt you pulled on my nephew, you're clearly ready." Gran's grin was as wide as the Bay of Fundy. "In fact, it was his idea."

~ ~ ~

Elorie leaned against the doorway and fumed at the laptops and cables overrunning her living room. "Ginia, there's a snack in the kitchen if you're interested."

Whether it was hunger or manners that drove Ginia out of the room, Elorie was grateful for the moment of privacy. Letting her simmering temper bubble to the surface, she glared at Marcus, who had yet to acknowledge her presence. "It's an interesting form of revenge you chose."

"And what would that be?" He continued to tinker with a laptop.

"Setting me up as spellcaster for a full circle."

"Most would consider that an honor."

"From anyone else, perhaps."

He shrugged. "So don't do it."

Elorie snorted. "Fat chance. You've managed to convince Gran it's a good idea."

"She didn't take much convincing, but feel free to blame me if you like."

Elorie paused, and then asked what she'd truly come to find out. "Do you expect me to fail?"

Marcus finally looked up. "Certainly not. I expect you to uphold the fine tradition of Nova Scotia witching and handle your circle competently and well." He squinted at her. "Wait, you're serious."

She nodded mutely.

He sat there for several moments, saying nothing. "It took two hours and five witches to undo that spell you cast on me, niece. It was a very impressive piece of magic. You're a witch of uncommon strength, and that kind of talent shouldn't go wasted."

He turned back to his laptop. "And if you tell anyone I said so, I'll seriously reconsider my plan to turn you into a frog."

She was pretty sure he couldn't do that. Then again, he was cozy with a four-year-old who probably could.

However, they'd talked for two whole minutes without her temper boiling over, and much as it galled her to do it, she had a favor to ask. A really big one. Now might be as good a time as any.

"Will you teach me?" she blurted.

Marcus turned around, a pained look on his face. "Teach you what, exactly?"

Cripes. She was going to live to regret this. "To spellcode."

He looked even more pained, if that was possible. "I thought Ginia was giving you and Kevin lessons."

"She is. And Kevin is catching on faster than I can blink."

Marcus shrugged. "The young ones are digital natives. For us, it's a second language; we'll always be slower."

"I'm awfully tired of being slower."

"I can't help you with that. You've got a good brain, and you'd be a lot faster if you stopped hating that computer of yours."

"I don't hate it." Elorie stopped. Lately, she pretty much did. "Well, I don't entirely hate it. I'm hoping that if I learn to be halfway competent, I might hate it a little less." Since it seemed like she was stuck with a permanent computer appendage, she was hoping to make peace with it.

Marcus raised an eyebrow. "None of my students are permitted to be only halfway competent."

She was definitely going to live to regret this. But it was clear that if she didn't at least attempt to master this side of her power, the under-ten crowd was going to leave her in the miserable, technology-challenged dust. And darned if she hadn't discovered a bit of her inner competitive witch. "You'll teach me, then?"

Marcus grinned, an unusual and somewhat scary sight. "I will. All I require is that you keep it entirely secret."

Elorie frowned. That was a really strange request, but considering the source, it could have been worse. She nodded in agreement.

"Excellent." Marcus rubbed his hands together. "Warrior Girl won't have any idea what hit her."

Jeebers. Who was Warrior Girl, and what had she just agreed to?

~ ~ ~

A Fisher's Cove lobster bake was an *event*. Add the greater Nova Scotia witching community to most of the population of the village, and there were more than three hundred people on the beach.

There were three bonfires, a cauldron-sized pot of baked beans, a cooking pit for the lobster, all the local fiddling talent, and a herd of kids playing chicken with the waves. So far, the ocean was winning.

Nell inhaled the tangled smells of smoke and salty air and settled into a chair beside Moira, who looked very content. "You love this, don't you?"

"I surely do. It reminds me very much of the best of home. There were no beaches or lobsters at our Irish gatherings, but the feeling of it is the same." She winked. "Not quite enough babies, though. If this group were truly Irish, there'd be a babe in every set of arms."

Nell grinned. "Who are you pressuring for grandbabies at the moment?"

"It's not pressure. Just encouragement. I think my sweet Elorie might be getting close, although she's had a lot to distract her of late."

"Babies come, whether you're distracted or not. I should know."

"Aye." Moira snugged a blanket around her shoulders. "And we both know that sometimes magic opens more than one kind of channel in a woman."

Oh, yeah. Her triplets had been conceived after a particularly stupendous full circle. Daniel still teased her about that. Aervyn, oddly enough, hadn't been the result of magical aftershocks—just a particularly cuddly Friday night date.

They watched in companionable silence for a moment, the quiet roll of waves in the background providing the heartbeat for the evening.

Lizzie's parents were taking care of the lobster bake part of the evening, with many willing assistants. They had uncovered the shallow, rock-lined pit long used for this purpose, and started a roaring fire that was now burning down to coals. Assistance from a couple of resident fire witches had sped the process up a fair amount.

Nell motioned toward the fire. "So what's with all the garbage cans?" There were about twenty large aluminum containers lined up behind the fire.

"That's the food. There will be corn on the cob soaking in salt water in a few. The rest will be mussels and lobster."

Lizzie's momma, who had been pushing around some of the fire's coals, was now in deep conversation with her daughter and Aervyn. As Nell watched, the two witchlings held hands and faced an enormous pile of seaweed. Aervyn's fingers wiggled slightly—whatever they were up to, it was clearly a fairly tricky spell.

Slowly the seaweed pile levitated, and then floated toward the pit. Nell looked around, a little surprised by such a visible display of magic with so many non-witches present.

"Relax, dear." Moira patted her hand. "People around here are well used to magic. They'll be thanking the young ones for saving them the trouble of shoveling all that seaweed, and we'll be eating faster for it."

Once the seaweed was layered in the bottom of the pit, willing hands opened the garbage cans and quickly added layers of mussels and corn on the cob. Lids clanged, steam hissed, and the iodine-laced odor of cooking seaweed caught a ride past Nell's chair. She sniffed in appreciation.

Moira laughed. "If Aervyn's not careful, a lobster's going to catch his nose."

Her son was leaning over one of the garbage cans in fascination. "How do they get the lobsters onto the fire?" Nell figured it wasn't by sticking their hands in the cans, the way they'd done with the corn.

"Well, there's the easy way, and the hard way." Moira giggled. "Looks like they're going to give the witchlings a go at the hard way first."

By now, Ginia, Sean, and Kevin had arrived. Nell was pretty sure it wasn't manners that had them volunteering Ginia to go first. Ginia, being no dummy, pointed at Aervyn. And Aervyn, being only four, grinned and got ready to do magic.

A lobster floated up out of the garbage can and headed toward the pit. Unfortunately for her son, the path to the pit floated right by his face. It was a hard call who was more surprised—the witchling who almost lost his nose, or the lobster who got teleported twenty feet up in the air.

The rest of the witchlings eventually got their giggles under control and began to help with the floating lobster parade. Aervyn kept a very respectful distance from their claws.

Nell turned to Moira. "So what's the easy way to get the lobsters to the fire—teleporting?"

Moira chuckled. "Pitchfork."

That figured.

Distracted by the antics at the lobster pit, Nell realized she had missed a lot of other activity on the beach. She pointed toward a large platform. "And what's that?"

"Oh, it will take an hour or so for the food to be ready. There will be some dancing while we wait."

Three hundred people were going to fit on that platform?

Moira got up from her chair. "The platform's for the old ladies like me. The young ones will dance on the sand. Come, now—we've been sitting long enough."

In California, dancing involved some swaying while jammed up against many other bodies in a very small space. Nell rapidly discovered that it meant something entirely different on a Nova Scotia beach.

She watched, jaw dropped in awe, as Moira shed her blanket, climbed up on the platform, and began some kind of rapid-fire Irish step dance.

She danced on her own for a moment, matriarch and star of this little part of the world. Then she motioned, and several others joined her on the makeshift stage. Holding Elorie's hand, she led a group of dancers through an age-old Irish celebration of life and the joy of having feet that could move on the earth.

The inner circle of the dance, the outer circle of witches and villagers clapping along with the music—it was its own kind of magic.

When they finished, Moira was escorted to a waiting chair like a triumphant queen. Elorie grabbed Ginia's hands and began to walk her through some of the simpler steps.

Nell walked over to take a seat by Moira again. Moira just laughed. "You haven't earned old-woman status just yet, my dear. Go on and dance. Anyone will be happy to teach you."

Sophie spun by and grabbed her hand. "We'll have you dancing all night long."

Nell learned two things in the next few hours. One, the people of Nova Scotia had the stamina of Ironman triathletes. And two, nothing on earth tasted better than beach-baked lobsters in the moonlight. All five of them.

Chapter 15

It was a very bleary-eyed crew of witches who gathered at sunrise the next morning. The mists floating in from the ocean hid some of the yawns, but not all. Elorie handed out coffee and hoped for the best. The witchlings, many of whom had fallen asleep in the sand in the wee hours of the night, seemed relatively cheery. That was good—for many, it would be their first full circle.

Mike was huddled with a couple of their local fishermen who had done early reconnaissance on the current location of the algae bloom. The goal was to push it gently out to sea to be reclaimed by the ocean's natural recycling systems. That was easiest to do if you knew exactly where the bloom was.

Each of the experienced point witches gathered up their trio. Moira cuddled Lizzie under her long wool cape; water witches got cold easily—something about their affinity with the chilly ocean waters. They chatted easily with Gwen, the third member of their trio.

Aervyn had somehow gotten Uncle Marcus laughing, which was a feat of magic unto itself. Air and water had the toughest jobs of the morning, so Elorie was happy to see a harmonious start. With Uncle Marcus, that couldn't be taken for granted.

Mike motioned that he was ready to begin, and the circle started to assemble. The outer circle would be light this morning—too many witches sleeping off the aftereffects of the night before.

Nell, Sophie, Moira, and Marcus stood in the cardinal directions, flanked by the other members of their trio. The young ones were all excited, but the face that drew Elorie was Ginia's. She looked so proud, standing tall in the earth trio, wind whipping her hair. This was her first full circle, and she was soaking in the full import of the occasion.

She was going to be an amazing woman one day.

She surely will be. Lauren stepped up beside Elorie. "She's already an amazing witch. I've helped with her training a fair amount, and she's so confident in her talents."

Elorie smiled in welcome. "That's what happens when the trainers do a good job."

"Maybe. Nell doesn't raise scaredy-witches either, but something about Ginia is special. A lot of witches fight with their magic, or at least brute force it a little. She's so in tune with her power. It's inspiring."

Hmm. This was beginning to feel like a non-accidental conversation. "And what do you feel in my mind when I do magic?"

Lauren blushed. "Not subtle enough, huh? Sorry about that. Usually I keep my nose out of other peoples' magical business."

Elorie snorted. "We stink at that around here. Go ahead and tell me what you see."

"Part of you feels like you're resisting. Not the power itself, exactly—more the process. I'm not describing it very well, but it hampers your magic."

"You describe it well enough." She looked toward the full circle. "I want what they have. A power rooted in tradition, practiced by generations. Ginia has the heart of a pioneer. I don't. I feel like I'm tied up in the back of the covered wagon, heading west whether I want to or not."

And wow, where had that come from? She sighed and scuffed at the pebbles under her feet.

Lauren gave her hand a comforting squeeze. "If I can help with untying a knot or two, let me know."

She needed to think a bit first. Her pioneering spirit might be lacking, but her sense of obligation to her craft wasn't. Lauren was the second person in two days to point out that resistance was hampering her magic.

She looked on the gathering circle and sighed. Still yearning for what she couldn't have. That had to change, and today seemed like a good day to begin.

As Gran's lilting voice began the call to water, Sean stepped up to Elorie's side. "Wanna watch? I can link you in so you can see the magic."

There was nothing wrong with Sean's heart, but as cool as it was to watch magic from the inside, right now she needed the comfort of her usual observer role. "I'll link in for your circle tonight, sweet boy, so I can see your fancy spellcasting. For now, I just want to watch with my eyes."

She drank in the sight of witches, young and old, joining in the age-old ritual of a full circle. Gran in her cape, Sophie and Ginia in matching long green velvet dresses, Kevin in jeans and a hoodie, Aervyn with chocolate smears on his face. Fine witches, all.

She gave thanks once again for Gran's presence. She had stood as point in the water trio for as long as Elorie could remember. The day would come when she would step aside, probably for young Lizzie, but it hadn't come yet.

Nell completed the final call to the elements, and Lizzie's eyes went big as the power pulled by twelve witches surged around the circle.

Elorie watched Kevin, cheering him on silently. They'd all been surprised and pleased when he had tested as the obvious choice to partner Mike—normally channelers only worked well with one or two spellcasters—but he was young to channel a full circle. Far more experienced witches had panicked when it was time to link into the circle's massive energy.

He's okay, Lauren sent. *He's nervous, but he's handling it.*

It was nice to have a monitor who worried about the trainers in the outer circle, too. Uncle Marcus was a skilled monitor, but he never spared a thought for trainer nerves.

Mike laid a hand gently on Kevin's shoulder. It was time.

Kevin closed his eyes and slowly reached his arms out. Wind and misty light whipped around his body as he called the elemental powers in to the circle's center. Elorie gasped as his feet rose slightly off the ground.

He's doing beautifully. Marcus connected in with quite the thunderbolt—he's not used to having Aervyn in his trio.

Kevin reached his arms to the sky, and moments later, so did Mike. Hand off. Now the power was in Mike's hands, and he could go to work moving the algae further out. Finicky but straightforward work for an experienced spellcaster.

Elorie waited with quiet patience. She was so very proud of her two witchlings.

They're very well trained, Lauren sent. *Lizzie held steady, and Kevin handled the channeling absolutely beautifully. Mike's almost done, I think.*

Done? Surely not. The last circle they'd done to move the algae had taken almost an hour.

Moments later, Mike dropped his arms, and the shimmering energy hanging over the circle dimmed and disappeared. He lifted Kevin to the sky and spun him around. "That was some superb channeling, my young friend. I'll work with you again—any day, any time."

Then he looked toward Marcus with a half grin. "Were you trying to blow us all up there?"

Marcus flushed. "My sincere apologies. I asked Aervyn to push me more power, and I couldn't fully control the surge."

Aervyn looked dismayed. "Did I do too much? I'm really sorry. Lauren says I have to be carefuller about that."

Marcus rubbed his head. "You did exactly right, my boy. You should always do exactly what your trio point asks, and you did. It was my fault for not remembering how much power you have."

"It was all to the good," Mike said. "Kevin handled it cleanly, and thanks to Aervyn and Miss Lizzie over there, we finished the spell in record time."

The circle broke formation as everyone moved to hug the various witchlings.

Lizzie beamed as Elorie walked over. "Did I do good?"

Moira leaned down and kissed her head. "Child, I haven't had that much energy in my trio in a very long time. It was a beautiful thing."

Lizzie grinned and wandered off in the direction of her parents. Moira reached out for Elorie's hand. "I think she should take point in the trio this evening. She's well used to working with our Sean, and I'll be right at her shoulder, should she need me."

Gran was passing the baton. Elorie's heart ached at the thought. Then she realized Gran's face shone with something akin to joy. "I've waited all this time, darling girl. And now there's a child of my heart, young and strong, ready to stand in my place."

Elorie hugged her tightly. She wasn't sure she could accept the change with nearly so much grace, but she would try. For Gran's sake, she would try.

~ ~ ~

Lauren snuck into her room at the inn and quietly closed the door. The place was overrun by witches and their families, and privacy was at a serious premium.

She grabbed her laptop and debated one last time. It wasn't that long ago that *she'd* been a new witch, fighting to accept the change and responsibility that came along with her power. Smoothing out a bump in Elorie's road wasn't necessarily the best way to help her.

Then again, it wasn't always necessary to leave obstacles in place when they could be easily fixed. At least she hoped it would be easy. Only one way to find out. She pinged Jamie on instant messaging.

Jamie: You called?

Lauren: Hey, you got a minute?

Jamie: I do. Shay and Mia took Nat shopping for gooey baby things, so as long as you don't need me to shop, I'm your guy.

Lauren: Ha. You've bought more cute baby things than Nat has.

Jamie: I buy necessary things. She buys frills.

Lauren: Really. iPods are essential for babies, are they?

Jamie: Music is good for their brain development. I read it somewhere. Besides, I think Mia may have co-opted the iPod. She can't resist anything red.

Lauren: Speaking of iThings, I need a favor. So far, Elorie has been stuck with a laptop to access Net power, and it's restricting her freedom.

Jamie: Not a lot of Wi-Fi hotspots in rural Nova Scotia?

Lauren: Exactly. But Ginia used Nell's iPhone when we first got here. I wondered if we could set up something like that for Elorie.

Jamie: By "we," I assume you mean "me."

Lauren: Pretty much. I'll bake you cookies.

Jamie: That's a suitable bribe. I can probably soup it up a little, too, so it has a wider range than normal. Give me a couple of days.

Lauren: Any way I can talk you into sending it for tomorrow? It's her birthday.

Jamie: Taskmistress. That'll cost you more cookies.

Lauren: Deal. And thanks. I think all the technology is getting in the way of her sense of belonging.

Jamie: She lives on the wrong coast—most witches out here spend half their life online. But yeah, she's not used to leading a wired life. An iPhone in her pocket should be a lot less intrusive.

Lauren: Exactly. She's casting for a full circle in a couple of hours, and the front lawn looks like a gamer convention. Ginia's having a blast, but I don't think Elorie's going to find it quite so cool.

Jamie: She was raised in Moira's world. Tradition's going to matter a lot to her. And speaking of full circle, you're going to need more than one phone to truly free Elorie from her Wi-Fi jail. Net witches don't work alone.

Lauren: Crap, I didn't even think of that.

Jamie: That's what I'm here for. I'll send a dozen or so overnight express so you can equip everyone, and then I'll go buy a new freezer for all the cookies you're going to bake me. Make some of them a kind Nat doesn't like, okay? She's on a bit of a food rampage right now.

Lauren: You'd think a teleporting witch could manage to hide a cookie stash.

Jamie: Nope. I swear she can smell them, even in the attic.

Lauren: It's only another six months. You'll live.

Jamie: Maybe. In the meantime, it sounds like I get to go shopping today after all.

Lauren: Stay away from the iPods. You're on a mission. iPhones—focus.

Jamie: When did you get to be such a bossy witch?

Lauren: Ha. I was always bossy. Only the witch part is new, and that's your fault. Gotta go, I'm being paged. Thanks, Jamie. I owe you.

~ ~ ~

Elorie sat on the grass behind the inn and wished she hadn't eaten quite so many of Aaron's pancakes. Or sausages. Or berries and whipped cream. None of it was sitting gently in her stomach at the moment.

Sophie sat on the grass beside her. "Nervous?"

That didn't seem like an adequate word to describe the state of her insides. "And then some."

"As I'm sure you've reminded many a witchling, that's totally normal. It's your first full circle, and you're spellcasting, no less."

She didn't need to be reminded. "Is everyone straight on their spells?" Unlike normal spellcasting, where the caster shaped the spell, Elorie needed the right spells in place to blend for the final result she wanted. That meant each member of her circle had a really specific job to do.

Sophie nodded. "Mike's walking the young ones through it one more time, but yeah, I think everyone's got it. Lots of mind witches in the group, too, so we can adjust in mid-circle if necessary."

Elorie frowned. "Maybe I should have tried something a lot simpler."

"Absolutely not." Sophie reached for her hands. "A caster's first spell is supposed to be a memorable one, and it's such a wonderful gift you've planned. It's a truly beautiful idea, Elorie. Aunt Moira will be so proud."

"She doesn't know what we're doing, right?"

Sophie shook her head. "Nope. The witchlings are sworn to secrecy, on threat of kitchen duty if they fail, and Lauren will make sure she doesn't figure it out during the circle."

"You've sorted out where to put it?"

"Yes, and where to move all the flowers. Fitting something that big in her back yard will be no easy task, you know."

Oh, but it would be so worth it. Elorie hugged her knees and smiled. It had taken a lot of careful thought to come up with a spell special enough for her first full-circle spellcasting.

She was really proud of her idea. She'd considered the unique strengths of her circle, and split the tasks into manageable parts neatly matched to the power of each trio. The only one she was suddenly doubting was herself.

Ginia spoke up from behind her. "The network's all connected and ready to go." Elorie took a deep breath before she turned around. She'd been trying to avoid looking at the sprawl of laptops and cables all over their lawn. They were a stark reminder that she was about to conduct the first full circle in Fisher's Cove's history that hadn't happened down on the beach. While most witches could pull their power from anywhere, Net power required a Wi-Fi bubble—and even Ginia and Nell couldn't make that reach to the ocean. They'd tried.

It was almost time.

A flood of witches came out the back door of the inn. Scratch that; it *was* time.

Fortified by food and naps, the witchlings bounced around, checking out the cool toys Ginia had set up. Marcus scowled and tried to protect as much of the equipment as he could, while most of the rest of the adults took the exuberant kiddos in stride.

Moira walked over to Elorie. "I'm so proud of you, my darling granddaughter. You'll have this now." She held out her hand, a simple silver ring with hand-etched Celtic symbols lying on her palm.

It was a ring Elorie knew very well. It had been on Gran's finger for as long as she could remember, a gift that had been passed from witch to witch since time unremembered. It was one of Gran's most treasured possessions.

Another passing of the baton.

Her heart wobbled as Gran slid the ring on her finger, but her resolve strengthened. However weird and modern her powers might be, she would try to be the witch Gran's legacy deserved.

Gran nodded in approval at whatever she saw in Elorie's eyes, and turned to the group with the opening words of ritual. "May the circle begin."

Elorie watched as the circle—her circle!—took shape.

Ginia, Sophie, and Mike on earth trio had the heaviest lifting to do for her. Their spell was both complicated and demanding. Aervyn had moved to the fire trio with Nell, and he was supremely excited about what he would get to do.

The air and water trios had an easier job this time, which was a good thing. Sean and Marcus were always a little rocky together, and Gran needed a break after her hard work of the morning.

Mike helped Moira settle at a chair and table, and the rest of the group assembled on the grass, laptops and mice in their hands. Jeebers. It looked like computer class, not a working circle.

Doesn't matter what it looks like, girl, growled Marcus. *It only matters what you can do with it.*

Elorie looked down at Gran's ring. Traditional or not, this was her circle, and they had a job to do. Raising her head, she smiled reassurance at Kevin, and then nodded to Gran. Ready.

Moira raised her hands, steady and confident, and began the call to the elements. As each trio followed in turn, Elorie felt power beginning to swirl. She nodded to Kevin and felt his mindlink click into place.

And that's when she truly realized the difference between a prank with a couple of friends and a full working circle. It felt like the eye of a hurricane—and they hadn't done anything yet.

She felt the magic inside her rise up to meet the swirling power. There was no room for fear. This was her birthright, and she intended to claim it.

The spell forming to her left was the earth trio at work. She marveled at the intricate, patient work of three minds shaping a literal bulldozer of a spell. Their spellshape oozed confidence and power.

To her right sat a single, uncomplicated shape of white heat. She didn't doubt Aervyn could get the job done—Nell had said the rest of the trio would just be holding on for dear life. And she was very glad for the containing spells spun by the air and water trios.

Their job was to keep everyone safe. You didn't let loose the fire witch of the century without some firefighters standing by.

Kevin nudged her mind. Earth was finally done shaping their spell. Elorie studied the shapes one last time before she began to work. With Kevin supporting and steadying the lines of power, she very carefully reached out a tendril of Net power to the earth trio's spell.

She jumped in shock as tendrils reached out of the spellshape, and then calmed as the questing fingers met and easily linked. Ah, Ginia's Net power. They'd hoped having her in the earth trio would make power blending easier. This was *much* easier.

Next she reached to Uncle Marcus and Gran, and the containing spells their trios had readied. No, wait. Those needed to layer over the outside. Visualizing as clearly as she could for Kevin, she backed the two containing spells away and reached for the fire trio's spellshape.

It's not a bomb, she reminded herself. It won't go off until you tell it to. Still, she pulled it toward the earth spell with infinite gentleness. When the two linked, the power jolt was sharp and bright.

It's just Aervyn again, Kevin sent, apparently an old hand at dealing with their super-witchling now.

Layering the containing spells around the final shape was quick and easy. Elorie paused for a few seconds, appreciating. This moment would never come again.

Each trio had included a trigger in their spell, and Elorie began the release. For this, at least, she had insisted on tradition—her very first rhyming spell.

"Fire, water, air, and wind.
Shaped and melded, bent and twinned.
Guide our magic to its place.
Form a gift of earth and space.
With our magic, four times three,
As we will, so mote it be."

As she finished, she let go the hold on her Net power and pushed. This would take everything she had.

No longer was she sitting in the eye of the hurricane. She was the hurricane. Power blew around the circle, through her and Kevin in the center, and into the gigantic spellshape that connected them all.

Fourteen witches held steady and created a gift from their hearts.

The spell dimmed, and Elorie felt herself swaying. Uncle Marcus's gruff voice came in her ear. "Next time, save enough to keep you standing." She might have been irritated if his hands, holding her steady, hadn't been so very gentle. Slowly, she opened her eyes and looked at Aervyn. Had they done it?

His eyes closed for a moment, mindspeaking with Lauren, who was at the site where their spell should have formed. When he levitated in glee, it was all Elorie needed to know.

Thirteen witches looked entirely delighted. Moira was utterly mystified. "Whatever did you do, my sweet girl?"

Elorie laughed. "It's a surprise, Gran. The best surprise ever. But we can't tell you until tonight."

Chapter 16

"Well," Nell said, "this qualifies as my oddest hot-tub experience."

Sophie handed down sandwiches and lemonade into the empty, rock-lined pit. "You just need to have a little imagination."

Nell grinned. "It'd have to be pretty active to turn you into a steamy guy." She nudged Elorie. "You're going to be sneaking over here at night with Aaron."

"So he tells me. I hope Gran will enjoy it." Elorie frowned, looking around. "Do you think it's going to work? I don't want to put too much pressure on Sean."

It was Sean's job, in the last circle of the day, to turn the empty basin into a beautiful, magically hot-springs-fed natural pool.

Nell laughed. "Relax, girl. You did most of the heavy lifting with your circle earlier this afternoon."

Sophie nodded in agreement. "Totally. Gran and Lizzie are up taking a nap together, Aervyn passed out on the back porch, and Ginia's snoring in the hammock."

Nell patted the rock beside her. "My fire punk did nice work melting these rocks together, but it's the earth trio who did the really heavy lifting. Why aren't you sleeping too, Soph?"

Sophie leaned back, appreciating the sun-warmed smoothness, and grinned. "Apparently, pulling a nice layer of rocks to the surface of the earth is an aphrodisiac for some." And how. They'd burned off plenty of energy, and then Mike had gone out for a run with his leftovers.

"Dang," Nell said. "Next time I wanna be in the earth trio."

Elorie giggled. "Then you'd better bring Daniel with you."

Sophie quirked an eyebrow, glad to see Elorie in a nice, uncomplicated moment of happiness. "How about you, spellmistress? I bet Aaron's a pretty happy guy right about now, too."

"He was, until he discovered several witches trying to cook potions in his kitchen. Now I think he's busy making 'Keep Out' signs and trying to convince the twins to cast hexes for him."

Sophie wondered lazily whether she might talk Aaron into giving Mike some cooking lessons. For some reason, all her potions on the stove tended to make him a little nervous. Silly witch. She almost never got them mixed up.

Nell looked over at Elorie. "Yup. She's a goner."

Sophie blinked. "Who—me?" When they both grinned, she laughed ruefully. "Well, yeah. But I was mostly thinking about potions, actually."

"Yeah, right." Nell snorted. "However, speaking of potions, how's it going with that girl of mine?"

"She's got the patience and precision. Yesterday, we mixed up a nice batch of belly butter for her to take back to Nat. We embedded a calming spell to help the baby sleep."

"Awesome. Nat will appreciate it as those baby arms and legs get longer and start keeping her awake at night."

Sophie held back a yawn. Maybe she really did need a nap. "Aervyn's sure there's still just one in there?"

Elorie almost dropped her lemonade. "Aervyn can see babies?"

Nell nodded. "Yup. He saw Nat's little bean just a few days after conception. It's an awkward talent, though. He popped the news to a total stranger in the grocery store last month."

Sophie watched Elorie try to get her expressive face under control, and she knew. She leaned over and gently touched her friend's hand, hoping to offer without intruding. "So can healers, with a scan. And we have a bit more discretion than most four-year-olds."

Elorie gulped and nodded. "Not yet. But soon, I hope. And please don't tell Gran. She's already knit way too many baby blankets."

Sophie grinned and reached for one last sandwich. She could keep a secret.

She realized Nell was watching her with a suddenly calculating look. "That's an impressive snack you just ate, even for a witch. When's the last time you scanned yourself?"

Sophie stopped with the sandwich halfway to her mouth. "That's impossible."

Nell laughed. "Not. Trust me—I know how babies are made."

Through her brain freeze, Sophie realized one thing for sure. She had to know. Oh, God. Reaching for power, she ran the basic self-scan that was every healer's first lesson.

And she found life.

A tiny little presence nestled deep in safety. Carefully she checked blood flow and oxygen supply, tissue health and hormone levels, and the healthy division of cells. Then the healer paused, and the brand new mama marveled. There was a baby in her belly.

When she opened her eyes, their empty hot tub was rimmed in daffodils. Nell and Elorie each plucked one, long the witch community's welcome for new life.

Elorie grinned and spoke through tears. "I know where you can get a large supply of hand-knit baby blankets."

Nell beamed and hugged Sophie tight, and then handed her a daffodil. "Go tell Mike before Aervyn finds out and spills the beans."

~ ~ ~

Demon wings and bat dung, would the girl never stop messing with him? Marcus glared at his laptop screen and the top-secret location of his Realm high-mountain keep. Since all his guards were currently sporting pink chest plates and fluffy bunny slippers, it obviously was top secret no longer.

Were three circles in one day not enough to keep Warrior Girl busy? He'd just seen her giggling together with Aunt Moira in the garden, not a care in the world. Probably discussing love potions or something.

He needed a break. When this day was over, he was heading back to his nice, quiet home. Not quite a mountain keep, but it was private, and an excellent place for a solitary witch.

Elorie strolled into the parlor. Perfect—just who he needed. "That was nice work earlier this afternoon. I trust you've had time to rest and recuperate. I'll be heading home tomorrow, so let's see if we can get a little more spellcoding through that thick head of yours."

She raised an eyebrow. "Such a lovely invitation."

Anyone who expected him to dither around with being polite was going to die waiting. He was a witch, not a social butterfly. "Just sit down, girl. We have bunny slippers to deal with."

"We have *what*?"

"The evil Warrior Girl and her minions have attacked my keep, and cleaning up her mess is a challenge appropriate to your spellcoding skills." He hoped. Warrior Girl's spells tended to be fairly devious.

Elorie sat down, lips twitching as she caught sight of his screen. "Sounds like serious business."

They both looked up in astonishment at a loud thud. Mike stood rubbing his forehead, having clearly just walked into a wall.

Marcus only knew of three things that could make a grown man forget where the walls were, and of those, he only considered alcohol a reasonable excuse. "The door's a foot to your left."

As Mike turned to face them, it was clear he wasn't drunk. Splendid. That meant the man was either bespelled or stupid in love. Marcus reached out with a quick mental probe and sighed. Witchling pranks could be reversed. That kind of love-struck tended to be terminal.

One more decent man lost.

Elorie elbowed him and spoke under her breath. "You can't possibly be that big a curmudgeon."

Marcus grunted and stretched a hand out toward Mike. "Congratulations, son, and good luck. You'll need it."

Mike grinned, the dopey look of a man who'd lost his way. "I'm having a baby. Well, Sophie's having a baby. We're having a baby."

Any man who repeated himself three times was already underwater.

As Elorie jumped up to hug the father-to-be, Marcus tried to hold on to his sense of superiority and ignore the slide of fear in his heart. Most witchlings lived long, happy lives. Almost all of them.

This was the problem with coming out of his cave. Too darn many things tugging at his heartstrings.

~ ~ ~

Elorie held tight to Aaron's hand as they hurried down to the beach. An accidental after-dinner nap had the two of them running very late for Sean's full circle.

She couldn't believe they'd actually made it to the evening without Gran discovering the sizable hole in her back yard. It would be a masterpiece of beauty and warmth when Sean was done, but right now, it was a frightful disturbance in the well-tended order of Gran's garden.

She'd never seen several dozen witches keep a secret for ten minutes, never mind an entire afternoon. Somehow, Gran managed to bring out the best in people, even when she wasn't trying.

Kicking off their shoes in the sand, they ran over to where everyone had gathered, inner and outer circles already formed. Moira looked up and smiled. "And that's all of us. You look well rested, my dear. Let the circle begin."

Elorie dropped into place in the outer circle next to Lauren and picked up her flute. Breathing deeply, she began to play the slow melody to the moon that had begun every evening circle she could remember. Haunting and sweet, the notes rose over all who gathered.

Other instruments in the outer circle added harmony and quiet echo, an offering of peace and love, and an invitation to belong—to the magic and to each other. Memory poured in, of the first full circle when the flute had been hers to play. Hesitant child's fingers moving carefully through the notes Gran had taught, and then pausing in wonder as those notes were picked up and magnified.

Witch or not, this had always been her place.

As she finished, Lauren reached for her hand. *That was the purest kind of magic. You weave hearts together as beautifully as you weave spells.*

Elorie looked on the moon and the beach, the familiar faces. She loved being a very small part of this great whole.

And now her students would take their places, too.

Her trainer's heart beat proudly—they looked so competent. Kevin and Sean, channeler and caster, ready in the center. Lizzie on point for water trio, with Gran standing just behind her. That one made Elorie's heart lurch a little, but then she saw the pride on Gran's face. Some changes were happy ones.

Lizzie stepped forward, holding a bowl of water, and Elorie gulped back the lump in her throat. Gran beamed as Lizzie lifted the bowl moonward and began the call to water in her young, clear voice.

"*We of the West call on Water,*
Of life-giving stream and cleansing rain.
We of the West call on Water,
The ocean's reach and drops under our feet.
We of the West call on Water,
With voices three.
As we will, so mote it be."

Many murmured the familiar words along with her, and Elorie felt the breeze of gathering power. She also saw Gran's eyes open wide.

Lauren laughed quietly beside her. *She's got some serious power, that little one. Here, Aervyn has me linked in. I'll share so you can see.*

Elorie felt Lauren's link, and then she could see the flowing spiral of water power for herself. Unlike previous mindlinks, she could also still see with her eyes. No, wait—with Aervyn's eyes.

Yup, Lauren sent. *He's a tricky little witch. You're seeing what he sees, magic and non-magic.*

Elorie watched in fascination as the other elements were called, adding sparking fire, swirling air, and solid earth flows to her field of vision. Then Kevin, steady and sure, began to gather the power. After experiencing the hurricane for herself, she could only applaud his quiet self-confidence.

When he had the energy streams neatly collected, he threw a huge power line toward his brother.

Elorie sensed Lauren's surprise as it was neatly caught. *I guess they've done that before. He was a lot more careful with Mike this morning.*

Everything seemed ready, and Elorie wondered at the pause. Then she heard Kevin's calm mental voice. *More.*

Water's power stream suddenly quadrupled in size. Then she felt Aervyn's glee, and the walloping dose of power he let fly toward Kevin. Mother of God!

Breathe. Lauren squeezed her hand. *Your twins are handling it just beautifully. Can you sense Kevin's mind?*

She couldn't sense anything but seething power. And then—the quietest of undertones, the flute in the marching band—she could hear it. The focused joy of an artist at work.

With a fierce competence that astonished her, he grabbed everything Lizzie and Aervyn had thrown at him and piped it to his twin.

Then they all steadied and waited for Sean to do his work.

Now familiar with spellshapes, Elorie had even more reason to be impressed as she watched Sean cast his spell. Working primarily with water and fire, he wove together a beautiful form of dancing light. Then, quickly flicking his fingers, he layered earth and air over top of the main shape. Tonight, it was those elements adding containment and safety.

As the spell readied, every witch present held their breath. The point of release was the most difficult for a spellcaster, and Sean had never handled a shadow of this much power before. Elorie had one last desperate surge of regret for asking this much of him.

Then power flared, and the entire circle glowed in the impossible light of magic unleashed.

As she watched with pride running over, Sean waited for the light to dim, neatly tied off the loose ends of power, and checked in with each member of his circle. Only then did he burst into an impromptu tap-dance.

Elorie laughed. Only a bunch of underage witches would have the energy to dance around like that after a full circle.

She made her way over to Moira. "How are you feeling? It's been a long time since you've done three circles in one day." And one was often enough to leave Gran exhausted, although no one was willing to admit it.

Moira snorted. "I'm not dead yet, child. It was the easiest day of magic in a long time, with Lizzie carrying most of the weight in my trio. I must say, though—this is the second circle of the day where I've no earthly idea what we did. Surely it's time to let the cat out of the bag now?"

Elorie grinned. This was going to be the best gift ever—and it was finally time for the giving. She pulled out a chair and motioned Gran to sit. "The rest are going to meet up by the surprise, and then Aervyn will give you a little ride."

A very eager crowd flowed up the hill toward Moira's yard. Elorie was pretty sure Aervyn provided an assist to several of their more elderly members. He was a more than a little excited. Then he popped back down, stood in front of Moira, and reached for her hands.

"Are you going to teleport me, sweetling?"

He nodded. "Uh, huh. But I'll be really careful about the flowers, just like Elorie said. She said we better not mess with any more of them, or you'll be really mad."

Gran's face was absolutely priceless. "You messed with my flowers?" That was all Elorie got to see as Aervyn, realizing he'd almost let the secret loose, ported the three of them into Moira's yard.

It was a picture-perfect landing, right next to the beautiful hot-spring pool that now graced her garden.

No one breathed. They had indeed messed with Gran's flowers, and Elorie dearly hoped it hadn't been a mistake.

Ever so slowly, Moira stood, her face absolutely unreadable. Then she removed her cloak and shoes and stepped into the pool, still wearing her summer dress. She spun around slowly in the center, and then sank in up to her chin.

Her face spoke her utter joy.

Elorie, for the first time, knew the true power of magic freely given, and her soul sang with it.

Sean bounced to the side of the pool. "Do you like it, Gran?"

Moira looked to Elorie a long moment, eyes full of astonished love. "How did you know?"

Elorie shrugged, suddenly very uncomfortable with fifty sets of eyes on her. "I remembered the stories." Gran had always been full of stories of her childhood Irish home and the wonderful, magical spring tucked into the green hills.

"Such a gift, child. Such a gift." Moira touched the waters reverently. "Magic lives in these waters, and oh, so much love." She looked at the faces gathered around. "Thank you. To each and every one of you, thank you."

Then she turned back to Sean. "Sweet boy, this is the very best bit of magic I've ever seen. A spellcaster's first spell is one that will always be remembered, and that you chose to make this gift for me—well, I feel like just about the most loved Gran ever."

Sean looked down sheepishly. "It was Elorie's idea, not mine. But I thought it was a really good one…"

Moira reached for his hand. "The idea matters, but so does the doing. You did magnificent magic tonight, and you should be very proud."

"We only did half," Sean said, more than willing to share the credit. "Elorie's circle pulled the rocks out of the earth and melted them together. They even made seats out of the rock and stuff so you'll be really comfortable, and fixed the flowers so you wouldn't get too mad. My circle just added the water. I guess Elorie did most of the hard stuff." He stumbled to a halt.

Marcus stepped to his side. "Not at all, my boy. Her spell required sheer power. Yours was about elegance. Imagine if you'd added a little too much heat and boiled Aunt Moira like a frog."

Sean turned white. Clearly that possibility hadn't occurred to him.

Moira rolled her eyes. "Marcus, go make me some tea and stop scaring the children." She held her arms out to Sean. "It was wonderful magic, and it will keep giving every time I visit this pool with my aches and pains and creaky joints. Come, join me."

Every witchling in the garden took that as an invitation, which was probably as she had intended.

Elorie wondered how many witches they could fit in the pool. She suspected they were about to find out.

Chapter 17

With delicate moves and sure fingers, Elorie finished attaching the clasp to her first creation since she'd returned from California. Paperwork, magic, and visitors had all conspired to keep her away from her studio far too long.

Her fingers and her heart had needed to create again, even if it was 5:30 a.m.

She'd walked past Gran's new soaking pool on the way to her studio. With the number of witches waiting a turn last night, she'd been mildly surprised not to find anyone asleep in the warm water. The temptation to crawl in again herself had been high, but her glass had beckoned. The pool would wait; her need to create wouldn't.

She'd dipped into her most special jar of treasures for this one. The violet glass was a color she'd never seen before or since finding this particular bit of loveliness. Obviously hand-blown, it had streaks of red and blue running through the depths of the glass, making it look almost alive, and somehow, its eons in the ocean hadn't marred the perfect heart shape.

She held the small glass heart in her hand and felt, as she always did, like it beat for her. A flat rim of silver wrapped around it now, and attached to a chain of delicate handmade links.

It wasn't often she claimed a piece of her own artwork. This one would be hers; it always had been.

She had just done up the clasp when a sound at the door had her turning around.

"Good morning," Sophie said, two cups of tea in her hands. "Is it okay to interrupt? Aaron thought you might be ready for a little breakfast."

Elorie looked longingly at her jars of glass. She wasn't quite ready to leave yet.

Sophie smiled. "He knows you well. Don't worry—if I'm not back up there in a few minutes, Aervyn will port us some breakfast. If you throw me out, he'll send down breakfast for one."

Elorie's stomach let out an audible growl. She laughed and motioned to her other chair. "Apparently, breakfast sounds good."

Sophie grinned. "Breakfast will be delivered to Aunt Moira's pool."

Excellent. It looked like she was going to get a morning soak after all. She picked up her cup of tea and followed Sophie out of the studio and down the path to Gran's garden.

Mists were still rising off the pool, and it was miraculously still unoccupied. Some of their travelers had headed home, but there were plenty who remained, guests in nearby homes. Not everyone was a morning witch—she'd have to remember it was a good time to wander over for a dip.

"Good morning, my lovelies! Come to have a soak in my pool, have you?" Moira walked out her back door, wearing a light robe.

She set her cup of tea down on a convenient flat stone and unbelted her robe. Elorie felt her eyes fall out of her head. Gran was naked!

Moira laughed. "In deference to the climate here, I don't work skyclad like I did as a girl, but trust me, it's the very best way to experience a hot spring. Nell's playing gatekeeper in the kitchen. We won't be disturbed."

Sophie shrugged and peeled off her bikini. Elorie paused, trying to wrap her mind around the idea that Gran had ever done magic wearing only moonlight. However, the blissful sighs of the other two as they settled into the warm waters got her moving again.

If Gran could skinny dip, she surely could too.

As she settled into the water, a tray with fragrant scones and strawberries materialized at the side of the pool. Bless Aervyn. She could get used to having a teleporting witchling around.

"Aaron's such a good man," Moira said, handing out scones. "Here, Sophie—you first, dear. As I remember, pregnant bellies aren't very patient."

Sophie blushed. "I had three before I left the inn. For someone the size of a pinhead, this is one very hungry baby."

"There's more than just the baby to grow. You've been monitoring yourself, I hope?"

Sophie grinned. "Of course. I'm a well-trained witch." Then she held out a hand. "Would you like to look?"

Moira smiled in delight and moved to place her hand on Sophie's belly. Elorie watched in fascination as a few moments later, Gran's other hand touched Sophie's temples, and then the back of her neck. She'd seen the same done for a headache or two, but not for a pregnant woman.

Gran caught the question in Elorie's eyes and smiled. "It's a wee bit of a hangover is all."

Elorie stared. Sophie wasn't a big drinker.

Moira laughed. "Not that kind of hangover. A touch of wine is fine for a babe, but nothing more. This is just some aftereffects of yesterday's magic. We all worked very hard."

Pride blossomed again as Elorie looked around at the pool. They had done some very good work.

Moira touched Sophie's cheek. "All fixed up, although I think these marvelous waters were taking care of most of it for you."

She glided over to Elorie. "Are you feeling any aftereffects of yesterday, sweetling?"

Elorie shook her head, wanting to dodge a healing scan. She wasn't at all sure what Gran might find, and not quite ready to know the answer. However, she had a question that had been niggling, and this might be a good time to ask. "Will magic affect Sophie's baby at all?"

"Affect? Of course," Moira said, her eyes twinkling. "Babies are very elemental creatures, and I think they feel the power flows more readily than we do. But harm? No. It would have to harm Sophie first, and she's well-trained enough to prevent that in anything other than the worst of circumstances."

She touched Elorie's hand gently, her eyes more serious now. "A witch with less training would want to be sure her channels were being cleared regularly. Otherwise, power remnants could cause a babe some distress."

Elorie nodded. Messaged received, Gran, loud and clear.

~ ~ ~

Marcus looked around the parlor of the inn. Such a motley crew of students. He had insisted on another spellcoding lesson. His reinforcements in that area were heading back to California in two days, and he wanted as much of their help as he could get.

That, and the longer he kept Ginia training, the less trouble she could heap on him in Realm. It amused him that she was currently helping to train his secret weapon. It wasn't an easy task. Elorie wasn't a dumb witch, but when it came to spellcoding, she was a brick-headed one.

"Stop scowling, nephew," Moira said. "You'll scare your students."

"I wish. Have you gotten that login spell working yet?"

"Not at all," she said, shrugging. "It wiggled a bit, but I'm just too old for this, I think."

Ginia giggled from the other side of the table. Marcus shot her a suspicious look, but refrained from a less-than-ethical mindread. She was up to something, but darned if he knew what it was.

Moira put down her mouse. "She's an excellent trainer, our Ginia. The young ones are coming along very nicely."

There was truth to that. Kevin was developing into a solid coder, and even Lizzie, who had only the small-sparks kind of Net power, appeared to have some spellcoding talent.

Aunt Moira, however, was a dead loss, and Elorie was far too resistant to use her magic effectively.

"It's not what she wanted," Moira said softly, following his gaze. "Give her time. Yesterday helped, but she has some steps to travel yet."

"She's wasting a prodigious talent."

"No, my dear. She's learning to live with it. Some of us move to acceptance more slowly than others."

He glanced at her sharply. Aunt Moira was fond of making her point in roundabout ways. She had never entirely approved of his isolated life. "Some things are not meant to be accepted."

She raised an eyebrow. "Oh, really now. And would that be a tolerable answer from Elorie?"

That was entirely different. He'd lost a brother because his magic wasn't strong enough. Elorie was denying the full potential of her magic.

He felt the black mood creeping in. It really was time to leave this place and go home.

A small hand slid into his. Aervyn. The black mood backed off, just a little. "I wrote a spell. Will you come watch while I set it off? Ginia says I need supervision."

Since Aervyn hadn't been able to string together three lines of functional code so far, Marcus doubted supervision was required. But for some reason, it wasn't in him to resist the tugs of the small boy who looked so much like Evan.

He sat down and glanced briefly at Aervyn's code. Well, hallelujah. Five lines of a login spell, with only one small glitch in line four. The child might actually get into Realm this time. "Go ahead, set it off."

Aervyn focused and clicked on his mouse. Then everything went black.

Marcus felt a strange sucking sensation and a moment of dizziness. "Who goes there?" said an oddly familiar voice. He opened his eyes and saw the head guard of his Realm mountain keep, still wearing his bunny slippers. Those had been unusually resistant to any and all reversing spells.

"What manner of infiltrator are you?"

Marcus realized he was lying on his back contemplating bunny-slipper spells while an armed man pointed a sword at his neck.

What in the heavens was he doing inside Realm? And evidently not in costume.

The guard suddenly toppled over and curled up, snoring. "We can do real magic here," Ginia said, dusting off her hands. "At least I can. I hit him with a sleep spell. So, how come we're in Realm?" She seemed very unconcerned.

"I don't think we're the only ones," Marcus said. "Aervyn activated a login spell right before I got dumped here."

Ginia's eyes opened wide. "Aervyn got spellcode to work?"

Marcus frowned. "It appears that way. And I guess this is what you get when someone with his level of power manages to pull off five decent lines of code." Although clearly that glitch in line four had been rather more serious than he'd realized.

"So, where is he?" Ginia looked around, a lot more worry on her face.

Marcus opened his mouth to yell for Aervyn, and then closed it again, realizing that was a waste of air. If real magics had come with them, then he and the witchling were both mindreaders. He cast out with his mind. *Aervyn. Where are you?*

The reply was strong and happy. *I'm in a castle with a princess. She's feeding me bread and honey. Am I asleep?*

Don't think so, my boy. I think you pulled us all into the game.

Wow, are we like superheroes now? Awesome!

Hardly awesome, Marcus thought. But the first step was to gather the troops. *Can you port to where I am? Ask the princess if you can have the bread to bring.*

Moments later, Aervyn thunked into place beside him, carrying a good-sized bag with several loaves of bread and a pot of honey. Clearly the princess was generous.

"Are we gonna rescue the princess?" Aervyn asked, his mouth still full of bread.

"Ha," Ginia said. "I've met her. She doesn't need to be rescued."

The princess in question was one of Marcus's stealth warrior creations. She had strong magic, excellent fighting skills, and a blessed lack of the almost universal female need to talk all the time. His perfect woman. If she'd caused Warrior Girl some consternation, all the better.

Aervyn swallowed the last of his food. "Should we go help Sophie? She's fighting pretty good, but there are two more big guys coming."

Marcus spun around in disgust. This was why amateurs shouldn't be spellcoding. "Which way?"

They all ran down the trail after Aervyn. Sophie wasn't far away, but one of the fighters attacking her had laid down a silencing spell, presumably so no one would come running to her aid.

Marcus took a fraction of a second to appreciate Sophie's extremely impressive kung fu moves, and then borrowed Ginia's trick and knocked out all three fighters with a sleep spell.

Aervyn hopped up and down. "Can I get the last two? Pretty, pretty please?" Two big warriors crested over the hill, approaching at a dead run.

Nell was going to have his hide for this. "Just a sleep spell, youngling."

Marcus was pretty sure the two warriors would sleep for a century. Aervyn's magic was not subtle when he got excited.

"Thanks," Sophie said, gasping for breath. "I was about out of tricks there. What are we doing here?"

"Aervyn ported us in," Ginia said. "Marcus didn't check his code well enough, I guess."

Aervyn grinned. "I told you I needed supervising."

Gah. It really was his fault. That fourth line of code had definitely looked wonky.

"Are Aunt Moira and Elorie in Realm too?" Ginia asked.

"Nope," Aervyn said, shaking his head. Marcus cast out mentally to double check. Good. Two less people to worry about.

Sophie grabbed a hunk of Aervyn's bread. "So, Super Boy, can you get us out of here?"

Aervyn shook his head. "Nope. But I bet Mama can. She knows all about reversing spells."

Sophie looked up at Marcus. "Nell went berry picking with Aaron, Mike, and the twins. They're not going to be back until after lunch."

It just got worse and worse. "In that case, let's go to the castle and see if the princess can scare us up some more food. We're going to have a long wait, and I don't want anyone getting cranky."

Ginia giggled and held out a loaf. "Have some more bread, Gandalf."

He scowled. No one was taking this seriously. "We could be stuck here for a long time, little fighter. Have you thought of that? Aunt Moira and Elorie are hardly going to be coming to our rescue." Neither of them could code their way out of a paper bag.

Sophie grinned along with Ginia. "Oh, I think you may be underestimating the two of them."

"Hardly. I've been training Elorie myself. She's not capable of coding a reversing spell. She's barely capable of coding any spell."

"Sometimes, nephew," said a strange voice, "you think too little of others." He spun around. The voice belonged to the Xena lookalike he'd heard was training with Ginia.

Ginia ran over and hugged the new arrival. "Aunt Moira, you're so smart."

Aunt Moira?

"I'm sorry to spill our little secret, my dear, but it seemed like it might be the best way to get you out quickly. Marcus is correct—neither Elorie nor I can solve this with coding, so we've another idea."

Good God. It was Aunt Moira. In the highest level in Realm, and clearly this wasn't her first visit.

One of the guards started to stir, and Moira calmly zapped him with a new sleep spell. "Elorie is going to use Net power to pull us out, and she needs us to shape some spells for her. It's handy that all of your magic seems to be working."

Marcus was still trying to process Warrior Girl's sheer deceit and trickery. Training Aunt Moira as her secret weapon was daft. Insane. And brilliant.

Sophie tapped him on the shoulder. "Focus. You can contemplate the likely magnitude of your defeat later."

Impossible. He wasn't going down to a nine-year-old girl and a woman in her seventies. The he realized Sophie hadn't been surprised when Xena had shown up. Good God. Maiden, Mother, and Crone. They were going to take over Realm.

Ginia met his gaze, supreme confidence in her eyes. Oh, yes. He was going down.

Moira picked Aervyn up and twirled him around, clearly enjoying the vibrant youth of her Xena avatar. "Perhaps we'll just take you home, and leave these three who aren't paying attention."

Aervyn giggled and shook his head. "Nuh, uh. I like it here. I wanna stay."

Moira tossed him in the air. "Aaron left Monster Mac and Cheese for lunch."

"Okay," he said. "I'll go, but I wanna come back and play again sometime."

"Let's see about getting out first, my dear boy, and then we'll see about a return visit." Moira turned to the others. "Ginia, Elorie needs for you to form a link between real and game that she can grab. My sweet boy here needs to ready a teleporting spell strong enough to carry four people. Sophie and Marcus, whatever power you can feed to either of them would be helpful."

Marcus nodded. It was a surprisingly reasonable plan. "I think we're most useful supporting Ginia's outbound link."

Aervyn frowned, counting on his fingers. "Why only four, Aunt Moira? Am I staying?"

She laughed. "Not today, sweetling. My lovely young warrior body will stay here. It's not real, remember. I'm really sitting in my chair, looking at my computer screen and wanting to tickle your belly."

Aervyn covered his belly and giggled. "Okay, but I'm coming back to play sometime."

Whatever complaints Marcus had about his companions, they were all well-trained witches. Within moments, they had the necessary spells ready to go. Now it was up to Elorie. She had the raw talent. It was her training and her will that were sometimes in question, particularly when computers were involved.

Slowly the spellshape in Ginia's hand began to shimmer. Then it gently expanded and settled over all of them like a dome. He looked up at the glowing light. Aye. The girl had talent.

Aervyn held steady as his spellshape began to move next. It wove and darted, linking into the dome of light in hundreds of places. Marcus shook his head. Elorie was overbuilding the spell, a common error of inexperienced spellcasters.

Then came the dark, and a deep sucking sensation. When he opened his eyes, his niece had her nose three inches from his face, and she didn't look happy. "Don't doubt me again. It weakens the magic."

Anger flared and died, guilt hard on its heels. She was absolutely right. "It's your training I doubted, niece, but even that was wrong. My apologies. It won't happen again."

She looked at him in absolute shock.

"That was awesome cool magic," Ginia said, oblivious to the undertones in the room. "Maybe after lunch we could try it again. Uncle Jamie would be so jazzed if we could zap everyone into Realm."

"Let's have lunch before we contemplate such things." Moira touched Marcus's arm and spoke quietly. "For a man who never apologizes, that was well done. Take the witchlings now—I'd like a word with my granddaughter."

Marcus did as he was told.

~ ~ ~

Moira chuckled as Marcus walked off. She wondered how long it would take him to realize he was wearing pink bunny slippers. Ginia's doings, she imagined.

She turned to her beloved girl. "Ginia's right, sweetling. It was wonderful magic. Now tell me what's wrong."

Elorie's expressive face was a tangle of frustration and hurt. "It doesn't feel like me, Gran. Every time I do magic, there are wires and computers everywhere."

"Aye, child. And you've done lovely things with that magic. My pool is the envy of every witch living, and probably a few who've passed, as well."

Elorie's face softened even as tears threatened. "That's just it. Making your pool almost felt right. I was part of a working circle, and we did magic that mattered."

She paused, taking a couple of jerky breaths. "But then we had Sean's circle on the beach, and part of my heart wished I could go back to being Elorie who plays her flute in the outer circle. Elorie of no magic."

Elorie who knew how she belonged. Moira settled in a chair. This called for careful handling. "I think I was nine the first time I wanted to give my magic back. My friends were taking a trip to the beach, and I had to stay home and study witch history."

Elorie sighed. "Is that what this is? Just a witchling tantrum? It feels bigger than that."

Moira reached for her granddaughter's hands. "It's not always convenient being a witch, my sweet girl. I hope you will continue to be Elorie the flute player, because you're wrong—there is a great deal of magic in that. But you are a witch, and even when that responsibility lays heavy, it's not one to be ignored."

"I know. You've taught me well."

Such sorrow. Moira's heart ached. "It appears that what I haven't taught you nearly so well is the joy of magic. It's such a gift you have. Magic is not always a burden."

Elorie shook her head. "It's not that. Weight I could handle. But why do I have magic that works best in some game? You heard Ginia. I don't want to be a shuttle service for witches who need a ride into their computer."

Ah. Still seeking her purpose, too. Moira ignored the petulance and dug for what mattered. "What *do* you want?"

Elorie sniffled. "I want to sit in the garden with you and help the flowers to bloom."

Some wishes were more easily granted than others. Moira picked a flower bud out of the table vase and prepared a simple blooming spell. She held them both out toward Elorie.

Her granddaughter touched the flower gently, smiling as it opened under her fingers.

Moira leaned over and tucked the flower into Elorie's hair. "Such magic you have in you, my love. Every witch must find their own path. If yours doesn't involve transportation for Realm players, that is for you to choose."

She paused, debating whether to go on. "But think on this, granddaughter. I haven't been able to toss a witchling in the air in thirty years. You brought joy to me and that sweet boy today. It's not all wires and technology. The hearts and minds are as real as those on the beach under the moonlight."

She touched Elorie's cheeks. "It's love that is at the very core of witch tradition, my darling girl. The rest is just trappings."

DEBORA GEARY

Chapter 18

Elorie tried not to grumble as she settled onto the inn's back porch. Witch lessons were putting a serious dent in her studio time, and her fingers still yearned to create. She touched the heart hanging around her neck.

Beckoned by some silent call, witchlings flooded up from the beach with Mike and Sophie in tow. Marcus, Moira, and Nell followed Aaron out of the kitchen, bearing glasses of milk and lemonade. It was the chocolate cake in Aaron's hands that had everyone's attention, though. Now Elorie knew why the witchlings had arrived in force. Sean could sense any freshly baked goods in a three-mile radius.

Lauren walked around from the front of the inn, a FedEx box in her hands.

"What do you have there, my girl?" Moira asked.

Lauren smiled. "Freedom."

Borrowing a knife from Aaron, she opened the box and pulled out several iPhones. Elorie tried not to scowl at yet more technology. She was working on changing her attitude. Really she was.

Lauren met her eyes. "The Net witches amongst you will be happy to know that you are each now the proud owner of one of these. Jamie shipped them out, and he's adjusted them in some ways he hopes will amplify your power."

Ginia grabbed the nearest phone, touched the screen a few times, and closed her eyes. Moments later, she beamed. "It's awesome. Uncle Jamie totally amped it."

Elorie assumed that was a good thing.

Marcus handed her a phone, and then rolled his eyes when she looked at all the screen options blankly. Her cell phone was of the no-frills variety. Evidently her first official witch lesson of the day needed to be how to access the Internet on an iPhone.

It was mildly embarrassing that Aervyn figured it out faster than she could. It was mortifying that Gran did.

All that was forgotten when Ginia had them lay hands on their screens and call up Net power. Elorie felt the rush blaze through her mind. Her eyes flew open, mirroring the shock she saw on Gran's face.

"Oh, my," Moira said, looking at her phone in awe. "That was quite something."

Elorie could see Uncle Marcus and Nell exchanging glances. She couldn't blame them. Any sane witch trainer was innately cautious, and a ramped-up power supply probably wasn't the greatest idea with a porch full of half-trained Net witches.

As one of those witches, however, she reveled in the power under her fingertips. Okay, maybe this was a piece of technology she could learn to appreciate. It was small enough to carry in her pocket.

Lauren touched her hand. "It's more than that. Jamie fiddled with the way these phones access the Internet in ways I don't understand, but you should be able to use it pretty much anywhere."

Ginia grinned. "Totally portable Net power."

Elorie paused in an agony of hope, wanting to make very sure she understood. "Even on the beach?"

Ginia nodded, engrossed in her phone. "Sure."

It *was* freedom. Elorie stroked the phone reverently. She would be able to call her power standing where land and sea met, like witches since time began. It was a gift beyond measure.

She looked up at Lauren, heart on fire. "This was your idea?"

Lauren nodded. "Jamie did all the work, though."

Elorie reached into her pocket and turned off Jamie's other gizmo, the one that kept her head from leaking. She wanted them to feel how much this meant to her. Mind-witch heads snapped up as the full force of her gratitude swept across the porch.

"Thank you," she whispered. "Just—thank you."

~ ~ ~

Nell grinned as Aervyn ported himself out of the way of a sizable wave. Given the wet state of his rolled-up pants, either he was mostly losing his game of magical chicken with the ocean, or he wasn't trying very hard.

The iPhones had been a great idea, but sometimes it took a mama to add the important details. All witchling phones were now equipped with waterproofing spells. Marcus had declined her services, but if he spent much more time giving witch lessons at the beach, he might live to regret that.

Lauren and Marcus were currently coordinating a lesson that blended some Net-power experimentation with projected mindspeaking. They were testing to see how distance impacted Net power, so pairs of witches had spread up and down the beach. Hence Nell's role as lifeguard.

Each training pair had a mind witch who was receiving instructions and reporting back to Lauren. Sean, for all his nonchalance, was able to mindspeak over impressive distances. His twin, paired with Elorie, was clearly stretched to the limits. Nell was pretty sure Lauren was gently augmenting Kevin so she could still hear him.

Aervyn could have made them all deaf from half a mile away, but he was showing surprisingly good manners in not making that clear to Sean. Her punk witchling had shown some signs of maturity lately that made her a little wistful. It was good that he learn to be less innocently overwhelming, but it also meant he was growing up.

Nell moved down the beach a little closer to Lauren and Marcus. Her own weak mind-witch powers didn't extend to long-distance conversations. *Elorie looks happy*, she sent. *Those phones were a brilliant idea, Lauren.*

More importantly, she's opening to her power with far less resistance, Marcus sent. *We might manage to make some progress here yet.*

Trust the grumpy old man to think happiness didn't matter, Nell thought. She tried to ignore the fact that he was only a few years older than she was.

They all watched as Elorie tried again to blend two simple spells, one from Lizzie and one from Sean. They'd spread further down the beach for this second attempt, and the spell merge failed. *She hasn't got Ginia's range*, Marcus grumbled, *and I can't figure out why. Ginia can blend spells from the other end of the beach, but Elorie has to be within a few feet.*

Nell was surprised the issue wasn't obvious to Marcus. *Kevin's her limit—she can't blend spells if she can't see them, and his mind magic isn't all that strong. He can't visualize it well enough for her when they get farther away.*

Hmm, Marcus sent. *That's going to make him a lot less useful to her.*

Nell gritted her teeth. She'd show him just how "less useful" Kevin could be. She had a theory about Elorie's Net power, and now seemed like an excellent time to put it to the test.

With careful precision, she sent a message to Lauren only and asked her to relay it with equal care to the trainees. When Aervyn burst into hysterical giggles, she was pretty sure her idea had been shared.

Elorie looked skeptical at first. A moment later, she looked a little mad and a lot focused. *What'd you tell her?* Nell asked Lauren.

That Marcus thought she and Kevin were kinda wimpy together.

Nell snickered. Lauren was turning into a very effective trainer.

Marcus was still oblivious. The man couldn't read emotions around him unless they knocked him on the head or he paid full attention, and right now, neither was happening.

Elorie and Kevin headed to the far end of the beach, closer to where the other witchlings were gathering. Nell grinned as Aervyn, Lizzie, and Sean all began forming spells as they walked. It looked like a little more than what she'd asked for. Clearly they were improvising.

What are they up to now? Marcus was getting testy. *We've already experimented in close proximity. They're just wasting time.*

They're kids at a beach, Nell sent. *Let them play a little.* She meant it, but she also needed to distract him for long enough to let her evil little plan come to fruition.

We're ready, Lauren! Aervyn, as the strongest mind witch, was clearly on messaging detail. She hoped he'd remembered to exclude Marcus.

Mama! Nell nearly laughed at Aervyn's indignant protest. He was probably rolling his eyes, too. *If I told him, it wouldn't be so funny, would it?*

Lauren stepped back from Marcus and made a big show of waving her left arm around. Nell snorted. No self-respecting spellcaster did that kind of hocus-pocus stuff. Maybe she was just trying to distract Marcus from the fact that her other hand was in her pocket, on her iPhone.

Then Lauren started rhyming.

"I ask the Water and the Air
Make a raincloud hover there
Above the head of he who doubts
Moans and grumbles, whines and pouts.
Let him the power of happiness see
As I will, so mote it be."

Nell gave up and dropped to the sand, holding her ribs. Lauren was milking her moment as an elemental witch for all it was worth. And damn, the girl could rhyme. As she watched in breathless laughter, a storm cloud of monster proportions formed over Marcus's head and let loose a torrential downpour.

Marcus appeared to be raining curses down on all their heads, but no one could hear him over the thunder.

Moments later, the cloud dissipated, and Marcus's clothes instantly dried. Nell rolled her eyes. Aervyn had a soft spot for the man. Her son was the only fire witch present with enough power to do a quick-dry spell that fast. Oddly, he never thought to do it on his own wet clothes.

Marcus glared at Lauren. "I assume you were just the decoy for that little stunt." He turned and stormed down the beach, muttering epithets under his breath. Nell sighed. No point letting some poor witchling take the blame.

She called after Marcus. "Lauren wasn't the decoy. She did the magic."

He spun around, eyes sparking. "She's no elemental witch."

Nell kept quiet, waiting for him to put it together. He might be an arrogant ass, but he was a very smart witch. She saw when it hit him. His anger vanished, replaced by total fascination. "Elorie sent the spell to Lauren?"

Aervyn popped up at Marcus's elbow, having ported his entire tribe of troublemakers back from the far end of the beach. "She totally did, Uncle Marcus. Did you like the thunder? That was my idea."

Sean poked Aervyn. Being a little older than four, he was wiser in the ways of not owning up to your part in witch pranks quite so quickly.

Marcus ruffled Aervyn's head absently and turned to Nell. "How did you figure it out?"

Sheer genius, Gandalf. My daughter comes by it honestly. Nell shrugged. "I took a guess. It seemed reasonable that if Elorie can download, she could upload, too."

Elorie looked confused. "Download and upload what? I just used Net power."

"Aye, niece," Marcus said. "But this time you didn't pull magic to yourself. You pushed it to someone else. Someone without those powers."

Ginia's eyes got big. "You're right. That's so cool. I wanna try." She jumped up and motioned to the others. "Let's go make another spell for Lauren to catch."

As a herd of witchlings ran down to the other end of the beach, Elorie moved away from Marcus. "Just in case you're about to get wet again."

Marcus snorted and waved a hand briefly in the air. "I don't think so. Any witchling who tries is going to discover the meaning of counterspell."

Nell wondered if Elorie had any idea of the implications of her newly discovered ability.

Not a clue, Marcus sent. *She still thinks this is fun and games on the beach.*

And you don't?

Nell's heart cracked when Marcus replied. *With this, I could have saved my brother. I wasn't strong enough on my own, and we couldn't get a circle together in time.*

~ ~ ~

Elorie held her breath as Ginia finished drilling a tiny hole in a piece of green sea glass. She wasn't at all sure that equipping a nine-year-old with a power tool was a good idea, but Ginia had been sweetly insistent.

Her temporary apprentice looked up. "So now I do the same thing to the other one?" Elorie nodded. Ginia had found a couple of small bits of green sea glass on the beach, and she wanted to make them into a birthday gift for Lauren.

Elorie rummaged in her wire collection. She had some thin copper wire that would go well with the green glass and Lauren's gorgeous hair.

Finished with the drilling, Ginia took off her safety goggles and looked at the wire with interest. "Now what?"

This was the fun part, if you had any artist's calling. "Now you dream a little. You need to ponder the glass and the wire, and think about how they might look nice together." She started pulling some half-done samples off her shelves. "You can hang the glass from a simple hoop, like this, or wrap the wire around to make a curly nest for the glass. That would look nice with the copper."

Ginia contemplated for a few moments, and then looked shy. "What did you do for the heart one you're wearing? It's really beautiful."

That caught Elorie by surprise. She'd expected Ginia to go for the curls. Her heart pendant had a hammered silver rim, which looked very simple, but required time and precision. "That's tricky to do with copper, and it would take quite a while, sweetie. I'll be happy to show you, though, if that's what you want to do."

"Yes, please." Ginia grinned. "Lauren's worth lots of time."

Elorie messaged Aaron to let her know when dinner was ready. They would be a while.

She picked several pieces of glass out of her baskets. Ginia's idea was a good one, and her inventory was in dire need of replenishment. She might as well work while Ginia labored. Her fingers blissed out with the normal routine of it all.

~ ~ ~

Moira giggled as Mike threw a pebble at Nell's window. She felt about ten years old again, sneaking around at midnight.

Nell stuck her head out the window and spoke in a stage whisper. "They'll be right down. Don't lose either of them."

Mike grinned back. "I won't. You just make sure Sophie doesn't decide to take a moonlit walk on the beach."

"Ha. I have chocolate ice cream. She'll never get past me." Nell ducked back in the window as Aervyn and Ginia came bouncing out the back door of the inn.

Aervyn looked very alert for a small boy at midnight. "I was really sneaky. I didn't wake up anyone." His sister shook her head. Clearly a small boy's standard for sneaky wasn't all that quiet.

Elorie came out next, yawning and holding up a bag. "I have cookies. We ready to go?"

Three generations of witches sneaking off to the beach on a top-secret mission. Moira had no idea what they were up to, but she was absolutely delighted. When Mike had recruited her, she'd taken a nice, long afternoon nap to be prepared. Who said an old witch couldn't be ready for anything?

Mike offered his arm for her to lean on, and she wasn't too proud to take it. The walk to the beach seemed a little longer these days.

When they reached the sand, she kicked off her shoes. It was a glorious night to be barefoot in the moonlight. This close, she felt Mike call earth power. "I found the perfect spot this morning," he said. "I left a marker so I could find it again."

Seven-and-a-half decades of life hadn't dimmed her curiosity any. What was the dear boy up to?

They walked a little way down the beach, just past the traditional place for full circles. Mike stopped and grinned. "This is it."

He squatted down in front of Aervyn. "Remember, this is top secret."

Aervyn nodded solemnly. "Just until tomorrow, right? I can do it."

Ginia grinned. "If he can't, I think I've figured out Mama's silencing spell."

Aervyn looked affronted. Moira nodded in approval as Mike intervened before his troops turned on each other. He would make a very good father.

Mike looked at Elorie first. "I asked you to come as an artist, as a witch who can blend spells, and as Sophie's oldest friend."

Then he turned to Moira. She looked in his eyes and saw love shining there. "I asked you to come as the keeper of traditions and the grandmother of Sophie's heart." Moira could feel her eyes misting over. She began to understand what they were about, standing here under the moon.

Aervyn grabbed Mike's hand. "Why are Ginia and I here?"

Mike grinned. "Because I need your firepower, superdude. We're going to make Sophie an engagement ring."

Aervyn frowned. "A what?"

Ginia elbowed him. "It's a ring you give somebody when you're gonna get married."

"Oh." Aervyn looked at Mike. "Is that because of the baby? Uncle Jamie and Nat got married right after their baby showed up in Nat's belly."

Mike laughed. "That's a good reason, but the best reason is because I love her."

Aervyn nodded. "Okay. Does that mean you're going to kiss her, too? Kissing's gross."

Elorie giggled and leaned over to Moira. "I think he's been hanging out with Sean and Kevin a little too much."

Moira smiled. She'd seen a lifetime of ten-year-old boys turn into young men mooning over the very girls they'd scorned for years.

Mike called his troops back to attention. "There's a lot of earth magic needed to make a diamond, and that's what the three of us will do," he said, motioning to the two children. "Can you feel the big chunk of carbon down below us?"

Aervyn scrunched up his eyes for a moment. "Yup, but that's awfully big for a ring, and it's kinda ugly."

"That's cuz it's not a diamond yet, silly." Ginia looked at Mike. "We're gonna squish it, right?"

Mike nodded. "Aervyn, can you see the picture in my mind? We're going to squish that big rock down to this really tiny shape, and then it will get all sparkly and pretty."

Moira hadn't known such magic was possible. Aervyn closed his eyes for another moment, and then nodded. Clearly he didn't have any doubts.

Mike looked next to her granddaughter. "Elorie, I'm hoping you can visualize a setting for the diamond." He held out a thin band of gold. "This was my grandmother's ring. We'll give you the power you need, but if you can shape it into something pretty, I'd really appreciate it. I'm no artist."

Elorie's eyes shone, ready to make a gift for the sister of her heart.

Ah, the boy was well rooted in tradition. Such a wonderful partner he would make her darling Sophie. Perhaps she was simply here to stand in witness.

Mike reached for her hand. "And if you would, I'd like for you to bless the ring."

That she could do, and with a heart abounding in pleasure. "I can do that when you're done, my dear. I've the blessing spell of my grandmother in my heart—I think that one will do nicely."

"I was hoping..." Mike paused as emotion swept his face. "I was hoping you could cast a blessing as we build the ring. Elorie could meld it right into the diamond and the gold."

Moira's heart wobbled as she realized what he wanted. The oldest of traditions, and the oldest of blessings, united by the newest of magics.

She readied an old Irish blessing spell, and then pulled down a bit of moonlight. It would make Sophie's diamond shine just a little brighter.

Chapter 19

Marcus could feel giggles tickling his mind channels. They were rather at odds with the dark and stormy book he was reading, so he sent a quick probe out to see who the happy troublemakers were.

It surprised him to discover Aervyn. Four-year-olds got involved in all manner of silly things, but this one usually had rock-solid mental barriers. He must be highly preoccupied to let stray giggles escape.

Curious, Marcus reached out a little further and discovered why Aervyn's mind was leaky. The little scoundrel was eavesdropping. Nell, Sophie, and Elorie were having iced tea in the garden, and the two youngest witchlings were spying on them.

All things were fair when a witchling wasn't minding his mind-witch manners. Picking the easier of his two targets, he linked quietly with Lizzie's mind and listened to their conversation.

"See," Aervyn said, in a whisper that sounded very loud to Marcus's enhanced channels, "they're the same. And Mama doesn't have one, cuz she says I'm all the trouble she needs."

"Not exactly the same." Lizzie was a highly precise witchling, a trait Marcus normally appreciated—when he knew what she was talking about. "Sophie's is bigger."

Marcus looked at the three women, trying to puzzle out the mystery. What did Sophie and Elorie have that Nell didn't? The only answer he could come up with was bikinis, and he was pretty sure swimwear fashion wasn't the cause of idle witchling conversation.

"Can you look again?" Lizzie said. "I want to see if the other one has a penis, too."

Aervyn's giggles should have been heard in the next county. "That's not a penis, silly. It's a tail. Mama says babies have tails when they're really little."

Babies? Marcus scowled, book forgotten. What on earth were they doing? Halfway out of his chair to nab the troublemakers, the mindlink he shared with Lizzie blazed, and Aervyn's incoming link clicked into place.

Hey, Uncle Marcus, said Aervyn, clearly unconcerned to find him lurking in Lizzie's head. *Do you wanna see the babies too?*

What babies? There were plenty of babies to be found in Fisher's Cove, but none of them appeared to be hanging out with the trio of women in question.

A very clear picture came down the mindlink. *That's Sophie's baby,* Aervyn sent. *Elorie's babies are newer, so they still look kinda strange.*

Marcus gawked at the small, alien creature on his mental screen. *That* was a baby? It looked a lot more like the shrimp he occasionally pulled in off his boat. *Are they supposed to look like that?*

More mental giggles from Aervyn as Marcus belatedly realized that was an eternally stupid question to be asking a four-year-old.

With small drips of sanity leaking back into his brain, he also realized Aervyn was doing something most trained healers would walk over hot coals to be able to do. And as far as he knew, healing wasn't on the boy's very long list of talents. *How are you doing that?*

Mind magic, Aervyn said. *Lauren can do it too, once the babies get a little bigger. She can see Nat's baby now. Can you see them?*

Marcus didn't bother to try. He knew when he was hopelessly outclassed. *Not at all, my boy. I wait until they show up on the outside to take a look.* That might not be entirely true, but he surely wasn't going to peer into a pregnant woman to find out. He began walking toward the flowerbed that hid the two schemers. Time for *them* to stop invading everyone's privacy as well.

Aervyn grinned as he arrived. "Let's go tell Elorie about her babies. They're kinda ugly, but don't tell her that. Mama says that makes girls cry, so I gotta use good manners and skip that part."

Marcus was pretty certain that eliminated any comparisons to shrimp as well. He sighed. "Let's go fetch Aaron first, shall we? I imagine he'll want to know too."

~ ~ ~

Elorie grinned at Sophie. "You think Gran's ever going to put her knitting needles down?"

"Are you kidding?" Sophie leaned over for another treat. "With three babies on the way, she's threatening to teach Lizzie how to knit too. Here, have a brownie. Chocolate's good for babies."

Elorie quirked an eyebrow. "Is that the healer witch talking, or the pregnant mama?"

"Does it matter?" Nell sat down beside Sophie, grabbing a brownie on the way. "Although I swear I craved chocolate more when I was pregnant with the girls than with my boys. Boys just don't have the chocolate gene."

Elorie giggled and pointed at Aervyn, currently running around the inn's back yard with a face smeared in chocolate. She wasn't convinced.

Nell laughed. "So it's not a perfect theory."

Mike walked out into the yard and snagged Aervyn, deftly avoiding the chocolate smears. "I need your help, kiddo. Can you be a witch megaphone?"

"Sure. What's that?"

"I need you to call everyone back now. It's time for presents, and some people went down to the beach and into the village. Can you mindspeak a call that far?"

PRESENTS! COME BACK FAST!

Elorie clapped her hands to the side of her head as Aervyn's very loud mental call rang out. Well, that ought to bring every able-bodied person in a hundred miles.

Mike, standing at ground zero, pretended to fall over dead on the ground, grabbing Aervyn on his way down. The tickles would have been funnier if Aervyn wasn't still mind connected with everyone. As a lot of people around Elorie discovered, covering your ears just wasn't that helpful when someone was mind giggling at top volume.

Aervyn! Lauren's mind voice was a lot quieter, but very insistent. *You're hurting our heads, Super Boy.*

The giggles shut off abruptly, followed by a much more quietly broadcast apology. *Sorry. I think I got a little excited. I'm a'posed to be working on that. But you should all come, because there's some really cool presents. Not for me, cuz it's not my birthday. But there's chocolate cake, even if it's not your birthday.*

Moira beckoned Aervyn. "You did a lovely job, sweet boy. Come sit by me. I'll share my chocolate cake with you. Ginia, love, would you run inside and get my bag?"

Elorie looked around. Witches had literally come out of the woodwork. There were almost a hundred people finding places to sit on the porch, the steps, or a spare patch of grass.

A hundred faces she knew and loved. She touched a hand to her belly. These were the people who would know her children and love them well. In Nova Scotia, villages still raised children—and in the witching community, they always had.

Aaron's hand reached down to cover hers. "Getting used to the idea yet?"

Elorie reached up for a kiss. Used to it? She was already figuring out how to squeeze two bassinets in her studio. Not that sleeping babies in Fisher's Cove ever seemed to make it to a bassinet. There were lots of arms willing to rock a baby, and they'd have to get past Gran to do it.

Ginia was back with Moira's bag, and a hush settled on the waiting crowd. Gran's presents were legendary. She pulled out two boxes, handing the larger one to Lauren, and the other to Elorie.

You first, Lauren sent.

Elorie shook her head. She knew what Lauren's box contained, and how very special a moment this was for Gran. *You first, my new sister.*

Lauren slipped the lid off her box and looked at the contents in mystified silence. Then she looked up at Moira, confusion all over her face. "Is this what I think it is?"

"Aye, lass. It's my great-grandmother's crystal ball. She sent it with me to travel across the sea. It's waited more than a century for new hands, but it began to glow when you arrived. It's meant to be yours now."

Lauren stared at the box in her lap like it contained eye of newt or something. "Sophie got here at the same time I did. Maybe it's really for her." She looked at Moira in consternation. "I'm so sorry—that came out wrong. It's one of your family treasures. It should stay in your family."

Marcus snorted. "Do they teach you new witches nothing?"

"Hush, nephew. What she doesn't yet know is our lacking, not hers." Moira leaned forward and took Lauren's hand. "In every way that matters, child, you are family. I would be delighted for you to have one of my treasures, and this one chose you."

Elorie watched love and utter discomfort tangle on Lauren's face. "But don't crystal balls show the future? That's not one of my talents."

"It's a tool, my dear. Nothing more. It will only speak to a witch of uncommon empathy and good judgment." Moira raised an eyebrow at Marcus. "None before you have passed that test."

Aervyn grabbed Lauren's arm. "Take it out and ask it a question. That's how it works. Don't worry. It's only a little hocus-pocus."

Lauren's face turned crimson as laughter swept through her audience. "I guess I figured crystal balls were a myth, just like cauldrons and pointy hats."

Fortunately she didn't look up and see all the glances exchanged at her comment. Elorie could count at least a dozen faces in attendance who'd polished Gran's cauldron as a result of some misdeed or another.

Lauren reached gingerly into the box and lifted out the clear glass ball. And then nearly dropped it as it started to glow.

Moira beamed with pleasure. "For a century now, it's been waiting for the right hands. Great Gran said it was a beautiful thing to see lit, and indeed it is."

Lauren looked completely gobsmacked. Nell snickered and leaned toward Sophie. "Modern witch, meet really old-fashioned magic."

As she watched the crystal ball with wonder and a smidgeon of jealousy, Elorie tried to put herself in Lauren's shoes. Oh, to hold such a piece of history in her hands and see it light up. "Is she really so uncomfortable with the old ways?"

Sophie smiled. "I suspect she feels like a very traditional witch I know, the first time she got handed an iPhone."

It took Elorie a moment to make the connection. "Did I really look as terrified as she does?"

"Oh, yeah." Nell nodded. "Like someone had handed you a small bomb."

Elorie tucked that little revelation away to think about later.

Aervyn was doing his bouncing thing again. "Ask it a question, Lauren!"

Lauren looked at Moira. "What do I ask?"

"That's why the crystal ball chooses those with empathy and good judgment, my dear. You have the wisdom to know the right questions to ask."

Lauren closed her eyes for a moment, and then stared at the ball very seriously. Dozens of eyes watched intently, but nothing happened. Elorie heard several sighs of disappointment, but Gran just watched with a gentle smile.

Then Lauren's eyes filled with tears, and she spoke very softly to Moira. Moments later, she closed her eyes, and Elorie felt the nudge of mind connection.

Tears ran unheeded as they all shared what Lauren had seen in the crystal ball. Gran, sitting in her garden rocker, with a babe in her arms and two more asleep in the basket at her feet.

Elorie felt the lifting of a weight she hadn't known she carried. Gran will rock our babies. Bless you, Lauren.

Sophie let out a trembling breath. "I guess we're coming to visit next year."

Lauren gently laid the crystal ball back in the box. This time she touched it with reverence.

Then she grinned at Elorie. "Your turn."

Elorie looked down at the small box in her hands.

Taking a deep breath, she opened the lid. The birthing stone. Oh, Gran. Clutching the stone, she crossed to Gran's waiting arms and buried her head in the shoulder that had always brought comfort.

"It's your turn now, sweetling. May it help your little ones into the world as it has generations of babes since time unremembered."

Elorie gripped the moonstone tightly. "Sophie will need it first."

Gran stroked her head. "I don't think so, child. Twins come a little earlier than most."

Two babies. Jeebers. As reality suddenly hit, Elorie melted to the porch floor. How on earth was she going to manage that?

She watched in a daze as more gifts were handed out. Lauren delighted in the earrings Ginia had worked on for several painstaking hours. Gran giggled over the bright pink shirt that said

"World's Best Grandma." And everyone sang along when Aervyn bespelled the flowers into a round of Happy Birthday.

Then Ginia handed Elorie another small box. From the sudden quiet attention around her, this one was important.

Elorie wasn't sure her emotions could take any more. Gran patted her hand. "Go ahead, dearest girl. This is the best gift of all."

One more time, she opened a box. And frowned. It was her new heart pendant. *That's* what had been niggling at her all day—the missing weight of it. She touched a hand to her neck, and Aervyn giggled. "I ported it this morning. Mama says it's okay to be a witchling thief if there's a really good reason."

Elorie began to understand why someone might look suspiciously at the contents of a box. "And what else did you do to it, sweet boy?"

"Wasn't just me." Aervyn had somehow found another brownie. "Lotsa people helped. We needed almost a whole circle. Shrinking stuff is hard."

The heart looked the same size as the last time she'd seen it. She looked around in confusion. All her witchlings looked very proud. Something was definitely up.

Ginia stood up. "Let me put it on for you."

Elorie held up her hair as Ginia attached the clasp, and then stepped back, eyes bright. "Now turn on Net power."

Elorie reached into her pocket for her iPhone, and discovered it was missing as well. Aervyn giggled again. Add "pickpocket" to his list of magical skills.

Ginia shook her head. "You don't need your phone. We put it inside your necklace, along with a couple of other cool spells."

Aervyn still danced in excitement. "Yup, we got the idea from—" He stopped speaking abruptly as Ginia's hand clamped over his mouth.

Nell jumped into the sudden silence. "Jamie says it's heresy to shrink something as cool as an iPhone, but you should basically have a permanent Internet connection around your neck now."

Elorie struggled to imagine an iPhone inside her sea glass. Then Nell's words sank in. A permanent Internet connection? Her eyes widened as hope and fear both hit. She faced the fear first. "Will it harm the babies?"

Nell shook her head. "Nope. Ginia embedded a couple of spells while she was tinkering in that glass heart of yours. You have one of Moira's best protection spells in there, and a sweet little spell to visualize elemental power. You should be able to see power flows now, even if Kevin's not around."

Elorie nodded, trying to take it all in. Her babies would be safe, and she wore a microscopic computer around her neck. Or something like that. If what Nell said was true, the details didn't matter.

Closing her eyes, Elorie reached for Net power. Her heart soared as her magic replied. It was hers to call, whenever she needed it.

Just like every other witch.

She clutched her pendant and looked at the faces around her. These wonderful, marvelous people had figured out a way to take down the last barrier between her heart and her magic.

They'd set her free. There was no greater love.

~ ~ ~

Sophie leaned back against the comforting rocks of Moira's hot pool and sighed. Bliss. She'd been waiting for this all day.

Moonlight shone on the garden, sending the mists dancing. It was a night for magic. Or perhaps for something a little different. She snuggled closer to Mike.

He tucked her into the curve of his arm and laid his free hand on her belly. Sophie smiled. "Our Seedling's fine. Nothing's changed since you checked ten minutes ago."

Mike chuckled quietly. "I'm not really checking. Just feeling, I guess. It's a miracle every time."

Sophie resisted the urge to drop into light healing trance with him. They needed to talk. Two people with a baby on the way couldn't live thousands of miles apart. And though her heart ached at the idea of leaving her Colorado haven, she would if that was the right next step.

Mike laid a finger on her lips. "Shh. I know we have plans to make, but I have something for you first."

She smiled as he reached for a nearby flower stem. Blue hyacinth. A profusion of small buds with a big message—flower-speak for constancy and steady love. It had always amused her that such a delicate flower represented the sturdiest of emotions. A gentle reminder that the man she loved had a steadfast heart.

Accepting his gift, she held the flower gently in her hands and reached for a gentle trickle of earth power. She cuddled into his shoulder as the petals unfurled.

She had just a moment to wonder at the racing of his heart, and then the flash of light in the petals caught her breath. "Oh. Oh, Mike."

Gently she reached in and pulled out a simple and stunning ring, diamond gleaming in the moonlight.

Mike slid it gently onto her finger. "Marry me, Sophie."

She tried to find words.

His hands gently cupped her face. "Seedlings need roots, and solid ground to stand on, and so do we. Make that together with me. I love you."

Sophie beamed at him. Roots and foundations weren't the stuff of most marriage proposals, but from one earth witch to another, they were everything.

She covered her hands with his. "Yes." It was the only word she could get out. And the only one that was necessary.

Chapter 20

Elorie slumped into the porch swing and took a deep breath. The silence was almost deafening. Aaron had just left with all their guests who needed a ride to the airport. Lizzie's father had taken the local witchlings out on his trawler for the day.

Gran was tucked into her garden, dealing with the profusion of flowers Mike's marriage proposal had left behind. Elorie grinned. Sophie's magic didn't run amuck for very many reasons. Gran had walked into her garden in the early morning and squealed loud enough for half of Nova Scotia to hear.

It was a joy that would help ease the partings somewhat.

Elorie swung gently. In a few minutes, she might get the energy to wander over to her studio, or have a visit with Gran. For the moment, swinging was about all the energy she could muster.

"Don't get too lazy there, niece." Marcus stepped out of the door of the inn, a cup of tea in his hand. "I've a spellcoding lesson planned."

She raised an eyebrow. "Even witches get the occasional day off."

"Not when their trainer is leaving in a few days. The faster you learn, the sooner I'll be able to go."

That was a mildly motivating thought. "Can we at least wait until after lunch? I was about to head to my studio." It was only a slight stretching of the truth.

Marcus shook his head. "Jamie will be joining us, and he's online, waiting. Come inside. I already have our laptops set up."

Elorie touched her heart pendant and sighed. Even its jazzy new abilities couldn't save her entirely from the curse of the laptop. Fighting off what she knew was a fairly irrational attack of laptop hatred, she hauled herself up from the swing and followed Marcus back inside.

She'd go sea-glass hunting later. That was the most effective reward she could think of to keep her bottom in a chair long enough to get through whatever Uncle Marcus had planned.

When she saw the Realm logo up on both computers, she mentally added chocolate to her self-bribe—an entire bar of the really good stuff.

She sat down in front of her screen and discovered it was only half Realm. The other half was Jamie's face on video chat, and that was a welcome sight, even under the circumstances.

"Good morning, Jamie. How's Nat doing?"

He grinned. "Still sleeping. Growing babies must be hard work. Congratulations, by the way—I hear there's a baby outbreak happening in Nova Scotia."

Elorie laughed. "I think Sophie's may have been conceived in Colorado, but Gran is happy to take credit. She claims her garden is full of fertility this year."

Suddenly Marcus's face popped up on her screen below Jamie's. It was eerie to have him both across the table and on her computer. "When you're done with baby talk, perhaps we can move on to our lesson for the day."

Jamie rolled his eyes. "Be nice, Marcus, or I'll tell Warrior Girl about your sleeper spell outside her secret garden."

Elorie had no idea what that meant, but it was very effective in improving Uncle Marcus's manners. Perhaps this Realm game had some benefits after all. "So, what is it we're doing today?"

"We're going to try to stretch what you did on the beach," Marcus said.

Elorie's eyebrows lifted. "Got an umbrella?"

"Not quite that literally," Jamie said. "Marcus said you were able to push magic to Lauren at a distance. We're going to see if you can push magic to me while I'm in Realm. We know you can pull it out, so in theory, this should work."

"Okay, but I need something to push."

Marcus grinned—not a pretty sight. "That would be the spellcoding part of the lesson, my dear. Why don't you give that protection spell another try?"

Sigh. For a moment, it had actually sounded like they were going to have fun. Elorie put fingers to keys and started to painstakingly craft the lines of code that would create the beginnings of a spell.

Jamie watched in disbelief. "You've been making her code from scratch? Marcus, that's evil."

Elorie froze. "There's another way to do this?"

Marcus glared in disapproval. "There are shortcuts, but I believe there's good value in learning to properly code a spell from the ground up."

Jamie winked at Elorie. "Well, since your method has her ready to dump half the ocean on your head, let's give my method a try, shall we?"

A couple of icons on Elorie's screen started to flash. "See those? They'll get you to some menus that let you pick up some precoded spell chunks. Stick enough of those together in the right order, and you can build a pretty decent spell."

"Or a train wreck," Marcus growled.

Jamie laughed. "It's not that hard to handcode a train wreck either. This way, you get to learn the logic of a spell first. When you want to get fancy, then you can work on handcoding."

She and Uncle Marcus were going to have quite the chat later. Following Jamie's clear instructions, Elorie had a protection spell assembled in just a few minutes. Then two warriors appeared onscreen. "Mine's the one with the blue helmet," Jamie said.

"When I look like I'm losing the fight, I want you to activate the protection spell and push it to my guy there."

Elorie jumped as an all-out swordfight broke out on her screen. How the heck was she supposed to decide when someone was losing? One good swipe of the sword and it could all be over. Even virtual beheadings weren't something she really wanted to witness.

"Lose faster," Marcus said dryly, "or I'll send over a couple of my men to help."

Suddenly Jamie's avatar fell to the ground, sword tossed uselessly to the side. Elorie grabbed her mouse and threw in the spell. The red-helmeted warrior's sword swung down like the wrath of God— and turned into a flower as it crashed into the protection spell.

Jamie looked stunned, and Marcus laughed like Elorie had rarely heard. "Didn't proofread her code well enough, did you? She used one of Ginia's spellchunks. You're lucky not to be flittering like a fairy. That girl leaves all manner of silly magic lying around, and she insists on adding most of it to the spell libraries."

Maybe she should be getting Realm lessons from Ginia—they sounded like a lot more fun. And Uncle Marcus didn't sound nearly respectful enough of her skills. Elorie looked pointedly at the flower. "The sword's hardly a threat now, is it?"

Jamie laughed. "Only to the male ego. Can you reverse the spell?"

Elorie reached for her mouse and quickly pictured the reversing spellshape in her mind. She pushed it at the warrior with the red helmet, and then squealed and covered her eyes as blood spurted out of Jamie's now headless avatar. "Ugh, gross! Do you have to make it quite that realistic?"

She uncovered her eyes to see two faces watching her in utter shock. "Oh, no. Did I do something wrong? It worked, didn't it?"

Jamie looked at his dead avatar and nodded slowly. "Oh, yeah. Worked like a charm. I just expected you to spellcode the reversing spell. How'd you do that?"

She blinked. "Well, it's mostly the same shape as the first spellcode. I just twisted it around a little."

Jamie frowned. "What shape? You see shapes in spellcode?"

Didn't everyone? "Sure. Just like any other spell."

Jamie looked at Marcus, and Marcus shook his head.

"Holy shit. Hang on a moment." Jamie started typing furiously on his keyboard. A couple of minutes later, he looked back up, victory in his eyes. "I just messaged Ginia, Marcus. She sees shapes when she spellcodes, too. That's why she can use Net power like Elorie, and we can't. They see the spellshapes."

Marcus groaned. "Warrior Girl can do this too? God help us all."

Why was she always the last one in the room to understand her own powers? "Why is that important?"

Jamie grinned. "Well, it seems that for you and Ginia, at least, it doesn't matter whether the magic is in virtual space or real space—you can see the power streams and manipulate them the same way."

She shrugged. So she was a virtual witch. That wasn't news.

Marcus sighed. "I hope Ginia appreciates the wonder of her talents a little more than you do, niece."

Elorie's frustration spilled over. "How can I appreciate it when I don't really understand why it matters? Doing parlor tricks in an online game doesn't seem like something to get all excited about."

Oh, jeebers. Realm was Jamie's baby, and she'd just mortally insulted it. Cheeks flaming, she looked at her screen. "I'm so sorry. This isn't about the game, really. I'm sure it's a lot of fun, but..." She trailed off. No point digging herself in deeper.

Jamie looked at her seriously. "Will you try one more test for me? I'm pretty sure that will help all of us understand why this is important."

He held up a flower bud. Elorie ground her teeth. More parlor tricks.

Jamie snickered. "That's the same look Aervyn gives me when he thinks I've asked him to do something dumb."

Elorie tried to get a grip on her temper, well familiar with witchling faces. Surely she could act a little more mature than a four-year-old. "What do you want me to do?"

"There's a blooming spell popping up on your screen. Can you activate that and push it to me?"

Easy, peasy. Elorie grabbed her mouse and shoved. Jamie laughed as petals flew off his flower. "I'd say that's bloomed."

Elorie blushed. Gran would have her head for de-petaling flowers, with magic or otherwise. There were no excuses for magical temper tantrums.

Marcus held up a spellshape on his palm. "I assume this is what you want for step two?"

Jamie nodded and held up a second bud. "Try the exact same thing, Elorie, but this time push Marcus's blooming spell to me."

Okay, she was still having a temper tantrum. Next time she bloomed flowers, she planned to be in a freaking garden. Looking at the off-screen version of Uncle Marcus, she yanked Net power, grabbed his spell, and hurled it through the computer at Jamie. He yelped as the flower in his hand exploded.

Oh, cripes. Temper evaporated as she realized what she'd done. What on earth had gotten into her? Control of magic was the first lesson preached to every witchling. "I'm so sorry, Jamie. I'm tired this morning, but that's no excuse. Are you okay?"

His smile was full of sympathy. "You've got a far better reason than that, little sister. Ask Moira about the joys of being a pregnant witch. Nell was a wreck with the triplets."

He glanced at Marcus. "Teach her how to cast a training circle. Pregnant mama magic can be a little unpredictable. No point scorching the furniture."

Her babies were the cause of all this? Already? Elorie laid a hand on her belly, overcome with emotion.

Jamie grinned. "Yeah. Nat says the upswings are pretty good, too. Keep Kleenex handy."

She sniffled. Her emotions hadn't been this much of a mess since she was thirteen. "Are we done with the magic tricks now?"

"It's about time we got back to that," Marcus said. "Do you have any idea what you've done, girl?"

She wasn't a total idiot. "Sure. I took magic from you and pushed it to Jamie."

She froze as realization set in. She'd pushed magic—real magic—across thousands of miles.

Jamie winked. "Not parlor tricks any more, huh?"

She shook her head slowly. "I can be a conduit for magic."

"Aye," Marcus said. "You can push or pull magic, real or virtual, and distance is no barrier."

No witch raised in Gran's sphere of influence could fail to understand the significance of that. Magic could only help what it could reach. If Uncle Marcus was right, the witching community's reach had just gotten a whole lot bigger.

The thrum of her pulse picked up speed. She could send magic to any witch, anywhere. As could any Net witch. Elorie felt the truth of it running through her veins.

Finally.

Joy stormed through her soul. Gran always said that witches didn't *have* magic—they *did* magic. Now, she knew what she was meant to do, why *she* had been gifted with this new form of magic.

She knew the witch she needed to be.

Until now, her magic had seemed to lean on her every weakness, push against everything she believed. But there was a reason she, even as a non-witch, had functioned as Gran's right hand. She was a born organizer.

She beamed at Marcus and Jamie. "We need to convene a meeting."

~ ~ ~

Jamie looked around Realm's new, hastily assembled witch meeting room. No castles or moats anywhere, just comfortable couches and some pretty cool art. Good thing he hadn't been in charge of decorating.

He'd heard rumors that Elorie had been having a tough time with the technology required for her magic. Whoever believed that hadn't spent the last several hours on the receiving end of her orders. When it came to organizing witches, he'd thought Nell was untouchable. He'd been wrong.

He leaned over to his sister. "This is the woman who is scared of the virtual world?"

Nell shrugged. "She didn't know how to power up an iPhone two days ago."

Jamie snorted. Elorie had taken over Realm, issued very polite orders for an online meeting space, and shuttled four-dozen witches into virtual reality. This was not a woman shy about using technology.

Or at least getting everyone else to use it for her. Shay and Mia had spent three very busy hours coding the new online witch hangout. And he'd kidnapped Ginia and Aervyn practically as they stepped off the airplane so they could figure out how to bottle a transporting spell. Good thing he had lots of minions.

Once serious witch business was over, he was so going to beam himself into the Realm gaming levels. Hot damn, that was going to be a game-changer.

For now, Elorie had a meeting room and a witch shuttle service. He couldn't wait to see what she did with it.

He wasn't the only one waiting. Moira sat on a comfy blue couch, Aervyn snuggled on her lap and the triplets at her feet, watching her granddaughter with pride.

Jamie knew the look—all witch trainers did. It happened when you watched your trainee step out of the nest. Whatever her path to get here, Elorie at this moment was a woman confident in her power and her purpose.

She stood up at the front of the room, and every head turned in her direction. "I wanted to thank all of you for coming. I know it was short notice and not much explanation."

Sophie smiled. "You asked, we came."

Jamie nodded, as did many others. It was the way of witches. Elorie had put out the call for spellcoders, and they had come. No questions asked.

"As many of you know, we've discovered a new kind of power source—and those of you who spellcode can all use it."

"But we can't do what you can with it," said Govin, one of Realm's best players.

"True. Some of us can use Net power differently, and we've spent the last week learning a lot about what's possible. I think Jamie and Uncle Marcus have briefed you on what we've learned."

Govin leaned forward. "You can push magic to any of us through the Internet, right?"

Elorie nodded, and murmurs started. She held up her hand. "We can also pull magic. It gives us a lot of freedom to put the right magic in the hands of any available witch. I asked you to meet here today to talk about how we can best use that in service of those around us."

Govin considered for a moment. "It would really help with witchling training. We often have a mismatch with available trainers, especially when new talents emerge quickly."

Moira beamed. "Just so, Govin. And you can definitely use it in your weather work." Govin and his partner spent countless hours working to minimize the devastation of some of the planet's harsher weather patterns.

Sophie spoke next. "There are things I can't do in Colorado because I'm a solitary witch." She touched Mike's shoulder. "Or I was. Last month, one of the little ones on my street got lost. It would have been a true blessing to call on Jamie or Aervyn for a seeking spell. It's not a talent I have."

Nell nodded. "We lack healers in California. There are times it would be very handy to have one available." She frowned. "This sounds like a pretty big organizational challenge, though. Hard to have the right people on call all the time to make the spells that are needed."

Elorie's eyes gleamed. "That's just it. For a lot of the things you've mentioned, we don't actually need to have the right people available at the exact right time. We just need their spells."

Ah. Jamie connected the last of the dots. Now he knew why she'd asked for spellcoders. She was freaking brilliant.

Her energy danced through the room. "Witches like Aervyn and Ginia and me can push magic to witches who need it, but we don't need a live witch making the spell. We can use one that's already spellcoded. That's what I'm hoping all of you can help with."

Jamie nodded, already making plans in his head. "You need us to code a library of spells." He could see the eagerness in the faces around him. Finding volunteers was not going to be a problem. He sensed a witch code-a-thon in the making.

Govin grinned. "We already have a pretty good library, but I'm guessing turning moat waters into fiery flames isn't what you had in mind."

Elorie laughed. "If any of you have moats in real life, we can give it a try, but no. Mostly I'm thinking about the everyday kinds of spells—simple healing, bringing rain, seeking—the ways most of us help our friends and neighbors now, but it will give us all a wider range of options."

Mike looked serious. "This could be used for more than just the everyday. We could save lives with this."

Elorie slowly swept the room. "Yes, we can, and we will. I'm hoping to start with the everyday aid. It will help us work out the kinks and the logistics, to figure out how to be a community in a different way than most of us are used to."

She took a deep breath. "But where we can bring small magics, we can also bring much larger magic." She looked straight at Marcus. "I dream of a world where far fewer are lost or hurt because we couldn't get the magic there in time."

She stretched her hands out to the group. "We are witches, and service is our highest calling. I'm asking each of you, as you wish and as you are able, to help."

Marcus was the first witch on his feet.

Chapter 21

Moira walked out into the early morning mists of her garden. Sleep had done a wondrous job of reviving her old bones. She was more than a little surprised to find her nephew taking a soak, and downright astonished when he smiled and stood to help her in.

"You seem rather cheerful this morning, my dear."

Marcus shrugged. "I woke up early. No idea why. I was up half the night working with Jamie to organize the new spellcoding library. We're already being pelted with spells. Witches can be a rather disorganized lot."

Moira hid a smile. "They're just eager to help."

"They could help by sorting." Marcus snorted. "And by using their heads. Young Sean's already uploaded a pirate illusion spell and an eavesdropping spell."

"How delightful." Moira laughed at her nephew's scowl. There was the Marcus she knew and loved. "You never know when a pirate spell might come in handy."

His eyebrows nearly crossed. "You can't possibly be serious."

"It's getting the witchlings involved in helping others, and that's a beautiful thing. An eavesdropping spell just needs a little reshaping to become a seeking spell that could find a lost child. Why don't you ask our Sean to work on that for you?"

He grunted.

She took that as a hopeful sign and pushed a little harder. "He's a strong and very imaginative spellcaster. It will take a creative trainer to get the best out of him."

"Hmm. Perhaps partnering him with Kevin will help. His twin shows a little more sense."

Moira had to turn away and gaze on her flowers to hide her smile this time. Elorie wasn't the only witch coming out of her shell lately. Marcus training witchlings, and with only token protests—who could have imagined?

"It's a very important responsibility Elorie has now," Marcus said. "You've prepared her well."

"I've helped her become the woman she was meant to be." And so very proud she was of who her granddaughter had become. The witching community had gained a new leader yesterday, one who would use her new magic to strengthen the old ways.

"She's got a firm grounding in tradition, and a strong sense of obligation to those around her."

Moira's heart twisted a little. "You speak of obligation and responsibility, but Elorie does this out of love. She has a truly magnificent heart." And perhaps a tiny ray or two of that love would seep into the fortress her nephew had built around his own heart.

He'd been such a sensitive boy. The day Evan had died, something in Marcus had broken. The healer in her had ached for that small boy for almost half a century now. Even for a witch steeped in tradition, that was a very long time to hold onto hope.

He'd smiled at her this morning. At the start of a glorious summer day, she was going to hold tight to that.

And she wasn't above meddling. "I hear that Jamie and young Aervyn are meeting in that lovely online living room later today to work on an alert system. I'm sure another mind witch would be a welcome addition."

Even Marcus couldn't resist Aervyn. That wee boy's most powerful magic was his contagious love of life.

~ ~ ~

Nell: This feels really old-fashioned after our new Realm meeting space.

Moira: Aye, but we can't be wasting transport spells to do that too often just yet. Maybe after we have more of them ready.

Nell: My triplets are working Aervyn and Jamie hard. Ginia says they're figuring out how to do more of it with coding and less with teleportation magic, so hopefully the Realm taxi service will be up and running soon.

Moira: I look forward to it. It was so delightful to cuddle your sweet boy in my lap. He won't be little enough to do that much longer.

Nell: Pretty soon you'll have far littler ones to hold.

Sophie: Yes. We need to get a rocking chair installed in that room. Aunt Moira's skills with fussy babies are legendary, and I, for one, would like to be able to call on them.

Nell: God, what I would have given for an instantly available virtual babysitter when the triplets were little.

Moira: And what I'd have given to be there.

Sophie: Well, Elorie and I will be happy to benefit from the wonders of modern technology.

Elorie: Indeed. Sorry to be late. Aaron's meeting with a friend of his to make some plans for our new house. I can't stay long, or they'll have added several thousand square feet for each child. Why do men always think bigger is better?

Nell: That, girl, is a question for the ages.

Sophie: Where are you building?

Elorie: Right between the inn and Gran's cottage. We want our own separate space with little ones on the way. I don't figure people on vacation want to hear babies crying, or stampeding little feet.

Moira: You might be surprised, my dear. However, I think it's lovely you and Aaron will be just a wee bit closer. I won't be minding the sounds of little ones at all.

Sophie: Can Aaron cope with two pregnant women in a month or so?

Elorie: Only if I get fed first :-). Just kidding—mostly. I'm suddenly starving all the time. Is that normal?

Nell: Oh, yeah. Enjoy it while it lasts. Hopefully you'll skip the nausea part, but eventually babies take up enough room that there's not much space left for food.

Moira: I used to swear my babies stole my food and fed it to the faeries. I ate like a farmer in those first months of pregnancy. So are you coming to visit us in the fall then, Sophie?

Sophie: Sort of. Mike and I were trying to figure out the wedding thing.

Elorie: Oooh, are you getting married here?

Sophie: Not exactly. Hang on...

Nell: Type faster, girl, and don't be so cryptic!

Sophie: Sorry. The thing is, we have family all over the place, and lots of places that are special to them and to us. Mike's parents have a beautiful sanctuary down in Mexico, Ocean's Reach where we did our first full circle together, and of course your garden, Aunt Moira. We tried to pick one, and we just couldn't. So we eloped.

Nell: What???

Elorie: You're married?

Moira: Ah, my sweet girl. Blessed be.

Sophie: We had a ceremony right here in my garden. It was very small, and so sweet. And now we'd like to come share our joy with all of you. We're going on a marriage celebration journey. We'll start in Mexico with Mike's parents, and then head up to Berkeley, if that works for you, Nell.

Nell: We never, ever say no to a party. Congratulations, Sophie. He's a wonderful man.

Sophie: Don't I know it. And then we'll work our way over to Nova Scotia for the finish, Aunt Moira.

Moira: We'll have ourselves a proper gathering and celebrate your joining, child. It's the way of the Irish—it's the party that truly matters.

Sophie: Nobody's mad?

Moira: You've always been a solitary witch, darling girl. You've had your private joy, and now you'll come celebrate with us. There's nothing but happiness here.

Elorie: I'm so thrilled for you, Sophie. Truly.

Sophie: I love you all, so very much.

Nell: The triplets might be mad that they didn't get to wear frilly dresses.

Sophie: Party dresses can be as frilly as necessary, by bridal decree.

Nell: That'll work. Aervyn would appreciate less frills on the small-boy front.

Sophie: Done. This bridal decree stuff is easy. How are the girls, anyhow? I know Ginia was missing her sisters by the end of witch school.

Nell: Yeah. They'd never been separated like that before, so they're awfully happy in each other's company right now. Jamie has them all hard at work coding for the new spell library.

Sophie: How's that coming? I got my latest assignment—it seems amazingly organized.

Elorie: You can thank Marcus for that.

Sophie: Seriously? Jamie said he was pretty involved.

Elorie: He's figured out this amazing tagging system that will search and match the closest spell to your needs. Even Jamie was impressed.

Nell: My girls think he's a genius.

Moira: He's kept that talent well hidden. Maybe I'll have to put him to work sorting my books.

Elorie: Kevin would be delighted to do that, Gran. He might never come out, though—you'd have to check on him every so often and make sure he doesn't starve to death.

Moira: I might just do that, but I'll wait a bit. He and Sean are preparing some interesting spells for your little project.

Elorie: Uh, oh. The last one I saw involved a cleaning spell that sings Bob Marley while it works.

Nell: Awesome. I'll take that one in triplicate!

Sophie: Me, too.

Elorie: You might want to wait until it does a decent job of cleaning. The singing part is pretty good, though.

Sophie: Have the cleaning spells been recategorized yet?

Nell: Yes. I think Warrior Girl gave Marcus a serious piece of her mind over that.

Moira: Whatever happened?

Sophie: Marcus put cleaning spells into a library category called "women's spells." I found them when I went to file a spell to ease menstrual cramps.

Moira: Oh, did he now.

Elorie: Don't worry, Gran—he got a piece of all our minds. I don't think it will happen again. Ginia's threatening to create a "grumpy old men" category if it does.

Moira: Well, I might just be adding a small reminder of my own. My cauldron's due for polishing.

Sophie: Sweet! I can tarnish it a little more, if you want.

Nell: Aervyn's added a rain spell that could take care of that. Marcus has a pretty thick head.

Moira: Do you all really think I don't have a good tarnishing spell handy? How do you think I've kept troublemakers busy over the years? It's wonderful that the witchlings are all getting so involved, though—a rain spell sounds like a lovely contribution.

<u>Nell:</u> It will be, if you're sitting outside when you access it. Some of the Realm players are having trouble getting used to real-life spells. I think Govin's living room is still soaked.

<u>Sophie:</u> Oops :-).

<u>Moira:</u> I have a request, if I may. Sophie dear, could you cast me a gentle sleep spell? It's getting harder to do for myself, and I do so appreciate a good night's sleep.

<u>Sophie:</u> That's a wonderful idea. I've also uploaded a couple of spells for joint pain—try those for your hands. I'd love to know how they work.

<u>Elorie:</u> Oh, I'll try one next time I've been working in my studio all day. My hands ache after that.

Moira stepped away from her computer for a moment to go fetch some tea. Witches helping each other wasn't a new thing—it was one of the oldest of things. But now they could get the right help to the right witch so much more easily, and oh, the generosity she was seeing.

Small gifts, freely given. It was the heart and soul of magic—and now it had new life. With her granddaughter at the helm.

Sometimes the rewards for a long life were rich indeed.

~ ~ ~

"Ouch!" Jamie said. "Wow, that's still way too loud. Aervyn, dude, we need to ratchet back the volume on that a whole bunch."

Elorie giggled at the antics on her computer screen, glad she hadn't been the guinea pig for this last test. They were trying to work out an alert system to page Net witches in an emergency. The spell library could meet an increasing array of needs, but there would always be situations where a real, live Net witch was required.

Coming up with the alert spell hadn't been a problem. Convincing Aervyn it didn't need to be as loud as a fire alarm was proving more difficult.

Ginia shook her head. "I think I can control volume in the code, Uncle Jamie. We might want it loud to get *some* people's attention."

Jamie considered for a moment. "So customize the volume depending on who we're trying to page?"

"That makes sense." Elorie fingered her heart pendant. "We might need to change the volume once everyone has pendants instead of phones, too."

She'd sent a batch of her biggest pieces of sea glass off to Jamie only that morning. He and Aervyn were going to work on shrinking iPhones into the glass. It was a more reliable method of portable Net power, particularly for the witchlings—sea glass was well used to getting banged up and wet. iPhones weren't proving quite as durable.

Ginia looked up. "Okay, I'm going to ping you. Lemme know if it's too loud."

Elorie squeezed her eyes shut. The last time had sounded like a monster gong inside her head. Fortunately, Ginia's idea of volume control was more precise than her little brother's. "Much better. A little quieter yet would be fine for me, but that's tolerable."

Jamie grinned. "Looks like we're ready to go, then. Do your troops have their emergency ready for us?"

Elorie rolled her eyes. "They've been ready since dawn." Nothing could have pleased Lizzie and the twins more than being asked to cause trouble on purpose.

She leaned out the window to activate their pre-arranged "go" signal. Uncle Marcus, lying in the hammock, raised his hand to the sky, and an ear-piercing whistle blasted through the air. Good grief. Aervyn wasn't the only witch who needed a lesson in volume control.

Moments later, Lizzie screamed, right on cue. Elorie looked over at her computer. "Emergency in progress."

Ginia grinned. "Excellent. I'm ready to rock."

Elorie walked outside to monitor in person. Uncle Marcus was still lying in the hammock. "Aren't you supposed to be keeping an eye on them, so Sean doesn't actually float out to sea?"

He tapped his head. "I'm mindlinked with Kevin. Not a problem. Lizzie's father has his boat out. Sean's not going anywhere."

Elorie shook her head. She knew all too well how much trouble Sean could get into even when you were watching him.

Halfway down to the beach, she spotted Sean in his inner tube, floating happily out in the waves. When he spied her, he screamed and yelled "Shark! Help!" She had to laugh. The last shark attack in Nova Scotia had been exactly never.

Kevin and Lizzie were on the beach, acting as the rescuers. Kevin had his iPhone out, shooting video so Ginia could see the problem. Smart boy. They hadn't discussed how best to communicate with the Net witch on call, and video was a lot faster than texting or talking.

Moments later, Lizzie, phone in her hand, started swaying slightly. She only did that when she worked with power. Elorie reached for her pendant, activating the fancy new visualizing spell that let her view elemental power streams.

Jeebers. Ginia had pushed a mess of spellshapes to Lizzie. Lots of air power, which made sense—that would be the easiest way to bring Sean back toward shore. But what on earth was the fire power for? There was also a third, more complex spellshape she didn't recognize.

Lizzie, all three-and-a-half feet of her, worked with the novel power streams like she'd been born to them. The spellshape containing most of the air power morphed out toward Sean and began blowing him back to shore. Routine rescue. Excellent.

Halfway back, Lizzie grinned and waved her left hand. Suddenly Sean was headed back out to sea, and at a fast clip. Then his inner tube flipped over. Elorie could tell from Lizzie's face—the change of direction had been on purpose, but the flip had been an accident.

It wasn't quite a real emergency yet. Sean was an excellent swimmer, and Lizzie's dad wasn't far away with his boat. But their carefully planned drill was now officially off the rails.

She converged on Lizzie at the same time as Kevin did. A quick hand stopped them in their tracks. They both knew better than to interfere with a witch holding a boatload of spellpower in her hands.

Lizzie took the spellshape Elorie didn't recognize and gently activated it. Suddenly the air was alive with a strange kind of music. Kevin listened in rapt attention, and then grinned. "Dolphins. She's calling the dolphins. Look!"

He pointed out to sea. Sure enough, a formation of three dolphins swam in from the north, heading straight for Sean.

Lizzie danced with delight, but never let go of the spell. The strange music changed slightly as the dolphins reached Sean.

Elorie watched in awe as Sean grabbed two dorsal fins and hung on for dear life. She could hear his maniacal laughter even over the crashing waves. The smallest of the three dolphins jumped into the air and landed with a splash. Elorie laughed. Another young one who didn't know emergencies weren't supposed to be fun.

Lizzie spun in a circle, just once, and the music changed a third time. The dolphins pulled Sean in a big circle, and then dropped him off about twenty feet from shore.

Sean treaded water for a moment, and then threw his hands up in the air.

Kevin leaned over to Lizzie. "Aren't you going to save him?"

Lizzie shrugged. "He can swim."

"Yeah, but we're supposed to be practicing, remember? What if he couldn't swim?"

Lizzie scowled. "Fine."

Two minutes later, Sean was on dry land and nicely warmed by the third spell Ginia had thoughtfully provided—now Elorie knew what the fire power had been for.

She wasn't sure her trio had taken the exercise seriously enough, but Ginia had shown creativity and forethought in the spell bundle she'd pushed to Lizzie. That had been very well done, and Elorie took careful mental notes. It would be her turn as the on-call Net witch soon enough.

Sharing the spells of the everyday was really the heart and soul of WitchNet, as their spell library project had quickly been dubbed. But the ability to network witches like this—with this, they would save lives.

Their emergency response team could use a lot more practice first, however.

DEBORA GEARY

Chapter 22

Elorie watched as the flower bud under her fingers bloomed and grinned in delight. In theory, she and Gran were testing a batch of plant spells Ginia had bottled for WitchNet.

In reality, for one small part of a morning, she was living a childhood dream. So many times Gran had said to her, "One day, you'll sit in my garden and we'll work magic together."

It had been a very long wait, but that day was today. They shared few words—just a love of tending, and the knowing that their hands did the work of witch hands down through the centuries.

For as long as she could remember, Gran's place had been her garden. Some of Elorie's earliest memories rooted here, along with her belief that magic was meant to be used for healing, for doing, for creating.

And that small magics, done well and often, were the true strength of a witch.

Moira stood up to stretch for a moment, and then beckoned. "Come, child. This patch of chamomile could use a bit of that potency spell Ginia sent."

Elorie held her hands up, trying to separate the potency spell out from the others she held. It was beginning to get quite confusing, and a couple of the spellshapes were starting to fade. That was one of the things they wanted to know—how long could a witch hold a pushed spell before it degraded?

About twenty minutes, she figured as she untangled what was hopefully the potency spell. Gently she touched the top of the nearest chamomile plant. When it started to dance, she had to laugh. "I'm guessing that's not the right one."

Moira chortled. "I don't believe so, but it's a lovely spell, nonetheless."

Feeling like a little girl on a summer's day, Elorie walked in a small circle, touching what flowers she could reach. Soon an entire bevy of flowers danced, much to Gran's delight.

They stood for a moment, arm in arm, and watched the flowers sway under the noon-day sun.

That was one of the other lessons she had learned at Gran's feet. Sometimes, magic was just meant to be enjoyed.

~ ~ ~

Nell lay back on her blanket and enjoyed the warmth of the morning sun soaking into her skin. Getting five kids packed up and off on a picnic was easier than it used to be, but she was still claiming the right to be lazy now.

Nat and Jamie could keep an eye on Aervyn. With a fire witchling on the way, they could use the practice. Besides, nothing bad ever happened at Ocean's Reach; the magic of the place had always felt protective to her.

She thought back to Aervyn's first weeks as a newborn and wondered if her brother was ready for what was coming. It was very unusual for an unborn babe to be playing with power streams, but if her son were to be believed, Nat's little bean had been doing so practically since she'd been conceived. They were in for an interesting ride.

Cracking open an eye to check on her herd, she realized Jamie wasn't paying attention to Aervyn at all. His hand was glued to Nat's belly, and his face was a mix of wonder and panic. "What's up, brother mine?"

"I can feel her." Jamie spoke in a hushed whisper.

Nell frowned. Nat wasn't far enough along yet for him to be feeling the baby kick.

Nat touched his cheek. "It's the power in this place. Even I can feel it. She's playing." She reached out a hand to Nell. "Lots of space on my belly, if you want to feel."

She squiggled over and laid her hand on Nat's belly, just beginning to round. Fire was Nell's strongest magic, a talent shared with her niece-to-be. She closed her eyes and let the power of Ocean's Reach sweep through her.

She could see several power streams—Jamie's close by, and Aervyn and Ginia playing farther off. And just under Jamie's hand danced a little ball of fire. Nell reached for what little mind power she had and shared with Nat. She was pretty sure Jamie was going to find his daughter's invitation irresistible.

Ever so gently, Jamie reached a tendril of power toward the dancing fire and wove around the edges. Nell could feel the love he sent, and the peace. The ball of fire nudged against Jamie's gentle web and then nestled in, dimming to a quiet glow. Totally content baby.

Nell felt the tears spill down her cheeks. She was pretty sure she wasn't crying alone.

~ ~ ~

Marcus sat down in front of his laptop and rubbed his hands together. Alone. Finally.

He might not be the best spellcoder in Realm, or the strongest Net witch, but he had age, experience, and sheer cantankerousness on his side. It was very obvious that Warrior Girl's world domination was only a matter of days away unless someone stopped her.

That someone was going to be him. He had an audacious plan, one that no one would ever expect.

He was going to make friends.

He'd been up half the night stockpiling a very nice cache of spells. Worthy alliance-building gifts. Or bribes. Whatever it took.

He planned to start small and stay under the radar. In Realm, that meant heading to the beginner levels. None of the top-tier witches bothered with the newbies—not enough of a challenge.

However, in a middle-of-the-night moment of clarity, he'd realized that the newest Realm arrivals had something he needed. Net power. Lots and lots of Net power. Earning your way to the higher Realm levels meant showing increasing proficiency with spellcoding—only the most rudimentary spells were permitted by the admin controls on the lower levels.

Most of the newest Realm players couldn't spellcode their way out of a paper bag yet, so they were still locked into the first level. And most of them were green enough not to realize what they could do with their Net power.

They needed a leader. An old, experienced, cantankerous leader.

Marcus grinned and sent out a level-wide invitation. He was about to turn the balance of power in Realm on its head.

~ ~ ~

Sophie tried not to laugh as Mike fell over for the third time in as many minutes. Post-run yoga was her way of getting even for his idea of a "gentle" run. Gracefully she reached behind her body, grasped her left foot with both hands, and arched it up behind her head.

Mike ogled her from the floor. "How much longer will you be able to keep doing stuff like that?"

"Nat says as long as I feel like it—my body will tell me when to stop." She grinned. "I just need to make sure that if I start falling over, I don't land on my belly."

"It might mess with your sense of balance when the baby gets bigger." Mike looked pleased at the thought.

Sophie laughed. Maybe he wanted company in falling over. "Nat says it helps with balance poses, actually. A bigger center of gravity. Jamie says she still does handstands—it totally freaks him out."

He reached for her hand and tugged her over on top of him, with an assist at the end for a very soft landing. "No freaking me out, okay? I watched a labor video last night, and I'm going to be scarred for life."

He was watching labor videos? That was so very sweet, but probably very misleading. "You know that witch births don't look very much like a typical hospital birth, right?" Some of those YouTube birth videos would scare anyone.

He grimaced. "This *was* a witch birth—mine, in fact. My mom emailed me the video."

"Really?" She lifted her head off his shoulder. "I so want to watch that. Or maybe I don't—why was it scary?"

"Scary's not the right word, exactly." He stroked her back. She wasn't sure which one of them he was trying to comfort. "My mom was amazing. They didn't have a full circle there, just my two aunts, but it was... let's just say I've never truly appreciated my mom enough."

She was confused. "And that scarred you for life?"

Mike shook his head. "Nope, not that."

Sometimes earth witches could take far too long to get to their point. She gently poked a finger in his ribs.

"It was the look on my dad's face. I've never seen him scared, Sophie—not like that. He was terrified. Mom was awesome, but Dad was a mess. What if that's me?"

She hadn't met his father yet, but Sophie knew her man. He'd hold steady to his last breath if that's what she needed. And according to Nell, birthing circles had evolved some in the last thirty years—now they supported the fathers-to-be as well.

"If anyone gets to be a mess, it's me." She laid his hand on her belly. "But that's a long time from now. Seedling's got a lot of growing to do first." Mike's breath slowed as he dropped into light healing trance to check on their baby.

Sophie grinned as the slight cramping in her left calf muscle disappeared as well. He really was a good guy to have around.

~ ~ ~

Sean looked around the beach. "We gotta find the prisoner, matey. No one is allowed to escape the great pirate Darth Vader and live to tell about it."

Kevin waved his new light saber in the air. "We'll find her, Captain. And we'll make her walk the plank when we do. Right after the great swordfight of doom. She doesn't stand a chance."

Sean cast out with mind power, trying to find their prisoner. His brother elbowed him in the ribs. "That's cheating, Sean—no mindseeking."

"We're pirates. We're supposed to cheat. Besides, Lizzie's using magic, or we'd be able to find her." The girl could make herself invisible anywhere near water, which is probably why she'd insisted they play on the beach. She might be small and kind of annoying sometimes, but she wasn't dumb.

"We could use stealth, Captain."

Sean sighed. Stealth wasn't nearly as much fun as swordfights, but when you were playing with a girl, you couldn't fight all the time or they complained it was *boring*. "What your plan, matey?" He growled for good measure. If he had to be a boring pirate, at least he could sound good.

Kevin grinned. "Mom sent chocolate cake for snack."

That would totally work. Lizzie was a sucker for cake. "Fetch the supplies, and let's have ourselves a pirate lunch."

"What about the prisoner?" Kevin spoke in a normal voice, but mindbroadcast just enough that Lizzie would hear.

"Har," roared Sean and waved his light saber. "No chocolate cake for the prisoners. Let them eat sand." He thought that was a pretty inventive line for a pirate.

Lizzie's head popped up from behind some driftwood. "I'm not eating sand. You hafta share; it's a rule."

Sadly, she was right, but Mom had probably sent enough cake for three. She was pretty smart that way. He waved his light saber at Lizzie. No point letting her off easy.

She just rolled her eyes at him. "Pirates don't use light sabers, silly."

"They do so. We're modern pirates."

Kevin held up two pieces of cake. "Eat. Fight later."

Lizzie reached for her cake, then sat down, clutching her head. "Ow. My head hurts."

Sean could feel her pain beating against his own mind. She wasn't kidding—it felt like someone had poked her with a light saber. A real one. He looked at Kevin. "Go get Elorie, quick!"

~ ~ ~

The sudden pain in her head had Moira stumbling off the path and into one of her flower beds. She lowered to the ground as quickly as she could, heedless for once of the plants she crushed.

Fear. Rolling waves of it mixing with the pain. This was very bad.

She reached for power and struggled to drop into healing trance. It hurt. Oh, her head hurt. Fighting through the pain, she tried to scan her own head. Feeble old witch. All she could see was the roiling red of pain. She tried to move her scan in closer and got washed away like a pebble hit by a rogue wave.

Her brain was fighting. And it was dying.

You can't fix this, old woman.

She could feel her hold on consciousness slipping. The pain slipped away as well, replaced by a numbness that was far from comforting. Time seemed to slow and she could hear the gentle breezes, feel the flower petals under her fingers.

The flowers. Her flowers. She'd spent a lifetime filling her garden with the magics of healing. With the very last of her power, Moira reached out.

Plants of life, plants of giving,
Hold me here, amongst the living.
What I've shared, give back to me.
As I will, so mote it be.

Gentle healing seeped in from the flowers under her fingertips. The frightening numbness eased, replaced by waves of pain that told her she was still alive. She lay very still, nestled in her flowers, and waited, and fought.

She wasn't ready to die yet. She had grandbabies to rock; Lauren had seen it in Great Gran's crystal ball. Please, let it be so.

~ ~ ~

Elorie didn't fly down to the beach quite as quickly as Kevin. The two little beans in her belly required more care, and the rocks down to the beach could be tricky to navigate. Kevin was clearly frightened, but she could see Lizzie sitting up and talking to Sean.

Sometimes the distinction between urgent and emergency wasn't terribly clear to a ten-year-old. She made a mental note—they probably needed to build that distinction into WitchNet as well.

She kept an eye on Lizzie as she hurried down the beach. No blood, but she was holding her head, and her slice of chocolate cake looked untouched. That qualified as serious.

Then Sean looked up, and Elorie's stomach knotted. He looked worried. Sean never looked worried.

She ran the last few steps and crouched down beside Lizzie. "What's the matter, sweetling?"

Lizzie cuddled into her lap. "My head hurts, and my eyes can't see very well. It's all fuzzy."

That sounded almost like a migraine. Those weren't infrequent in witchlings with a new power emerging. Elorie let out a deep breath. Migraines they could deal with—they just needed to take Lizzie to Gran. "Is it getting any worse, sweetheart?"

Lizzie shook her head. "No. But it's getting cold. I don't like the cold—it wants to take me away."

Elorie sucked a breath back in. That didn't sound at all like an emergence migraine.

Lizzie shrank into her lap. "Don't let it get me, Elorie!"

Was something external affecting her? Elorie looked at Kevin. Sean was the stronger mind witch, but Kevin had better control. "Can you barrier her? Make it so her mind is shielded?"

Kevin nodded and took Lizzie's hand. As soon as he did, Lizzie lifted her head and beamed. "You made it stop!"

Elorie let out her breath a second time. Okay, immediate crisis averted. Now they needed expert advice. She took Lizzie's hand. "Let's go find Gran. Maybe she knows a story about that nasty cold you were feeling."

Sean danced up the path ahead of them, waving his light saber and fighting off the great cold menace. Elorie wished it were that easy. Some of the symptoms of emerging power were terribly frightening for witchlings. Some were terrifying for the adults as well.

It didn't sound like fire magic, and that was a good thing. But the cold worried her. If memory served, that was one of the possible signs of astral travel. She held Lizzie's hand more tightly.

Suddenly, up ahead, Sean's light saber went crashing to the rocks. He turned around, ghost white. "It's Gran, Elorie. She's in awful pain."

For one terrible moment, no one moved. Then the earth tilted, and Elorie took off after Sean at a dead run. As she rounded the corner to Gran's garden, she saw Uncle Marcus flying out the door of the inn, face constricted in terror.

Then they heard Sean's scream.

Gran. Oh, God. Gran.

Chapter 23

The sight of Gran, lying pale and twisted in her flowers, nearly broke Elorie in two. She dropped down next to Gran's side, searching frantically for a pulse.

Marcus grabbed her wrist. "She lives. Just barely, and her head has had some sort of terrible trauma, but she lives."

Elorie gulped for air. Gran was their healer; the village had no other. Clearly there was no time to fetch medical help—getting emergency services to Fisher's Cove took far too long.

Emergency.

WitchNet.

She swung around to the witchlings behind her, all frozen with fear. "Go find every laptop you can. Run!" They took off, feet flying.

She turned back to Marcus. "Find Sophie. Use the alerts."

He was already typing frantically into his phone. "I'll get Jamie and Ginia as well—they can help round up any other healers. I think Meliya was in Realm."

"Hurry." Elorie held Gran's hand tightly. She felt so cold.

Sean was back moments later with a laptop. Marcus grabbed it and pounded furiously on the keys.

Sean looked down at Gran. "Why is she holding the flowers?"

Elorie's brain tried to follow his odd question. "What?"

"She's holding flowers," Sean said.

Elorie reached gently for Gran's other hand, clutching a crumpled blue flower. Her breath caught. "This hand isn't as cold." Then she recognized the blue. Cornflower. Healing.

Gran's garden was keeping her alive.

Elorie could hear Marcus barking commands to whoever he'd managed to track down. Her head snapped up. "Do you have Ginia?"

He nodded.

"I need her. I need all the plant blooming and healing she can push to me."

Marcus looked at her like she'd gone mad.

Elorie pointed to Gran's hand clutching the flower. "I think she's pulling healing from her plants." She waved her arm at the garden. "But look at them—they're weakening."

Marcus reached for the nearest plant. "I have a little earth magic. I'll help."

"No!" Elorie's voice snapped out, shocking even herself. "We have more powerful earth witches online, and spells already in the WitchNet library. I need you to find me healers. The plants are only life support; they can't bring her back. Find Sophie."

She reached for the laptop beside her. In the meantime, she could keep Gran's garden alive. Kevin touched her shoulder, pale, but determined. "We can do that part, Elorie. With the plants. I can pull the WitchNet spells."

Sean was already crouched in front of a flower bed, fingers waving softly. Lizzie sprayed a gentle mist of water from her fingers and crooned gently to the flowers.

Kevin was right. She would be needed to pull whatever healing spells they could find. She handed him the computer just as Ginia's face popped onscreen.

Marcus practically threw her his laptop. "I have Sophie."

Elorie nearly broke again when she saw Sophie's face. "It's bad, Soph. I don't know what's wrong. It's in her head."

Sophie was a study in anguish. "I can't heal what I can't see. Dammit, we haven't coded a healing scan for WitchNet yet." Her voice cracked. "That was on my to-do list for next week."

Elorie's eyes closed against the pain. So very close. They had a healer, and a way to pull the magic, but the healer couldn't see. Her head ached from twin waves of fury and impotence.

Headache.

She grabbed the computer screen. "Sophie. Would a new healer be feeling Gran's pain?"

Sophie frowned in confusion. "Yes. Any healer would."

Lizzie.

She whirled around. "Lizzie!" The child ran over, water still dripping from her fingers. "Kevin, can you let down Lizzie's shields, just a little?"

He nodded, fingers still flying over the keys.

Lizzie grabbed her head.

"I'm sorry, sweetling." Elorie pulled Lizzie into her lap. "We think you might be feeling the same thing as Gran. Can you tell Sophie how it feels?"

Lizzie rubbed her eyes. "Like a big pounding inside my head. It hurts most right here." She touched over her left eye.

Sophie met Elorie's eyes, fear growing. "Is the pain sharp and pointy, sweetie, or big and round?"

Elorie read the words Sophie had typed into the message box on her screen. *If this gets any worse, keep her tightly barriered. We don't want to lose two.* It was all Elorie could do not to scream.

Lizzie tilted her head, considering Sophie's question. "Mostly big and round, but sometimes it's pointy. It's a little better now, though. I think the plant spells are helping."

Sophie's voice wavered. "I hope so. I hope we have enough ready." Then she straightened up. "Lizzie, you can go back to watering now. That's a big help."

Elorie looked back at the screen, afraid to ask.

Sophie looked grim. "It sounds like a stroke. We're going to need to move her. You need to get her into Realm, little sister. That's the only place we can gather healers quickly enough."

Words caught in Elorie's throat as she clutched Gran's hand tighter. "Is it safe to move her?"

"No," Sophie shook her head, tears falling. "It could kill her. But if we don't move her, she'll die."

Jamie's face suddenly popped up on her screen, the soaring hills of Ocean's Reach behind his head. "We can help with that. Elorie, I'm going to push you a special transport spell. We'll use full teleportation—that will be gentlest for her. Aervyn's anchoring into rock here to help hold everything as steady as possible."

Elorie closed her eyes in desperate appeal for a miracle. She knew magic could kill. If hers killed Gran...

Uncle Marcus's hand landed gently on her shoulder. "We have a full circle waiting. You can do this. She would trust you with her life."

Holding onto the trust in his eyes, Elorie clasped her pendant and called her power.

"For Gran I seek, for Gran I call,
In power and love, do we stand tall
With magic steady and hearts all true.
Keep her with us, life renew.
There's love to give, and babes to see,
As I will, so mote it be."

If babies couldn't keep Gran with them, nothing would.

With a steadiness she hadn't known she could still command, Elorie reached for the transport spell as Jamie pushed. Even she could tell it was a work of art—delicate, complex, and rock-steady. Gran could be in no better hands.

Just as she readied to activate the spell, a second spellshape formed on the computer screen in Ginia's hand.

It's the healers, Uncle Marcus sent. *They'll help hold her steady as soon as she crosses into Realm.*

Elorie wrapped the second spell around the first. Gran's hand was getting colder again. They had no more time to waste.

She *pushed*.

When she opened her eyes, Gran lay on a low bed onscreen with Sophie at her head. Sophie's face creased in the focus of healing work, not the grief of death.

They'd done it. Gran was in healer hands.

Marcus took her arm. "Now we wait, and pray." And he whisked them into Realm.

~ ~ ~

Sophie tried to quiet her mind. Panic was no friend to a healer. She looked up into Mike's eyes. "You can feel it too?"

He nodded and glanced briefly around the room. "We all do. Stroke, and a bad one. Front left hemisphere."

"Her channels are badly blocked," said Meliya, the oldest healer in the room. "I've already started working on that."

Sophie nodded. That wouldn't address the worst of the damage to Aunt Moira's brain, but it would prevent any further damage to the rest of her body. Stroke could kill nerves and cause permanent paralysis.

Two of the younger healers sat at Moira's feet, perfusing her body with oxygen, clearing out the toxins. They had surprisingly little work to do. Aunt Moira's garden had breathed for her. The crisis was in her brain.

Mike touched her hands. "Ready when you are."

He was right. They had to get started.

Sophie dropped into healing trance and felt other healers gently joining. Surrounding them all, just outside the room where Aunt Moira lay, was the beating power of a full circle. Sophie drew on their strength, and their steadiness.

Then she began the delicate and tricky journey into her patient's brain.

There were two kinds of stroke—blockages and burst vessels. She was almost positive they were dealing with the second. Aunt Moira was an experienced healer, and any trained healer did regular self-scans. She wouldn't have missed a major blockage in her brain. Unfortunately, burst vessels were a lot more complicated to heal.

Partway up the middle cerebral artery, she found what she dreaded—a lake of pooling blood. She felt Mike's calm breathing beside her and steadied. She would do her best.

With quick instructions, she dispatched her team. Mike and Meliya would slow Aunt Moira's heart while they went to work on the burst vessel. Her job would be to grow the new artery walls. It was the type of magic at which earth-witch healers excelled.

And a battle she was very likely to lose. One witch could only do so much, and Mike couldn't be spared from his job.

She felt a hand slide into hers. Ginia. Earth-witch healer-in-training. Once more, Sophie steadied. With sure mental hands, she began to work. Grow a cell, stitch it to its neighbors. Grow another cell, repeat. It wasn't difficult work—it was a race. They had about two minutes.

When Ginia had the basics down, Sophie left her working at the easier part of the tear and headed for the worst of the damage. She could feel the younger healers siphoning blood away so she could see, but it was still making the work very difficult.

An errant thread of power caught her attention, and she turned around. Then she gaped in shock. Aunt Moira's torn blood vessel was growing toward her at impossible speed. The kind of speed that took twenty healers, not one trainee. There weren't twenty earth-witch healers on the planet.

No, said Jamie's mental voice. *But there's one, and Elorie's pushed out Ginia's magic to every spellcoder in Realm. We're replicating as fast as we can, and Ginia's coordinating. Can you use it?*

Oh, hell, yes. Sophie grabbed the growing blood vessel as it nearly knocked her over and began pushing it sideways. With this kind of growth, they didn't need to repair the tear. They could go around it.

Thirty seconds later, they had a new vessel ready to join above the tear. Sophie worked feverishly on the join, as did every other spare pair of healer hands.

They backed away with seconds to spare. Sophie signaled Mike and Meliya to speed Aunt Moira's heart back up.

Then she did what every healer does when life is on the line. She prayed.

~ ~ ~

Elorie lay with her head in Aaron's lap, drifting slowly out of sleep. Her eyes shot open as memory hit. "Gran?"

Aaron stroked her hair gently. "We don't know anything more. The healers are still working." He smiled in thanks as Nell bent down with a bowl of soup. "Eat. You did fierce magic to bring her here to Realm, huge magic to help heal her brain, and you need to keep your strength up."

Nell sat down beside them. "We've been feeding the masses. There were too many witches running on low gas tanks." She gestured toward the low building that held Moira. "The healers are peeling off one at a time to eat."

Elorie grasped her hand. "Any news?"

Nell shook her head. "No. They're working to repair as much of the damage as they can." Her voice softened. "She's alive, and that's a miracle."

Mia wandered over, bearing a tray of sandwiches. "Hungry? Or would you like a couch to sit on?"

"A couch?" Elorie tried to shake the fogginess out of her head.

Mia grinned. "Trying to keep everyone comfortable."

Nell gave her a big hug. "You do good work, kiddo."

Elorie looked around in growing shock. When they'd arrived in Realm, it had been in the middle of a huge grassy plain—the best Jamie could come up with on very short notice. Now it was a huge and lovely garden, with big shade trees, flowers, couches, food buffets—and literally hundreds of people.

It was a vigil. With every witch she'd ever known.

Then she looked at Mia and Aaron, and turning her head again, realized most of Fisher's Cove was present, too. Scratch that. Clearly there were plenty of non-witches present as well.

Words caught in her throat. "She'll get better for sure. Gran would never miss a gathering."

Mia nodded, eyes fierce. "That's the idea."

There were all kinds of magic. Elorie handed the rest of her soup to Aaron and stood up, grabbing Mia's hand. "I need your help. Can you find me a flute?"

~ ~ ~

Sophie's hands dropped to her sides. She was too exhausted to move them. They'd done everything they could. The rest was up to Aunt Moira and the strength of her spirit.

Mike nestled her into his shoulder. She could feel his shuddering tiredness too. Her entire team had given everything they had.

A soft snore in the corner caught her attention. Ginia lay curled like a mouse, quietly sleeping. She'd done the work of a fully trained healer, and then some. "She's going to be an amazing healer one day."

"She already is," Mike said. "That spellcoding idea was sheer genius."

Yes. If Aunt Moira lived, Ginia and Elorie's brilliant teamwork would be one very important reason why.

She stretched out a hand toward Ginia. Someone should check to see she hadn't gone into channel shock. Mike laced his fingers in hers. "Relax. She's fine, just sleeping. Every healer in the room has checked on her."

She laid a hand on her belly. The babe was fine too. It had been an anguishing line to walk, giving all she could to her healing without putting the life in her belly at risk.

"You did enough," Mike said. "And Moira would be the first to tell you that any more would have been wrong."

Sophie nodded. Her head knew that. Her heart had cracked in two at the choice.

Mike handed her a protein drink, and she sipped obediently. This, too, was part of keeping their Seedling safe. And there would be more healing to come. Months of it.

At least she hoped there would be. Aunt Moira still lay frighteningly still and cold.

Ginia sat up in the corner and rubbed her eyes. "Who's playing the music?"

Music? Sophie cocked her head to listen as gorgeous lilting notes floated into the room. It sounded like Elorie's flute at full circle.

Elorie's flute.

Sophie pushed off of Mike and stumbled to the door, opening it wide. Music wafted in, the moon floated high in the sky, and hundreds of faces circled the building, holding candles and softly singing as Elorie's music soared.

She waved urgently to Jamie. "Can you disappear the building? Put her in the middle of this."

Moments later, the building vanished, and Aunt Moira lay on a bed under the night sky. Flowers bloomed all around her, and the moon floated in a little closer. The coder and the witch in Sophie both marveled. It was magnificent.

Jamie touched her shoulder and spoke quietly. "Anything else we can do?"

One last thing. "Can you push the music into her head? Can you help her see this? Very, very gently."

He grimaced. "I'm not gentle."

Lauren stepped up beside him, clutching her new crystal ball, and took a deep breath. "I am. I'll do it." She closed her eyes, swaying slightly. A few seconds later, she smiled and broadcast. *She's listening. Just barely, but she can hear us.*

Sophie saw tears running down dozens of faces, but the soft singing never wavered. And Elorie's flute had never played with such star-touched beauty.

~ ~ ~

It was time to start the circle. That was her job. Moira could hear her granddaughter's flute playing, but something wasn't quite right. Where was her circle? Where was she?

She struggled to see, to swim through the heavy fog choking her mind.

The music. Listen to the music. She could see Elorie in her mind's eye, swaying gently as she played. The faces in the circle, a bond of love and community and magic. So many. It must be a very important circle.

And oh, the moon was marvelous tonight. It felt like she could reach up and touch it. Ever so slowly, the light melted away the fog, and she could see more clearly.

She also seemed to be lying down, and that was very strange indeed.

Then memories of the pain flooded back, the agony in her garden, and the awful, creeping cold.

She fought to open her eyes, and saw shadowed heads and the day-bright moon. It really did look close enough to touch.

"Is this heaven, then?" My, her voice sounded terrible.

Gentle laughter and kisses rained down on her forehead. "No, Aunt Moira, you're still with us. You've come back."

She wasn't dead? Moira looked around slowly, at the blurry moon and the shadowy faces. All was not as it should be. "Sophie, my sweet, I can't see very well."

Now tears fell on her face along with the kisses. "I know, and I'm so very sorry. We'll do what we can with that, and it should get better over time. For now, just know that we love you. You've come back to us. It will be a bit of a journey, but you'll rock our babies. I promise."

Moira felt the light touch of a sleep spell, and she gave in to the drifting. She would rock the babies. That was fine, then.

DEBORA GEARY

Chapter 24

Elorie looked up at the castle and smiled. Lizzie would be in heaven, sleeping in a turret.

The castle was the latest inventive solution produced by Realm's miraculous coders. When you had hundreds of sleepy witches, lots of beds were a good thing, and castles happened to come with rooms aplenty.

And to her eternal astonishment, Uncle Marcus was playing host. It was his castle Jamie and Ginia had transported into Gran's world, but they'd chosen it for its size, not for the owner's renowned hospitality. Even his virtual serving staff seemed shocked by his manners. He'd fed everyone, had them graciously shown to rooms, and promised a hot breakfast in the morning.

Which would be coming soon—if the Realm sky were to be believed, the sun was just peeking over the horizon. Elorie's stomach growled. She needed to find some food soon, but she was wedged into the corner of a really comfortable couch with Aaron's head pillowed in her lap. He hadn't made it as far as a bed. Judging from the snores she could hear, a number of the nearby couches were inhabited as well.

"Want some breakfast?" asked a quiet voice over her shoulder. Sophie slipped into the nearby armchair and laid a tray on the table between them. "We pregnant mamas can't sleep all day like some people I know."

Elorie smiled in welcome. "Mike's still asleep?"

"He is. Most of the healers are, but apparently Seedling here isn't as tired as everyone else." Sophie patted her belly.

Elorie picked up one of the breakfast pastries. It smelled divine, buttery apple and a tease of cinnamon. "Have you checked on Gran?" She'd briefly held Gran's hand late in the night, but the healers were keeping visitors to a minimum while she slept.

Sophie nodded. "She's still resting. Uncle Marcus's excellent kitchen staff has prepared some broth and herbal tea for when she wakes."

"How is she, really?" Elorie stared at her breakfast, afraid of the answer.

"It will be a long road." Sophie stirred her tea aimlessly. "Her speech has definitely been affected, and her vision. Both of those should improve with time and long-term care. Uncle Marcus says her mind feels fairly clear, though, so that's a hopeful thing."

When you practically grew up with someone, you caught the nuances. "What aren't you telling me, Soph?"

"There's a lot we don't know yet." Her eyes radiated distress. "She may not be able to walk. The right side of her body has been hit very hard, and sometimes that's hard to reverse."

Gran unable to walk, talk, or see? Elorie sucked in air, fighting the sudden lightness in her head.

"Don't you pass out on me." A touch from Sophie, and it got suddenly better. "She's alive, sister mine. She's alive, and she's the strongest woman I know. She's going to need us all to believe in her."

Elorie nodded. Gran had been her rock for as long as she could remember. If Gran needed to lean now, then they'd stand strong for her, for as long as it took. She looked around at all those gathered and waiting. There would certainly be plenty of help.

"I kept thinking last night about how lucky we were," Sophie said. "If this had happened just a month ago, when your magic was still hidden, we wouldn't have been able to bring her here, or do half of what we did to heal her. You saved her life."

"Getting her here wouldn't have mattered a bit without your skills." Elorie gripped Sophie's hand. "Gran always said healing was the most exalted of magics. She's right."

Sudden humor hit Sophie's eyes. "She only said that to keep us all stirring potions in herbals class."

Elorie grinned in memory. It felt good to think of Gran in those moments—strong, and alive, and giving witchlings a touch of grief for not paying enough attention.

So many had come to Gran's aid. Her witchlings, pushing love and life into those precious flowers. The coding geniuses of Realm. A four-year-old powerhouse and the gentlest of teleportation spells. Lauren walking around with Great Gran's crystal ball and encouraging hearts to believe. So many had given anything that was needed.

Such love for Gran. Peace settled into Elorie's heart, and gratitude that she'd been able to do her small part.

The door of Moira's temporary residence opened, and Meliya stuck her head out. "She's awake."

~ ~ ~

It was most unpleasant to actually feel your age. Moira tried to wiggle her fingers and groaned at the effort.

"Easy, Aunt Moira. We'll sit you up now." Sophie's voice was soothing, as any healer's should be. It grated at Moira's soul. Good. Grumpy patients made faster recoveries.

Gentle hands propped her up and tucked pillows behind her back. Moira realized it all seemed very dark. The blurry moon of the night before swam into her mind. Perhaps whatever had happened had taken her sight.

Elorie's soothing voice this time. "Can you open your eyes, Gran?"

Her eyes were still shut? Well, of all the silly things. No wonder it was dark.

"I think they're crusted shut." A moist cloth carefully wiped her eyes, along with the slight tingle of a light healing spell. "There now, give it a try."

Opening her eyes had never seemed like so much work. The first sights of light and shadow were still terribly blurry. Then efficient hands slid a pair of glasses into place. "Do these help? Meliya bespelled them for you to use while your eyes heal."

Moira blinked several times. Oh, yes. Those were splendid. She could see quite well now. She smiled at her beloved girls.

Sophie grinned back, the pleasure of a happy healer in her eyes. Elorie's smile was a lot more wobbly.

Sophie put a quiet hand on Elorie's shoulder. "It's normal, and quite temporary." She sat down on the edge of the bed. "You've had a stroke, Aunt Moira. It's affected the right side of your body, so your smile is a little crooked yet."

A stroke. So she had almost died, then.

She tried to call enough power for a healing trance to see for herself what had happened. Sophie rolled her eyes and shook her head. "There's plenty of time for that later. Save your strength."

She gently picked up Moira's hands. "Can you squeeze my fingers?"

Moira focused on her hands. The left one squeezed fairly normally for an old woman who had almost died. The right one moved and shook, but couldn't grip Sophie's fingers.

As a healer, she knew it was quite good news that it had moved at all. As a woman with a hand that didn't do as she asked—well, that was a wee bit scary. "I guess I won't be walking for a bit, then."

The raspy voice, she had expected. But even to her ears, her words had been garbled beyond recognition. Elorie laid gentle fingers on her lips. "Wait. I have an idea."

She walked out of Moira's field of vision. Sophie leaned in. "You'll be singing to this babe of mine. Just give it time."

Ah, Sophie. A good healer doesn't make promises she can't deliver.

Elorie slid back in the door, Lauren at her heels. Sophie's eyes brightened. "You're a genius, little sister."

Moira met Lauren's eyes. *If my mind's a vegetable, don't you be letting these two know it, now.*

Lauren burst into relieved laughter. "You sound just like your normal self in there. Hang on a moment while I put mindlinks in place so everyone can hear you." She glanced at Sophie. "Will that be okay?"

Sophie nodded, and Moira felt a mindlink click into place. *Hello, my lovelies. So tell me about this place I'm in, and how I got here.*

Three beaming faces started talking over each other. It was a delightful clatter. She listened for a while, and then held up a hand. It wobbled a bit, but did the job.

So let me be sure I have this right. I've been ported into Realm, saved by a team of the witching world's best healers, and no one's brought me tea yet?

Sophie grinned in delight. "There really isn't anything at all wrong with your mind, is there? Tea's on the way, along with some homemade broth."

Moira scowled. Ever since she was a little girl, she'd truly detested broth.

Elorie giggled. "Well, you made the rest of us drink it often enough."

That's because it's good for you, child.

Elorie patted her hand. "You just remember that when you have to drink cups and cups of it today."

Perhaps one of the witchlings could come to distract her. And maybe she could talk one of them into sneaking her a wee scone to have with her tea.

Lauren snorted and patted her hand. "Good luck with that."

Drat. Having her every thought heard was going to have some downsides.

Sophie's eyes twinkled. "That will be good motivation to practice talking."

Surely a sick old woman deserves a little spoiling?

Lauren grinned and looked at Sophie, who nodded. "If you're feeling up to it, there are a whole lot of people who'd like to lay eyes on a sick old woman."

And wasn't that the point of visitors, to distract the sick from the nasty things healers forced upon them?

Sophie pushed a button on the wall. "Jamie, can you take down the walls again? Aunt Moira's ready to see some friendly faces."

Moira gasped as the walls fell and the sky opened above her head. Perhaps the low-hanging moon hadn't been a dream.

Then she saw the faces, and the flowers. Dozens of people—no, hundreds. So many of those she loved—witch and non-witch, from the village and from the other side of the world. With the same message of love in every set of eyes.

And, oh. Every one of them clutched handfuls of irises and peach blossoms. For health and long life.

Her heart spilled over with the joy of it.

~ ~ ~

Sophie wandered through her herbals room, gently touching each jar and bundle of hanging herbs. The room smelled lightly of the lavender she'd harvested and hung at the last full moon. Aervyn had taxied her home to gather some things she would need to care for Aunt Moira.

She'd come to collect. She'd also come to say goodbye.

This house was her haven. While she loved the bonds of communal magic, in her heart, she was a solitary witch. Or perhaps, a solitary woman who happened to be a witch. Even as a small girl, she'd spent many happy hours alone, wandering the forests or the beach, or sitting quietly in a café watching the world go by.

This house in Colorado had been her retreat. Her solace. The place she'd planted herself when it had become clear Fisher's Cove couldn't be her home.

She loved it so much she'd built its double in Realm. Other players had castles and keeps, or sorcerer's cottages. She had an odd little mid-century ranch house with spectacular gardens. It would still be there to comfort her as she left the real home of her heart behind.

Gently she closed the door of her herbals room and left her gathering bag by the door. Her gardens called, one last time. She touched the dahlias and columbine, inhaled the lemony scent of sorrel, and laughed quietly at the mint, which had managed to take over half the garden in her two-day absence.

Hopefully the new owners would like mint tea.

She let her tears fall. There was no better place than a garden to soak up sorrows and turn them to good use. These were not entirely unhappy tears. Change was coming in her life, and much of it was very good.

A wonderful man awaited her and the child they had made together. And Aunt Moira was doing amazingly well for someone who had suffered a catastrophic stroke.

But she would need care. Long-term care from a trained healer.

There were others who would serve, others who would help. The witching community always took care of their own, and Aunt Moira was the most beloved of witches. It wasn't necessary for Sophie to go, to uproot and leave her home.

But it was right.

Even as tears fell and she said her goodbyes, her heart was sure. The next chapter of her life would be written in Fisher's Cove.

~ ~ ~

"She wants to go home." Elorie sat on the arm of Aaron's chair, having done one of her best things and convened a meeting. "Is that possible?"

"I hope so." Nell grinned. "She's getting as grumpy as Aervyn when he's sick."

Elorie sighed. That was the reason for the meeting. "I know. I keep reminding myself that cranky patients get better more quickly."

Sophie laughed. "I'm beginning to think she taught us that all those years to make a good excuse for her bad behavior now." She sobered. "We can definitely *get* her home—she's well enough to be transported. But she's going to need a lot of care once she gets there. Are we ready for that?"

Aaron squeezed Elorie's waist. "I can make sure she's got lots of bland, mushy stuff to eat. No broth."

Elorie giggled. Gran had practically thrown the last cup of soup at the poor witch delegated to get her to drink it. The good news was that she'd thrown it with her right hand. As a result, Sophie had ordered cups of broth sent in every thirty minutes. Throwing things was good physical therapy.

Nell shook her head. "You know you're truly loved when people are drawing straws for the chance to have you hurl pottery at them. Aervyn won the last draw, and he's all excited to go visit her."

Mike rubbed his head. "Tell him to duck faster than I did."

"Emotional swings will be a part of her recovery process," Sophie said. "Her brain is in remarkable shape, but it still has some serious recovery to do. Expect her to have a little more of a trigger temper than usual."

"Now you tell us." Elorie stood up and stretched, still kind of creaky from napping in odd places. "On that happy note, what else will she need?"

Sophie started to tick off on her fingers. "Someone staying with her round the clock, since she can't get out of bed yet. Regular healing to help her nerves and tissues recover, so she gains back some of her lost abilities. Soaks in that marvelous pool of hers. A reason to get up in the morning and function."

Excellent. Lists she could work with. Elorie started running through the possibilities. "A reason is easy. She has a new healer to train. Lizzie's clearly got at least some talent in that direction."

Sophie smiled slowly. "A trainee. That's absolutely perfect."

"She can have two," Nell said. "We couldn't figure it out in time to get healers to Moira without moving her, but Jamie and Aervyn have worked out how to shuttle someone through Realm to a different real-world location than where they started. We can send Ginia to Moira. California's very short of healers, so getting her some training would be a wonderful thing."

"That would be helpful," Mike said. "She's actually got some good skills already, and perhaps Moira would object less to monitoring from her own students."

Elorie loved watching a plan come together. "I'll stay with her for now, and the witchlings can help during the day."

Marcus shook his head. "No. I'll stay with her. She'll need lifting and carrying, and you shouldn't be doing that in your condition. I'll move my things to her guest bedroom."

Dead silence greeted his pronouncement. *Uncle Marcus* was going to move in with Gran?

He looked around. "What? You think I can't take care of one cranky old witch?"

Nell snickered. "Well, you've had plenty of experience with the cranky part."

"I know how to throw the cup back at her," Marcus said dryly.

"I think it's a good idea," Sophie said. She winked at Elorie. "It will give Aunt Moira lots of incentive to get better quickly."

It would surely do that. Uncle Marcus as nurse. Egads.

Elorie tried to remember the rest of Sophie's list and get her meeting back on track. "What about healing? We've got several healers in Nova Scotia, but Gran was the only one in our village. I can set up a rotation for people to come stay at the inn for a while."

"We can bring healers from farther away, too," Jamie said. "With the newly tweaked shuttle spell, Aervyn and I can taxi anyone in through Realm."

That would be amazingly handy, but it seemed like a big load for a small boy. "Isn't he tired from all the people he moved around yesterday?"

Nell shook her head. "Nope. We fed him cookies. He'll be fine."

Mike took Sophie's hand. "Help will be welcome, but Sophie and I can handle a lot of the healing."

Elorie shook her head. They were newlyweds, and just starting a new life together. Gran would have been the first to object to intruding on that very special time.

Sophie held up a hand to stall her protests. "Is that small cottage to the left of Aunt Moira's still for sale?"

Elorie frowned. "You mean that awful shack? Sophie, nobody could live there." It had been for sale for ten years.

"No, but we could build there." Mike kissed the top of Sophie's head, and then grinned at Elorie. "We figure Seedling will have built-in playmates that way."

They were going to move? Elorie's heart stuttered in shock and joy. Earth witches never moved.

Sophie smiled. "I love her too, and she needs us now."

It was an enormous gift of love, and not only for Gran. Elorie's mind swam with visions of shared dinners and little ones playing together, morning soaks in Gran's pool, and the everyday joys of a sister next door.

All that was left was a proper Nova Scotia welcome. Elorie held out her arms. "Welcome to Fisher's Cove, you two. We'll have a gathering. Nothing will get Gran well faster."

Her meeting dissolved into a cacophony of well wishes and celebration.

Elorie sat quietly as the noise swirled around her. The last few days had been a miracle of community—so many people giving whatever they could. Sophie's last gift, however, tugged particularly hard at her heart. Earth witches rooted deep and seldom left home. Anyone who knew Gran knew that.

And however much they would welcome her, building a house was a long process, one of chaos and upheaval.

It was the last thing Sophie needed, and Elorie realized it was in her power to help. She looked around for Jamie and Ginia, and motioned them over. "I have an idea."

~ ~ ~

Her idea took the next several hours, seventeen witches, three coders, and every person with a shovel in Fisher's Cove.

At the end of it all, Elorie stood in Gran's garden, happy to be back in the village she loved, and marveled at what they had done. Sophie's house—the Realm version, at least, and Jamie swore it was an exact duplicate of her real home—sat nestled in the grove of trees to the west of Gran's cottage. If it weren't for the freshly dug foundation—since apparently Realm homes didn't need those little details—it might have been sitting there for years.

It was the right welcome for a sister's homecoming.

The hordes of helpers had disappeared, leaving things quiet for Gran's return. They'd left behind baskets of flowers, housewarming gifts for Mike and Sophie, and enough food to feed the entire village for a week.

They were ready. She pulled a loaned iPhone out of her pocket and smiled at Aervyn's waiting face. "We're ready, sweet boy. Beam them home."

Moira's bed materialized in the clearing behind her garden, Sophie and Mike holding her hands. It had taken creativity and general bossiness to keep them away from the village all afternoon. She'd finally had to let Gran in on the secret to pull it off.

Sophie looked over with concern. "She's really tired today—I think we need to get her straight to her room."

"Nonsense," Moira said, sitting up with a grin. "I'm fine." It didn't come out entirely clearly, but no one mistook what she meant.

Sophie's face was absolutely priceless. "I thought you were exhausted."

Gran's lopsided grin was equally priceless. *It's not easy to fool a healer, my dear. I did a good job, if I do say so myself.*

"Fool a healer?" Sophie spluttered to a stop, a mess of frustrated confusion.

Gran reached up slowly to cup Sophie's face. Her right hand was a lot slower than her left, but it made the journey. "Welcome to Fisher's Cove, granddaughter of my heart. Look what they've done for you."

Sophie turned around, totally mystified. Elorie watched very carefully and knew the exact moment when she finally spotted the house. Shock and joy exploded on her face—and the entire village of Fisher's Cove exploded with flowers.

She clutched Mike's hand and turned to Elorie. "My house. You planted it here."

Elorie grinned. With the fresh dirt around the edges, that's exactly what it looked like. A house planted for a family to grow in.

Sophie had a home, and Gran would have so many babies to rock. The most traditional of joys, provided by the most modern of magics.

Elorie clasped her heart pendant, knowing that in Realm, hundreds of eyes and hearts watched along with her. It was a very good day to be a witch.

Thank you!

I hope A Hidden Witch was a good read. Please feel free to share it with a friend.

Want the next book in the series? Visit www.deborageary.com to sign up for my New Releases email list. The next books in the series are:

A Reckless Witch (late November 2011)

A Nomadic Witch (late May 2012)

And more in the planning stages!

Made in the USA
Lexington, KY
15 October 2013